Readers love STOLEN FUTURES Future Imperfect:

"This is the best book in the quadrilogy! Fast-paced, with twists and turns from start to finish - the action never lets up! A brilliant end to the series; pulling together all the threads from the first three books into one satisfying and explosive conclusion! The imagination and creativity in the *Stolen Futures* series is worlds apart - quite literally."

— Nic B., United Kingdom

"I have loved reading the *Stolen Futures* series."

— Hugo F., United Kingdom

STOLEN FUTURES

FUTURE IMPERFECT

M. Drewery

SPACEBOY BOOKS

Denver, Colorado

Published in the United States by:
Spaceboy Books LLC
1627 Vine Street
Denver, CO 80206
www.readspaceboy.com

Cover Art features Creative Commons Public Domain image by artvizual

First printed July 2023

ISBN: 978-1-951393-24-3

To my Grandparents

This book is dedicated to my brother who is always full of
encouragement.

THE FUTURE

Today was the beginning of my war against my own people.

All I could think about was *am I the worst traitor ever or a tool of universe's justice?*

"The key to having your ship not be detected is to make sure that you emit nothing that sensors can detect," the Mouth explained to me.

I was busy staring literally out into space through the viewscreen of my own space ship, barely thinking. His statement roused me and I turned to him and said, "What?"

He repeated his statement.

"Yeah, I know Mouth, so?" I replied.

"So how are you going to get us close to this Destroyer without being detected until the last, possible, moment? We fire the engines to get to them, they detect us, no chance of surprising them."

"Your people were space farers, right?" I asked.

"We were a long time ago. We left our planet on a giant ship we built, due to a non-Thief disaster, arrived on Pebbles'..." he trailed off as he thought of his former companion. "...homeworld and dismantled the ship to create a new city and start again. Three centuries later the Thieves arrived on our world! By then we only had small ships and few scientists well versed in the science."

"My people were exploring our solar system before their destruction. We had no ships that could save anyone, although one billionaire tried and died. Which was no loss. He thought he was Iron Man."

"Who?"

"Not important. Our craft were under powered, but there were ways to get ships around a solar system without engines," I said.

"Explain."

The console in front of me started flashing.

"Let me show you," I replied and grabbed an internal comm. "Everyone, it's happening."

Then the bridge of the *Vengeance* started to fill.

Antumbra was in first and took her place in the pilot seat next to mine.

Hippo took his modified seat, as did Lyger. Mantis and Ada hung at the entrance to the bridge and behind them were a number of different aliens.

"Callum?" Ada asked.

"The wormhole is fluctuating. Something is coming through," I replied. "Time for the engine burn. Is the cannon ready to mask our approach?"

Ada turned to a Ramothian next to her tapping away at a tablet. The Ramothian nodded. "Everything is set. Let's do this."

Lyger brought up a course on the main viewscreen.

It showed a solar system of eight planets. My ship was hovering inside the atmosphere of a moon orbiting the largest.

Behind us was one of the Ramothians' Black Hole guns, a giant weapons platform capable of firing a tiny black hole.

"Ok, get rid of the satellite," I said.

The Ramothian issued instructions into a communicator.

Then the cannon behind us fired. Two blasts in rapid succession. A black hole first, and then an antimatter shot. The black hole would strike the satellite feeding us sensor details through the atmosphere of this planet, since we couldn't see out. The antimatter would destroy the black hole.

On the viewscreen all the sensor details dropped to zero, the satellite was gone.

"Fire our engines, Lyger," I said.

Lyger nodded and the engines of the *Vengeance* flared up.

The ship left the planet's orbit shooting down at the gas giant below. We were going very fast closer and closer to light speed.

Right now, we were flying practically blind, everything had been worked out carefully by many scientists and I hoped no one forgot to carry the one.

"Computer will shut down the engines in five, four, three, two, one," the Ramothian said.

Lyger lifted her hands off the pilot's controls and the engines shut down.

"Now we're in gravity's hands," I said.

It appeared as if we were falling into the gas giant's atmosphere, but instead our ship soared around the planet using its gravity to speed us up further.

Nearly two thirds of the way around the planet, we were flung away, heading out into the edges of this solar system.

"That, Mouth, is how you remain undetected. We are no longer emitting anything."

"Callum, the Destroyer is breaching the wormhole," Antumbra said.

As we glided out of the solar system the wormhole we were approaching was getting bigger and bigger fast. Antumbra zoomed in on the swirling opening and, sure enough, a giant comet breached the surface.

"As always, the Thieves have covered their ship in ice. If the inhabitants of this system detect it they won't suspect that it's a giant spaceship here to destroy them," Antumbra said.

"They may never know what happened here," I replied.

"Wait," Antumbra uttered.

"What is it? Have they detected us?" I asked.

"No, it's just the size of the ship is too small. This vessel is the size of an Ark," Antumbra reported.

I sighed. "Not what we were hoping for, but maybe it will do."

"Callum, since it's smaller than anticipated we are off course."

"We planned for this," I looked over my shoulder at the aliens in the corridor watching the mission. "Everyone secure yourself in a room... decompression protocols."

The aliens ran down the corridor and secured themselves in lots of different rooms.

"I've never been on a ship that purposefully breeches its hull," Antumbra said.

"Thrusters would show up on a sensor sweep," I said. "But air escaping into space wouldn't, Lyger."

Doors behind me closed and Lyger replied. "All compartments sealed. Opening valve 1 now," she said.

Behind me my enhanced ears heard a mechanism open a small vent on the side of the ship then I heard the roaring of escaping air.

The viewscreen showed our course adjusting.

"Too much," Lyger commented and I heard one mechanism close and another open and more rushing air. "We're fine," the cat like alien reported as a mechanical clunk sealed the vents.

Antumbra looked at me. "Only you would think to carve a hole in our own ship's hull to use as thrusters."

"Well, there's no way the Thieves would sense it," I replied.

"Get ready," Lyger said. "One way or another we're going to fire the engine in a minute and hope the Ramothian cannon is faster on the draw than the Thieves."

"Ada get ready with the beacon," I said.

Ada tapped at some buttons and reported. "Ready to fire."

"You know what to do, Lyger," I said.

Lyger breathed in deep, purred, then steadied herself. Her hands lightly gripped the controls of the ship.

The giant iceberg in space loomed closer.

Her eyes narrowed, then suddenly the cat grabbed the controls and yanked them sideways, her tail slammed down on a button in front of her as she did so.

The engine fired and the *Vengeance* careered off to the left.

Through the ice was a dark object, the real ship beneath.

"Firing," Ada said.

The ship launched a missile down at the ice and it struck the surface, but didn't explode.

"Beacon set," Ada said.

"Full power!" I cried out.

The ship lurched forward again.

In front of us, ice erupted outwards. Lyger took the ship out into open space.

"Their weapons are locking on," the Mouth said.

I looked out and a double barrelled weapon installation was extending out of the hole in the ice, pointing towards us.

"They've locked on," Antumbra said.

A blast of energy shot from the vessel's weapons. However, it went wide as a second before a black hole struck the hull of their ship, wrenching a giant hole in the top part of the vessel. Then a fraction of a second later antimatter hit the black hole and detonated it.

The ship was sent spinning, the ice shell around it shattering completely.

The Mouth smiled and, considering the size of his mouth, it was a big smile.

"We have our doorway," he reported.

"Take us in, Lyger," I ordered.

As she turned the ship I turned on the comms, "Prepare for boarding," I said, and a cheer went up throughout the ship.

In the viewscreen, the ship curved around and then headed right for the Ark type vessel belonging to the Thieves, and into the gaping hole our cannon had left in its side.

"We're in."

•

"There," Antumbra said, pointing up past stacks of chimneys this Ark would normally use to suck water from the air, to a hole in the internal super structure, that showed corridors beyond.

"Give me a landing platform," Lyger asked.

Hippo readjusted some controls and the ship's weapons started firing.

The blasts peeled away walls and ceilings, creating a larger breech the ship could land on.

Once the space was cleared, Lyger took the *Vengeance* in, landing in our makeshift docking bay.

I unbuckled myself from my seat, "Let's go take this vessel," I ordered.

I was first out of the cockpit and down to the ramp leading out of the ship. Behind me Ramothians, my alien friends and lots of other volunteer aliens waited for me to go first.

I activated my kinetic shield, which not only projected around my body a layer of protective shielding, but a holographic projection hiding my features behind armour. Not real armour. Just a disguise. I had altered it to look like the armour of an old English knight, well, a sci-fi-ish knight.

As I left the ship, pulling out my gun and sword, which I flicked out straight, everyone followed me.

There were no Thieves to greet me at the bottom of the ramp, we had caught them totally by surprise.

"Ok, you all know your assignments. Get to them," I commanded feeling a rush as everyone behind me gave me a reply of, "Yes, sir."

I led a team consisting of Hippo, the Mouth, and a number of other aliens, towards the command centre.

We had to go slow; the corridors offered little in the way of protection. I led, since my shield would allow me to absorb the first couple of hits.

The Mouth followed behind and Hippo behind him.

We reached an intersection and I switched on the special feature of my gun, an x-ray function that allowed me to see right through the bulkheads and around a corner.

Waiting for us was a bunch of Thieves. Their mechanical parts showing clearly despite their soft, squidgy bodies.

I held up my hand to stop the Mouth and Hippo. I fired my gun and the blast of concentrated x-rays passed through the wall, and right through a Thief.

It toppled, dead, out into the corridor and this caused the other waiting Thieves to realise they could be picked off and they broke what cover they did have, weapons blazing.

I threw my arms out and the shield absorbed the first volley, then me and the Mouth darted sideways as Hippo hefted a giant gun and pulled the trigger.

The weapon sent out a stream of blasts that ripped the Thieves to shreds.

"Any more?" the Mouth asked.

I used my gun to scan the area: no more Thieves hiding.

We pushed on to the control centre, taking out a few more Thieves along the way.

When we reached the control centre I tried to scan the room but the walls were too thick, and the x-rays useless.

"Take out the cameras," I said, and we all blasted away at the domes on the ceiling. The Thieves inside the room wouldn't know what we would be planning.

I side stepped up to the door.

"Thieves, listen up, we control the rest of your ship. Surrender," I said.

"Callum is that you?"

I momentarily deflated; I had hoped this ship was only crewed by Thieves. Instead of hearing the slimy voice of a Thief it was a voice I knew well.

"Hello, Ogwambi," I replied.

"Not expecting to hear from me, were you?" the Ugandan representative asked. "After you gutted me."

"Weren't you trying to stab me?" I said.

There was a pause.

"You're not getting in here," Ogwambi said. "Not without significant casualties."

"Give up Ogwambi," I repeated. "There is no need for any casualties."

"I will not give up this ship to you or your alien friends. Why are you doing this Callum? You're human. You should be with us."

"I don't recognise any of you anymore," I said harshly.

"We don't recognise you, either," he spat back. "For what it's worth, all remaining humans in existence consider you exiled from humanity. Do your worst to try and get in here."

I sighed and came away from the door.

"How do we get in?" the Mouth asked.

"We could storm the room?" Hippo suggested.

"Anybody have a reflective surface?" I asked.

The Mouth handed his polished gun to me.

I held the barrel out past the door and moved it up and down.

My enhanced eyes took in the room. It was the size of the old human modified Ark, and inside were seven Thieves gathered around Ogwambi in the middle. Their tentacles held many guns pointed at the door. They even had shields to protect themselves.

Suddenly gun fire erupted at the door frame and I pulled the gun back.

"We'll definitely lose people if we go in, and we can't use grenades... We don't want to break the ring of computers around the edge of the room."

"How do we do this then?" the Mouth said.

I looked around trying to think.

I then turned around to face the wall.

I pointed my gun at the wall and used the x-rays to see behind it. It revealed that the domed control centre was in the middle of a virtually empty space, except for power conduits ringing the circumference where the computers were. I panned the gun upwards. The dome was just a screen and had no significant connections.

"Bring me a cutter."

In fifteen minutes, we had cut through the wall and I ducked my head through the empty space.

"Give me a grenade," I said.

"You said you couldn't use them in there."

"I'm worried about blowing up the consoles, however the dome is just a screen, we don't need all of it."

"What are you doing, Callum?" Ogwambi asked.

I whispered into a radio hanging on my chest.

"Get ready to breach after you hear the explosion," I said.

Hippo and the Mouth readied themselves.

I activated the grenade and tossed it up at the dome.

My throw was perfect and the grenade lodged in the support structure for the dome right near the top.

Three seconds later, it blew.

"Breech," I shouted.

I stepped out a little and saw that the dome had been blasted inwards, and shrapnel had rained down in the middle of the room, peppering the Thieves there with bits of metal. The ring of consoles was undamaged.

All the Thieves were down or writhing in agony.

As I and the Mouth breeched through one door, others came through the opposite one and we all fired downing the remaining Thieves trying to raise their guns.

I found Ogwambi in the middle of the room. His mechanical enhancements had protected him. But he had a nasty gash on his forehead.

He coughed and spluttered and sat up.

In his hand was a gun that he brandished through watering eyes.

I immediately grabbed the hand yanked it to one side, which cause his hand to droop and I took the gun from him.

He lay back, defeated.

"You traitor," he said to me through bloody teeth.

"I betrayed nothing. You betrayed our legacy," I said.

"Our legacy is assured, Callum. Humans are safe, our civilisation will endure now...forever," Ogwambi spat.

I turned my back on him.

"We don't deserve such safety," I said taking in the room, my eyes checking on the condition of the consoles. Thankfully they were undamaged.

I heard a shuffling behind me and turned quickly to see Ogwambi's arm rise, blade extending and I could do nothing to stop him.

Thankfully the Mouth shot Ogwambi in the hand blasting off the robotic one attached there. He screamed and grasped the charred stump.

My jaw clenched.

I had stabbed Ogwambi not long ago, I had pierced my old friend's flesh with my own blade. I had felt such guilt and shame at doing so. Now as I watched him cry at his lost hand, I barely felt anything.

It was like a part of me had died.

Every action I took against them was piece by piece erasing mankind from the universe, where once I been trying to save it.

"Thank you Mouth," I said.

The Mouth nodded to me and put away his gun.

"Get the bodies out of here, and lock up Ogwambi. Let's see if this ship has what we want."

Behind me the dead bodies were dragged away, I didn't even look over my shoulder when Ogwambi was unceremoniously dragged out.

I tapped at the controls, which were still able to bring data up on the damaged screen above me.

The Mouth sidled up to me, "Do we have it?" he asked.

"We do, we have our own wormhole generator," I said, and I turned to him with a big smile on my face. "We can now attack the Larceny homeworld directly."

THE PRESENT

1

APPROACHING HOME

The excitement on board the Ark was building every day.

We were getting closer and closer to our new homeworld and so everyone was starting to make plans, to dream, to wonder what it would be like to live on the surface of a world again.

It was such a bizarre feeling, like I'm still a teenager, my time on the Ark is a large slice of my life. I'd almost forgotten what it was like to walk on a planet, to feel the breeze on my face, to swim in water.

We would have to restart human civilisation as well. We had to land the Ark, then start building houses, roads, farms etc. Some of us would start families. If I lived a long life then I would see thousands of new humans be born.

I'm American, so this resonates with me. The history of my country is all about a group of people cutting ties with their old lives and starting again. Well, half my family history. The other half is living in harmony with the land and then fighting the people who after cutting ties then tried to cut people. I suppose I am all set. I can live in harmony with this new approaching land, and be ok with settling there.

Of course, we were going to do it a lot better than the English, Spanish and French. For one thing, we weren't going to genocide an entire population. Our new homeworld is people-free, so we won't repeat history's mistakes, mistakes that one half of my family tree had to endure.

We were going to start a colony. One day history books will be written about what goes on here. In a few centuries we hope to have cities, bowling alleys, maybe even cinemas again.

And I get to be one of the first to lay the foundations of all that.

I had a spring in my step every day as I thought about what I would do when we reached our new world. I started my morning by heading to the observation room and staring out of the window as we entered this new solar system.

I was not the only one. Many Arkonauts gathered for the same ritual, hoping to see one of the new planets in this system.

I joined Sanna by the window one morning. She stood watching the stars go by with her hands clasped behind her back.

"Anything to see?" I asked, stepping up next to her. I also took a moment to brush my hands against Nemo's tank and he swum over to me, and circled around the edge of the glass.

Sanna pointed upwards and sure enough a planet was coming into view. A gas giant with three rings encircling it.

"This is the first one. There are 8 planets in this system and as we approach this is our Neptune."

"I'm in the control centre for the rest of the trip. Our course takes us by three others," I said.

"Anything on the new homeworld yet?" Sanna asked.

"Today is when the Ark sensors can get some more info, we also hope to use the visual sensors to get blurry shots of the planet."

"I hope One chooses somewhere good to land," Sanna said.

"From what I can tell, it has to be one of the fertile regions. We want to be able to grow crops as soon as possible."

"It's only five weeks till we land."

"Actually, we're going to land in seven weeks. One says we have to take two weeks to do some projections, make sure that where we choose to land won't be covered in ice in the near future, or is actually a super-volcano or something."

"What? We have to wait seven weeks," Sanna growled to herself.

"Maybe we could use the small shuttle to get down to the planet, and walk around...shore leave?" I suggested.

Sanna brightened up. "Let's just hope it's safe down there," she added.

We then both stood quietly and watched the planet pass by.

After a few minutes I said, "Well I'm off to work for the day. Meet me in the cafeteria later, I'll let you know what the sensors find."

"See you later, Maiara," Sanna replied.

It was a short journey to the control centre, my morning commute. When I reached the room other Arkonauts were swapping out with the night shift.

I relieved Darma from Indonesia.

One showed up a little later than normal, carrying a tablet. He stood in the exact centre of the room, then looked up from his computer and glanced around smiling at the new shift rotation.

"Right, everyone, it's a big day today. Let's try and get some sensor readings and find out more details about our homeworld. Luciana, please start scanning."

Luciana nodded and immediately started pushing buttons. The dome above us and the floor displayed the details she was receiving. As the dome screen concentrated on visual sensors an image of the planet below started to take shape.

"It's just like we thought, Earth class, same atmospheric pressure, two natural satellites, two poles, just like home."

"Ok, it's time to launch the probe," One said.

We all smiled at one another. This was something we had added to this mission. Dr. Ghost had not thought of this, but we had and we had built it.

I activated a camera and the dome screen above us showed a device near the front of the ship.

"Bring it online," One ordered.

"Probe One online," Luciana reported.

"We should have thought of a better name," Oda said from across the room.

"What? Like Carlos?" Luciana replied.

"No, a space probe-y name like the Hayabusa or Sakigake," Oda suggested.

"How about the Exploradora," Luciana suggested, "Spanish for explorer."

"I honestly thought you were saying *Dora the Explorer*," Koyla said.

"Exploradora it is," One said over the laughter. "Activate it, Oda," he added.

I watched the probe come online. It was a modified missile; one we had found in the cargo bay. It had been provided just in case our new colony world boasted large animals we would need to fend off.

We had added small sensors to it and were about to fire it ahead of us towards the planet. It would beat us there by several days.

"All systems go, One," Sanna reported.

"Launch the probe."

We watched the missile/probe's thrusters fire and launched the thing ahead of us and it rocketed away. It was very powerful and in a few seconds it was out of sight.

"Ten seconds till engine shut down," Luciana said. She continued to count down and at one announced. "Shutdown."

"Is it still on course?" One asked.

"Checking...Yes, the burn was successful. It will reach the planet ahead of us by a few weeks," Koyla said. "Better than we hoped."

"Excellent. More time to gather data," One said, "Well done, everyone."

"One, shall we test the sensors?" Koyla asked.

"Yes, but only for only a minute though. We don't want to drain the battery, which we need to unfurl the solar panels when we get closer to our new homeworld," One agreed.

Oda tapped at some consoles. "Sensors online."

"Data coming in," Luciana said.

"Get the probe to double check its course for us," One ordered.

"Course matches our estimates, except there is an object in the probe's path that we haven't detected."

"What is it?" One asked.

"Sensors are detecting ice."

"Is the object moving? If so it's a comet and will probably move out the probe's path."

"It's moving, but not like a comet. It seems to be orbiting the star in the heart of this system," Luciana reported.

"Luciana, alter the probes course to go around it," One said.

"Done," Luciana replied.

"How big is this thing? Is it a small planet?" I asked.

"I've locked on one of the ship's telescopes. Shall we take a look?" Koyla said.

"On screen," One said.

The dome showed us the object the probe had detected.

It was not a planet or a comet.

It was a misshapen lump of ice, some parts clear, other parts dirty. As it drifted slowly in space it left behind a trail of particles.

"What is it?" One asked.

We all checked our sensors.

I could find nothing; it was just a lot of water.

"Erm, I'm detecting clusters of metal in the...thing," Koyla said.

"Metal, was it a ship?" Oda asked.

"One that became incrusted with ice?" I asked. "Like the Ark did when it reached our solar system?"

"How big is it?" One asked.

"330 million cubic miles," Sanna replied. "That's like the size of America."

"One, I think one of those pieces of metal is near the surface," Koyla reported.

"Can you show us?" One asked.

"It's blurry, in a few days we'll be close enough to see it properly," Koyla said and he put an image on the screen.

The metal shape was sort of long, tapering to a point at one end, and more rounded at the other. It appeared to have more metal sprouting off the top.

"Is it a ship? Maybe an alien vessel that crashed onto that ice ball?" Koyla suggested.

"Who knows, but let's not concern ourselves with it until we get closer," One said. "Shut down the probe. Let's conserve its energy until we need it."

●

A few days later, I was sent to retrieve One. I could have used the comms system, however I had never seen his quarters before, so I went in person. I knocked on the door to his quarters and he called me in.

I used to think that maybe he would stand in an alcove somewhere and recharge like a battery. However, he had a normal room, a little bit bigger than the rest of the Arkonauts. I didn't feel jealous about that, though. He was the captain, and he had to make sure humanity survived. I think allowing him some more living space was a decent reward for his hard work so far.

He had a bed, which I was surprised to see was a mess. Some personal effects were strewn across a desk in one corner.

Clothes littered the floor.

I chuckled to myself. One obviously didn't like tidying his room.

He stood with his back to the door, inspecting a bunch of scribbles he had made on the far wall. The blank wall acted like a whiteboard, and he had filled it with calculations and information. At the centre of it all was the piece of bloodied material that had been thrown backward through time, presumably from future Callum.

"Yes, Maiara?" One said, not turning around.

"Sensor details are coming in about that ship imbedded in the ice ball that was in our path."

"You could have called?" he asked.

"I wanted to see where you lived," I said looking around the room intently.

"Please don't tell me my room is untidy. I know. My father and mother used to tell me to clean my room over and over when I was a child. It's bothersome when people mention it now that I'm in my twenties."

"I thought grown-ups kept tidy places?"

One huffed. "Tidiness is just an organised mess. I know where everything is in this room. It's when people tidy it that I lose things."

I walked up to join him and stared at the wall of calculations.

"What is all this?"

"I spend some of my down time trying to figure out how a possible future version of Callum time travelled."

"Any luck?" I asked.

"A bit, the portal that opened on the ship was caught on internal sensors. The details were helpful. Of course, the fact of time travel actually being possible is not what interests me."

"How can that not be interesting?" I blurted out.

"Human scientists had already proven the existence of time travel. That scientific discovery got lost in the general chaos of the Ark and Destroyer's arrival. What interests me are two questions, questions whose ramifications also bother me. Firstly, is this future Callum still alive in the future, now that current Callum has unfortunately passed?"

"Oh yeah. I hadn't thought about that. If he was killed in the past, then how could he exist in the future to send a message in time?"

"I know how he could have survived the first time. It's the fact there is a new timeline that I don't understand."

"What's the second question?"

"Why hasn't he time travelled again? He didn't even rescue himself."

My heart ached when I thought of him, the way me and One causally talked about his existence and non-existence. I thought about his touch, his smell. My heart beat a little faster when I realised he might still be out there.

One traced his hand to a set of equations in the top right of his display. I think I have an answer to why he can't come back again. However, it is not conclusive." He then reached for his top pocket and pulled out a slip of paper with the same set of equations on it. "I keep a copy here to look at all day. It vexes me not to know."

"Why?"

"I guess it's because I have to be ready for anything, and I am not ready for another piece of bloodied clothing to be thrown back through time. I need to get this right."

"What does all that say?" I asked, gesturing to the bit of paper.

One chuckled, "Unfortunately, Maiara, you don't have the cosmologist and astrophysicist nanites that I have. You won't understand."

"Oh, gee... thanks," I said.

"A statement of fact. Not an insult. Anyway, let's go to the control centre and see if we've discovered a new alien species."

Once back in the control room, One ordered the sensors to focus on the big ball of ice once again.

The control room didn't just have the normal shift working there. We had been joined by some of the others who were off duty.

The connection with the probe was made.

"Is it in our way?" One asked.

"No," Koyla replied.

"Good. We can't afford to fire the engines and go round."

"I have a good sensor lock on that large piece of metal," Sanna said. "Focusing in now."

The display above turned to the big ball of ice. It was indeed massive, many times the size of the Ark a giant misshapen lump drifting in space.

"One, there appears to be many metal objects imbedded inside," Sanna reported.

"Zoom in on the largest," he ordered.

The probe's camera focused on a patch of the iceberg. At first it was a blurry blue, then the camera focused and everyone gasped including One.

Frozen in the surface of the ice were numerous ships, human ships. There was an aircraft carrier, a rusted oil rig, a submarine. All embedded and frozen in the big ball near its equator.

"I don't understand, those are human vessels," Sanna said.

"How did they get here?" I asked.

"There is only one way," One uttered.

2
THREE

"What's that?" Koyla asked.

"The Destroyer came this way," Luciana deduced. "And, for some reason, dumped all the water it held."

"Indeed," One said.

"Wait, how could the Destroyer have come this way? We saw it leave Earth in another direction," I said.

"But these are Earth ships. This is water from Earth. The Destroyer came this way definitely. It must have gone through the wormhole," Darma said.

"How could Earth scientists have got it so wrong?" I asked.

One started pacing, and the control centre crew looked at him as he strolled deep in thought.

"Maybe the Destroyer needed to take a different route from the solar system. It was nearly full of water, and even in space weight matters when you go from planet to planet," I said.

"Surely the scientists on Earth would have calculated that?" Luciana said.

"Scan the ice field again," One said.

I couldn't tell if he was finally rousing himself into action or just stalling.

Sanna scanned the field. "The probe has made more detailed scans, it seems as if we were right. The ships are human."

She put on the dome images of the various ships as the probe passed close to the ice. I saw battleships with human markings on them. There was even signs of sea life in the ice, frozen forever in the vacuum of space.

"One, the probe has moved beyond the ice and can now scan the new homeworld," Sanna said.

"Wait," One said.

"What...why?" I asked.

"If the Destroyer came through the wormhole then it did so for only one reason, to head to the planet in our path," he said.

"You mean it sucked up our water, and went to another planet to suck up its water after dumping all ours?" Koyla said. "Are the aliens who destroyed Earth just spiting us by taking away our next best option?"

"No, that's not it," Oda said. "The Destroyer came to Earth through the wormhole then it returned through it. Returned back where it came from."

"Back where it came from...y—you mean the homeworld of the aliens who sent it?" Sanna asked.

"Exactly. That planet could be where the Destroyer was sent from," Oda concluded.

"We're heading right for the aliens who destroyed Earth!"

"This is why I don't want to scan it. Scans can be detected and these aliens are certainly advanced enough to detect our attempts to scan them. Who knows what that might trigger?" One said.

"But we have to. We have to know," Luciana said.

"Maybe it's best we don't," Koyla said.

"And do what instead?" Luciana shot back.

"The only option would be to head back through the wormhole," I said.

"Then what? Earth is a field of debris?" Sanna said.

"Mars?" Koyla optioned.

"Non-viable as a planet; the Mars missions proved that," I said.

We all looked at One. The options did not sound good.

"Scan the planet. Let's be sure," he said.

Sanna conducted the scans and after a minute she reported.

"One, I'm detecting complicated communications, huge sprawling cityscape, and a dozen other Destroyers parked on the planet," she said.

"I don't understand. Why didn't Dr. Ghost see this?" Koyla said.

Suddenly, Luciana's console started flashing and she checked up on it.

"One, the computer just activated something in the ship," she reported.

"Do you know what?" he asked.

"Not the location. I can only tell you it was a command to deactivate and open a cryo-pod."

"A cryopod?" One gasped.

"Yes. Isn't the only person currently in a cryopod Two?" I asked.

"She is, although she's not in cryo sleep. It doesn't need to be deactivated."

"The computer sent the command automatically; it was set to deactivate and open the pod once..." Luciana began.

"Once what?" Koyla asked.

"Once we detected the planet ahead."

"The ship was waiting for us to scan the alien world. It knew it was the alien's world," I said. "Why would Dr. Ghost set this up? And who is in that pod?"

That's when we heard tapping of footsteps from the corridor. Someone was walking this way. We all turned to the door as the footsteps neared.

"I—is that them?" Luciana asked.

The tapping came closer. Strong purposeful steps. It sounded like the person was wearing heels.

Then rounding into view came a girl. She was probably 18 or 19 and dressed in a shimmering red dress that hung from strong shoulders, on which cascaded brilliant blonde hair. The hair framed an artfully made-up face with bright green eyes.

Something about her seemed familiar, like maybe I knew her as a younger person, maybe.

She stood at the door, finger tips together.

"Hello, my name is Three."

3
THE REPLACEMENT

Ten minutes later, I took my seat in the theatre, as did the rest of the crew.

One had ordered this. He wanted the whole crew to meet this... Three.

She went along with it, smiling in a way that looked like she was being as patient as she could, like an adult with a child they didn't have time for.

She stood on the stage, her dress casting dancing red lights ahead of her. She moved up and down the stage looking at all the Arkonauts present.

The whole room was whispering, gossiping. Rumours were flying around: who was this new person we had never seen before? She seemed both familiar as a human, yet as alien as...well, an alien.

I sat next to Sanna and Koyla, waiting for what presentation she was about to begin.

When the final Arkonaut sat down, the girl opened her arms wide and put on a big smile.

"It's so nice to be out of my cryopod. You have no idea how uncomfortable they are," she said in a jovial manner. Her voice boomed around the theatre; she had a headset wrapped around her head like she was giving a talk at a university. She paused, and I wondered if she was waiting for laughter. She hadn't read the room if she was.

Most of the crew weren't really looking at her. They were glancing at One who stood behind her, his back straight, a frown on his face.

Three brought her hands together and shook her head, and I think she mouthed the words *tough crowd* to herself.

"For those of you I haven't met yet, my name is Three. Actually it's Laine, but, you know, Dr. Ghost had a system," she said shrugging her shoulders. That joke got her a few chuckles.

"You're probably wondering who I am…" before she could continue hands went up and she ignored them. "Which I am obviously here to explain," she said loudly, and the hands went down.

"I am like One…and Two, of course, a contingency put here by Dr .Ghost to take charge."

"Take charge, really?" Koyla said, in a low voice meant only for me and Sanna.

Three's eyes glanced in his direction and her face stiffened for a moment. Her gaze then swept the crowd.

"Anyway, you're probably all wondering what this contingency is. Well, the ship's sensors have finally determined the nature of the planet ahead, in a day or two we'll reach our new home…"

"You mean five weeks," Luciana interrupted.

"Yeah it's not going to take two days," Illarion added.

Three paused in mid stride. "I'm sorry?" she asked.

"Yeah, we're five weeks out," Sanna confirmed.

Three rocked back on her heels. "No, the ship's sensors would only bring me out of cryo sleep when they gave detailed scans of the planet. I was told that was only possible when we were two to three days away," Three said.

One took a small step forward. "We outfitted a probe and sent it on ahead of us. We're getting sensor readings far earlier," he explained.

Three went a bit pale. "So, I have to watch over you for five weeks," she said to herself slowly. She rubbed her hands together as she looked down at the ground.

One stepped forward again. "Are you alright, Three?" he asked.

Three straightened up and took a deep breath. "Yes, yes of course, just re-calculating.

"Ok. So we're five weeks out. That's fine. I can deal with that..."

"Why were you activated when we discovered that the planet we're heading towards, is the homeworld of the very aliens who sent the Destroyer to Earth?" Moana asked.

"Well, Dr. Ghost always knew that of course," Three said.

"What?" dozens of people around the theatre cried out. Eyes went to One, who we knew to be Dr. Ghost's son.

I bet they were thinking what I was thinking: *why didn't you tell us?*

Three turned on her heels following the stares to One.

"Didn't he tell you?" She asked pointing a finger at him.

"No," was the reply from several Arkonauts.

"I did not know," One said. He uttered the words so matter of factually that I believed him...the question was *why did he not know?*

"Oh, I thought he would have told you, but if you didn't know..." Three said, and she turned back to the room.

"Dr. Ghost always knew that the planet we were heading for was the Destroyer's homeworld. He didn't tell you on Earth because of security concerns. Yes. I bet you all think you could have been trusted with the truth, however just one rumour, one slip up, would have meant the whole plan failing.

"I was told before I went into cryo sleep that One would reveal the truth so that you would be prepared, told the real plan."

"What real plan?" Moana asked.

"Dr. Ghost has secured us a place on this new world. Where humanity can start anew."

"A place with the aliens who destroyed Earth?" Sanna called out.

"It's not quite as simple as that...er..."

"Sanna," One said.

"Yes, Sanna," Three finished.

"It sounds like a terrible plan," Gerlinde said.

Three looked down and I swear she mouthed the words *five weeks of this*. She then raised her head throwing back her luscious golden hair.

"Ok, I'm starting off on the wrong foot here. You were supposed to know this. There is literally not enough power to get you to another planet. You were supposed to be prepped for this. I'm afraid that One has let you down."

"One has saved us multiple times," Koyla said.

"Anyway... let's get you up to speed."

Three raised her wrist and activated a device there. I thought it was just a piece of jewellery.

One stepped forward again raising a hand this time.

"What are you doing?" he asked.

"Just some more memories. I was really hoping that we would only be doing this for two days. Just have to activate them far earlier. Shouldn't be any trouble, though," Three said over her shoulder at him.

"Tell them what you're doing," he ordered.

"Children..."

"Arkonauts," One corrected.

"I'm just going to activate some Nanite memories in your brain that have been dormant, secret injections Dr. Ghost gave you. You may not know this but there he gave you a secret 18..."

"We know about the 18th," Koyla interrupted her.

"Oh, you do," Three said gritting her teeth. "Well...well done for figuring that out. I'm going to activate some just like that and deactivate a few you no longer have a need for."

"Wait you..." I started.

Then Three stopped tapping her device. Everyone's head in the room sort of twitched, except for mine and One's.

"There," she said letting out an exasperated breath and composing herself again.

"Let me restart this explanation."

"Dr. Ghost made a deal with the aliens who attacked our homeworld. It turns out that mistakes were made on both sides."

"Mistakes, they destroyed our world," Koyla said. However, he was not as angry about it as I thought he should be. I looked around the room expecting nods or at least a 'hell yeah's, but nothing. Everyone was waiting for an answer, like this was a reasonable conversation.

"The aliens in question send their ships out to collect resources, sometimes they malfunction. Unfortunately, Earth was attacked by a malfunctioning Destroyer.

"The aliens were really super sorry about that. Unfortunately, the Destroyer would not remotely shut down. One way or another it was going to leave planet Earth and its giant engines were going to destroy the planet. There was no way to stop it. But the aliens, to show how sorry they were, offered Dr. Ghost the chance to send to them humans who could live on. He choose you," Three said.

I looked around. That sounded plausible, however there seemed to be so many gaps, like why didn't One know this?

"This is obviously going to be a shock for you, and over the next five weeks..." she said those last few words through gritted teeth, "... we will prepare ourselves for this new reality.

"The aliens are sorry that this kind of mistake was made. Rest assured, they feel very sad that this happened."

"Sad? They destroyed a whole race," Luciana said.

"And rather sweep it under the rug, they instead are going to help humanity rebuild. They told Dr. Ghost to send them survivors and they would be taken care of. Has any country on Earth ever done that for those they hurt accidentally or on purpose? Did the Europeans or Americans ever give back to the indigenous people they hurt? Did companies who inadvertently caused global warming ever pay back for those accidental mistakes? No. But these aliens are they're going to help us. They are going to pay back."

Three sighed and looked at us all with sadness in her eyes.

"You have to look to the future now. You are still the remnants of humanity. You still a have tremendous weight on your shoulders. Please, please accept this slightly different future.

"They are no longer our enemy, they never were. They want to help us, though."

She let those words hang in the air.

Next to me, Sanna shifted uncomfortably in her chair and then looked at One. "Why weren't you told, One?" she asked.

One looked down at the ground.

"I don't know." He then stepped forward, passing Three on the stage. "Maybe I did know? Remember when I had to have my nanite memories replaced by Callum? Maybe I lost that knowledge? Maybe my father thought that to get you here this information would be a distraction? Maybe it would scare me and you? But we can't turn back now. We're locked in. Maybe my father wanted to make sure of that? So, I guess we have to trust this new situation.

"I know my father would not send this ship to do anything else, but secure the future of the human race," he added.

Three then stepped in front of him.

"You should all relax. Unlike before, you're not going to have to rebuild from scratch. The aliens are going to give us a head start. Everything will be fine."

Murmuring spread across the room.

Sanna turned to me and said, "I don't like the fact we weren't told, and I'm scared to meet these aliens."

"Me too," Koyla said. "But what choice do we have? Besides Dr. Ghost set this all up. We're still saved."

"You're right," Sanna replied. "At least we're not going into the realm of our enemy."

A thought came to my mind, and I stood up to get above the talking.

"Three," I began, and the room went quiet. "What is the name of...of our new hosts?"

She smiled at the room, "Our new friends, who are there for us, who are offering their homeworld to us, are called the Larceny."

4
NEW FRIENDS

The next five weeks were the strangest of my life.

That, in itself, is a strange thing to say. After all, I was on an alien spaceship. I had travelled through a wormhole and been attacked by a space squid, met a giant crocodile, and fought a fish man.

Maybe strange is not the right word... Awkward is.

Three seemed competent as a leader, but there was something off about her.

She held regular meetings with the crew, prepping us for life with our new alien friends, yet she didn't talk about survival on this new world, she focussed on what great things could be expected. She also repeated these talks with slight modifications. Padding it all out for five weeks.

These aliens had already prepared living arrangements for us and would help finding a new homeworld somewhere else.

The meeting where she showed us what these aliens looked like was the freakiest of all.

Turso, while being a walking fish, still looked vaguely human in his own way. These Larceny were unlike anything I had seen before.

They were basically walking squids and octopuses.

Both types walked on their tentacles. Their planet was almost completely urbanised, and separated into over a dozen families that obeyed an Overlord that controlled the species.

Three said that the Destroyers they sent out were to gather water from uninhabited worlds and return it to the cities. The civilisation apparently got its power from water, in some form of fusion process.

She encouraged us to get over our initial apprehensions of these aliens; they were, after all, generously enabling humanity to survive.

Of course, talk about the Larceny was everywhere.

"I hope this isn't some sort of Twilight Zone situation," Koyla said quietly at our table in the cafeteria.

Three was not there. She rarely ate with the crew. But Koyla was keeping his voice down all the same.

"What do you mean?" Ogwambi asked.

"My grandfather used to show me this old tv show called the *Twilight Zone*, basically a bunch of sci-fi horror stories. One of which was when aliens invited humanity to their homeworld and it seemed liked a cultural exchange. The aliens even provided a book describing what they intended for the humans who visited their world, the book's title was apparently *To Serve Man*."

"And?" Sanna said, her fork halfway to her mouth.

"Turned out the book was a cookbook for humans," Koyla finished.

"They gave humanity a cookbook?" Illarion asked.

"No, no... The book was a book on how to cook humans," Koyla said.

"Wait are you saying that these aliens are going to eat us?" Gerlinde asked.

Koyla shrugged.

"I don't like the sound of that," Moana said.

"Do you know someone who would?" Gerlinde asked her.

"Point is, do we really know what these aliens want?" Koyla said.

"Three doesn't seem to be lying, and if Dr. Ghost put her here surely it's all on the level," Ogwambi said.

"Dr. Ghost has kept things from us before," I offered.

"Only one thing, and it was to our benefit," Illarion said.

"But why activate Three now? Surely a year ago would have been better. You heard her. It was supposed to be two days before we reached the new homeworld that she expected to be released, not five weeks. Two days is not a lot of time to prepare us to be guests of another race. Something doesn't add up," I said.

"Calm down, Maiara. What's the alternative? Actually, this whole thing makes a bit more sense. We rebuilt the Ark as a livable spaceship in a few years. Couldn't have done that without these aliens help," Sanna pointed out.

"Why didn't the aliens just shut down the Destroyer, rather than let it destroy Earth?" I asked.

"Three said it was defective," Koyla replied.

"I guess..."

I trailed off because the cafeteria was going quiet. One had just walked in. Our conversations turned to whispers as he went to the food dispenser and grabbed his meal. He went and sat down alone. He tried to look stoic and unabashed by the silent treatment. He had experienced it before, during his first few days on the Ark, until he saved Callum and the others from those intruders. He had never sat alone since then.

Nowadays though, he was sitting on his own more and more.

I looked around the room wondering if someone join him. That's when I realised it would have to be me.

I stood up and picked up my tray.

"You finished?" Ogwambi asked me.

"No," I replied, and I walked across the cafeteria. At first, no one paid me attention... until I sat down opposite One.

His eyes widened in surprise.

"So how you doing?" I asked.

He slowly chewed his food and looked back at me.

"Hello, Maiara," he finally said.

I was aware of talking over my shoulder.

"You can hear them all, right?" I asked.

"I can, of course, but I try not to pay attention."

"Even for you, I bet the appearance of Three was a shock," I said.

"It's only twenty more days. Soon, we'll land on this alien homeworld and I'll have a new role," he said.

I paused for a minute as he stared down at his food.

"I don't like how this is handled One. You should have been told by your father."

One poked the food on his tray. "I think that too. However I believe there is a plan in all of this. I trust my father with these decisions."

"But he put you on this ship to captain the crew, and now you've been supplanted," I said.

"Maybe he had to change the plan after I was put on board. Don't forget I was stored here after I was modified. That was also before the Ark went into orbit. Maybe that's when these Larceny got in contact, and he had to change his plan."

He poked his food some more.

"It's still not right," I said. "Has Three told you what you'll be doing when we reach this new world?"

"She's very vague about it, actually. Something about being a liaison, talking to these Larceny, making sure Arkonaut needs are met."

He stared off into space as he chewed his food.

I wondered if maybe changing the subject would cheer him up or take his mind off the people talking about him in the cafeteria. "Did you solve that time travel issue?"

One smiled and turned to me. "I'm glad you asked. I've had more down time so I..." he trailed off as once again as his reduced position was brought back to him.

"Well, tell me!" I said.

He sort of snapped out of it. "Well, I finished my calculations and I know why Future Callum hasn't followed up with us. I think I've worked out a solution... It's pointless, though. I can't get it to him."

"So, what is it? And why hasn't he figured this out? How do you think he even got time travel in the first place?"

"There's no way he would have been able to figure it out, he must have met someone who can time travel," One replied.

"Why haven't *they* figure it out?" I asked.

"It's probably because this was unexpected. As far as I can tell, there is no way of determining what time travel will do to the universe. If it was impossible to predict, then whoever gave Callum the means to time travel couldn't be prepared for the fact that if you time travel once, you can't do it again to the same point in time."

"But you figured it out?" I said.

"Indeed, but I do have a different perspective."

"Were you always this clever?" I asked.

One put his fork down and then rested his elbows on the table hands together. "No, I wasn't. My father made me who I am today."

"How different were you?" I asked.

"I had what doctors called Rett Syndrome, a genetic disorder that basically affected my brain's development. I was so different to who I am. I had severe physical disabilities, and, in layman's terms, was stuck as a child, unable to mentally develop."

"That's when your father did all this?" I said gesturing to his muscular tall body.

One nodded. "I don't remember it, actually, the process. In fact, the nanites in my brain are what keep me mentally aware and at this level. Remember when Callum had to inject me with my nanite memories, when I was shot more times than my enhanced body could take? If he hadn't done that then I would have woken up a completely different person."

"Well, I'm sure we would have liked him as well. Plus, I think even that person would have been looking out for us."

One rubbed his hands together then looked away from me. "You know, I don't know about that." He then smiled. "You would have had a super strong adult with the mind of a child to deal with."

"We would have handled it. We've handled everything else that the universe has thrown at us so far," I replied.

One turned his head towards the corridor and a few seconds later Three wandered in, wearing a sparkly emerald dress this time.

Heads turned to watch her gracefully collect her food.

I couldn't see her face completely, but when the tray came out I could see a slight grimace on the side of her face.

When she turned around, though, she was all smiles and she got invites to come and sit at each table.

"I don't know if I could handle that, though... Certainly not for three weeks or more," I said to One.

That brought a smile to his face. "Like me, it's what she has been prepared for. Can't fault her for that."

5
THE DIVE

The day of our arrival at our new home was today.

I didn't sleep. Well, not properly. Maybe for an hour. I felt certain that everyone on board was the same.

This was it. We were going to step on a new planet after nearly two years in space. That, in itself, was exciting. To have that safe feeling of being on a planet we can breathe on. No more worrying about power or water loss. No more wondering if the hull would buckle and I would go flying out a hole and into space.

I rolled onto my side to stare at the white wall of my room. I took a deep breath and let it out slowly. My heart was racing. My brain flashed ideas and images at light speed through my mind. I thought about shaking hands with these aliens, if they had hands.

I realised, in that moment. that the rest of my life was going to be spent on this planet as a guest. I wouldn't be in school. Would I have to get a job and work nine to five? What were these aliens going to be like?

For the first time it occurred to me that I was not going to be as free as I thought. I would, if this was an empty planet that we could colonise. For the last year I had dreamt about building a house of my own; of studying a whole new world. I had dreamt of being a 100 year-old women surrounded by several generations of my descendants.

That was all gone, replaced with the fact that now I was going to have a more ordered, structured life. I was going to be in a city, living to the whims of these admittedly, nice, aliens for taking us in... but still under their rules.

I felt like I wanted to run away. The thought of taking the small scout ship and flying off into the wormhole again even crossed my mind.

But running away wouldn't help.

I sighed as I slid out of my bed to get dressed. I put on my Arkonaut hoodie last and zipped it up. I chose a deep blue colour today. As I admired the colour, and the feel of the fine stitching Two had done, it occurred to me that I might have to wear special clothes on this planet. These Larceny might have clothing preferences for us. I guess our clothes would fade and deteriorate over time, so that meant they would have to make us new ones. I shuddered at the idea of fashion choices being made for me. I closed my eyes, breathed deeply again, and left my room to face this.

Out in the corridor, the others Arkonauts were rising and heading out. There was no day or night shift. We were all up. Those not needed would sit in the theatre or the observation room as myself and others made sure the Ark landed safely.

I met Moana in the corridor, "Morning," I said as cheerfully as I could, despite my lack of sleep.

"Yah, yah..." she managed to reply through a yawn. "Morning," then she stared into space for a moment and shook her head. "Wow. This is it," she said wearing a nervous smile.

Koyla stepped out of his room as fresh as a daisy. "Today's the day, everyone," he announced to the corridor. "Finally solid ground," he almost cheered.

"Yeah, I hadn't thought of that," Moana said brightening up. "Grass, water, wind... It's funny how you miss the simple things."

Oda walked up rubbing his eyes. "Urrgh. What are you guys talking about?"

"Today's the day we finally land this thing," Koyla said.

Oda seemed to pause for a moment and then smiled. "Finally. And we don't have to worry about building houses or hunting for food. These Larceny are going to give it all to us."

I shrugged. "I was looking forward to the hard work of building our own place."

"But this way we're going to have more options. These aliens are an interstellar civilisation. Just think what possibilities we'll have," Moana said, and she led us down the corridor. "We won't have to rebuild our entire civilisation again. We'll be able have access to ships, maybe? Who knows?"

"We'll have electricity," Koyla said.

"We'll have running water," Oda pointed out.

"Comfy beds," I added.

Moana put her arms around me, "It will be great, Maiara. We're very blessed."

"Yes, blessed," I echoed, but deep down I was still apprehensive.

●

The control centre was almost full when I got there and I took my seat.

One was there, standing in the centre, arms behind his back. But he was not in charge here.

I gave him a smile and nod.

He returned the gestures, but weakly.

Three, meanwhile, walked around him wearing a regal dress. Her high heels tapped the floor. I winced every time she did, wondering if they were going to crack the floor screen, which showed us the world we were approaching.

The dome showed the same, but also plotted our descent. The world was much like Earth however it had one very large ocean and a single continent that went from the north to south pole. A world more water than land, which made sense given how much water these alien's ships gobbled up.

But, in various places over the planet,were huge, deep craters . In some of them were Destroyers, nestled in them and protruding from them like mountains. The plotted course for the Ark showed that the ship would head towards its own hole on the edge of the continent, which held a large city.

"Ok everyone, let's get this right," Three said. "It's time to flip the ship."

"Maiara, Luciana, this is for you to do," One said.

Three bit her bottom lip when he spoke to us. "Yes Maiara and... Luciana do what you know how to do."

I glanced at Luciana, who placed her hand over the controls. "Shall I take the lead?"

"Give the commands," I said to her.

"Thanks," she replied and briefly glanced at the readouts in front of her.

"Cut the engines," she said.

I put in the commands and the raging inferno near the base of the ship was reduced to nothing.

"Engine room reports total shut down. Power conservation in effect," Oda said.

"Maiara, south side thrusters fire. Keep them consistent and get ready to reduce on my command," Luciana said.

I switched on the thrusters and used a touch screen dial to slowly turn them up.

On a representation in front of me, the Ark started to roll. The base of the ship rose up. It was like someone had tapped the Ark on the top and flipped it over, and we were watching it in slow motion.

"Easy now," Three said.

I gave Luciana a sideways glance and managed to communicate in a single eyebrow raise, *Yeah, we know.* Then went back to work.

Once the Ark was ninety degrees from its previous position, Luciana fired up the north side thrusters. Their power countered what I was doing and she said, "Ok, Maiara, stop your thrusters," she said.

I slowly powered them down, watching the readings and seeing that Luciana was perfectly matching the power balance.

She fired up her thrusters just enough to get the base of the Ark pointing forward.

I looked up at the dome to see that our projected course was perfect and we were aligned exactly how we wanted to be.

"Job done," I said and sat back.

Three said, "Conduct a final scan of the planet below."

Oda obliged from his position.

"Scan running. Detecting millions of lifeforms, hundreds of cities and a dozen Destroyers, including the one that struck Earth," he reported bitterly.

"Can we shoot at it?" Illarion suggested.

"No!" Three snapped.

"I was only joking, Three," Illarion said crossing his arms.

She shook her head like she was trying to dissuade a fly trying to land on her. "Sorry. It's just that this is important. First impressions matter," she said. "I have been prepared to make this transition as smooth as possible."

I reached over my controls to take a look at the readings and get a sense of this planet myself.

Before my fingers could touch them the whole console shut down.

"What?" Oda said from the other side of the room.

I spun in my chair to see that every console was turned off.

"The Ark is turning," Luciana said.

Her console was dark too her fingers tapping uselessly at its surface. She swiveled in her seat to stare at the dome screen. I looked up and watched as the base of Ark turned sharply to point directly down at the planet.

"We've changed course," Luciana said.

"We're diving," I said.

"No. We're crashing," Oda said.

6
THE LEADER

"One, what's happening?" I asked.

"I'm in command here," Three interjected and she stepped gracefully forward and looked at the controls. "It seems as though the Ark has initiated a crash dive onto the planet below."

"What?" One said, suddenly rising from his docile state.

"One, be silent," Three commanded, reading the data on the screen. "This is nothing to worry about...however, you may well want to listen to what happens next."

The whole ship then jerked, as thrusters on top of the vessel fired. The lateral thrusters then started firing. I felt the throbbing through the floor.

"The engine is charging up, but not firing," Luciana said.

The Ark's base was now directed at the planet, as if it was going to land.

"This trajectory is too steep. The Ark's kinetic absorption shield has shut down. It won't survive the impact," Luciana said.

"Three, we need to stop this," One said.

She sighed and rolled her eyes.

"Try if you like," she said.

"What kind of spare leader are you?" Luciana said. "We're about to crash onto the planet."

"Yeah, shouldn't you be doing something?" Koyla added.

"I will do something in a minute. But, I want you to see what happens next," she said.

One stepped past her, and his fingers danced on the controls.

"It's not accepting my commands. There's an override in the system."

"Who put that in?" I said, and shot an accusing glance at Three.

"It was put in two years ago. Right before the Ark was put into Orbit above the Earth..." One said.

"Who did it?" I asked.

One paused as he read the information.

"One?" I asked.

Luciana slid her chair over and read the same information One was seeing. "It was Dr. Ghost."

Three sniggered as the Dome screen flickered, then changed from a view of the planet below to Dr. Ghost's face.

It couldn't be him, though. He was dead. Then I remembered that Callum had told me a recording of Dr. Ghost was programmed into the computer, as a sort of guide for One.

"Crew of the Ark," the recording began authoritatively.

"Here we go," Three said bursting into a wide grin then turning towards One. "You're going to hate this, but you won't be able to turn away."

"This is broadcasting all across the Ark," Illarion reported.

Dr. Ghost exhaled, "First, I want to tell you how proud I am of all you. You, teenagers, have got this ship to its destination. You've overcome many challenges."

Dr Ghost's recording then looked down away from the camera. He rolled his thin shoulders, then looked back at us.

"By reaching the point that this recording has been activated, you have proven yourselves. You are all that humanity could have hoped for as legacy bearers. You are tough, not only physically, but psychologically. You are determined and, best of all, together, as one.

"During the course of planning the Ark project, I discovered and recruited you all, and you all impressed me. It seemed that my plan to ensure the survival of our species was assured.

"Then, I unfortunately received some disturbing information. The journey through the wormhole will not take you to a new homeworld. We discovered that it will instead return you—this ship—

to its creators. The ones who sent the Destroyer to ravage our world. This, you must be aware of by now.

"The aliens on this world are called the Larceny.

"You no doubt have many questions, and I will do best to answer them in the short time we have."

"We're about to enter their atmosphere," Luciana reported.

"I want you to know that the Ark was meant to save you, and our race, "Dr. Ghost continued. "To give us a chance to start again fresh and new. However, I learned such things were not possible... I tried to find another direction for the ship to go to no avail.

"Then, I realised that sending this ship to this world was the only thing I could do. Your mission stopped being one of salvation and became one of revenge... No. Of justice... A chance to bring our great enemy down and end the destruction they wrought upon this galaxy for their own greedy ends.

"I sent you towards the wormhole with the hopes that you would get the ship to the other side and from there to the homeworld of our great enemy.

"The Ark is now under the control of a program designed to crash it into their world, creating an explosion that would either wipe them out, or bring them to the brink.

"This will, of course, end with the death of humanity. But there was no other way.

"I cannot ask you for your forgiveness. This is what needed to be done. Humanity's time must end to also end the Larceny's.

"I cannot save you. This is justice. The price must be paid.

"Sorry children," Dr. Ghost bowed his head. "There was no other way to save you... No other way."

The image of Dr. Ghost looked directly into the camera. Then faded away.

"Father," One said, and he looked close to tears.

"Oh, of course you were sent here to save them, yet you can't," Three said tutting. "I can though. Me and my father's plan is the only way forward for humanity."

Three walked up to the controls tapped in a few commands and the Ark slowed to a stop. The main engine then came back online and settled the Ark into orbit above the planet.

Luciana's console flashed.

"Er... Three, there is a signal from the planet below," she reported.

"Open the channel."

Appearing on the screen was a face that almost made me scream in surprise.

7

THE TRUE ONE

I saw a face that had become the most famous on Earth, the face of a man I thought was a hero. I thought back to the last time I had seen him, delivering a stirring speech when the Ark had been raised into orbit.

It was the Vice President of the U.S.

That's when it clicked. Where I remembered... Where I had seen Three before.

She was there, she was his daughter.

"Hello, crew of the Ark. Welcome to the homeworld of the Larceny, and the homeworld of humanity. By now an attempt by Dr. Ghost to murder you has been foiled by my daughter... known to you as Three.

"As a director of the Ark Project, I hereby take control of the crew and terminate the authority of Dr. Ghost's son, known to you as One.

"Please land the ship at the designated site. We will meet you there briefly before escorting you to the Citadel of the Overlord of the Larceny... to begin your new lives."

His face then disappeared.

"The VP. He's alive. He got here before us. How?" Oda asked.

"There is only one way," Luciana said.

"The Destroyer?" I asked.

"Exactly."

"But that means he met with the aliens, the Larceny, on Earth. Then he went aboard their ship and left humanity to die," Illarion said.

We all looked at Three.

She was smiling. "Well, yes, it is true. My father, the one who pulled humanity together and saved it, did get aboard the Destroyer at the behest of the Larceny."

"He left billions to die," Oda shot at her.

"The Destroyer was going to take out Earth regardless. He saved a few on that ship and, by the way, he still made sure the Ark project was completed.... Getting you here," Three pointed out. "It's just like I said, the Larceny are prepared to open their arms to us."

"Wait. This is all so confusing. Dr. Ghost programmed this ship to crash into the Larceny homeworld, but the VP made sure you were here to stop that? Why? How? Didn't Dr. Ghost know?" Illarion asked.

Three sighed. "This conversation is getting away from me. Look, I'm still in charge. Make sure the Ark lands at the..."

"No. We're getting out of here. This planet isn't safe," One said. "Luciana, fire the primary engine. Maiara, plot a new course out of this solar system. Oda find us another wormhole."

We all began to leap into action until Three squared up to One.

"You are not in charge here. My orders stand. No one touch anything. I'm sick of babysitting you all. We are joining the rest of humanity. Accept it."

"Ignore her. We need to get going," One said.

We didn't do anything. I looked into the eyes of my fellow Arkonauts. I imagined we were all thinking the same thing. How could we escape? It took this ship's total resources to get us here. Firing the engines again would mean less power. One didn't seem to have figured this out.

Three turned away from One. "Crew, Dr. Ghost just tried to kill you all. He just tried to sacrifice this ship, and your lives, to get revenge on the Larceny. Do you want to follow his son?

"My father has a place ready for us on that world. It's time to get off this ship and walk on solid ground again."

"You lied to us," One said. "These Larceny didn't accidentally destroy Earth."

"Yeah. They were in control of the Destroyer they could have just switched it off," Luciana pointed out.

Three stepped away biting her lip. "It doesn't matter. I'm in charge. I've been placed in charge. I've been bred to be in charge."

"And you've proven yourself incapable," One pointed out. "Follow my orders, everyone. We need to find a way out of this solar system."

That was when Three jabbed her arm forward. I heard the scrape of metal on metal and I gasped as a blade shot out from her forearm.

One was just quick enough to dodge and the blade only slit open his jumpsuit.

He didn't pause to dwell on this surprise attack. He grabbed her arm and forced it and the blade down to the ground where it snapped on the display screen floor, which chipped.

He then kicked her away.

We all got up from our seats.

Three retracted the remains of the blade into her hand, and from her other arm another shot out.

She swiped at him smiling. One ducked and dodged away. Never taking his eyes off her.

"Get out of here," he told us.

We made our way to the exits.

Three dived in with another slash, and One kicked the blade away, He then punched Three in the stomach and she went flying into the console.

Her smiled disappeared and she gritted her teeth.

As One came for her, she slashed at him, but he saw it coming and bent around the blade. He also anticipated the return stab, caught the arm, and drove it into the console, breaking that blade too.

He then grabbed her head and slammed it into the console.

Three backhanded him and he went flying across the room.

She leapt from her console and kicked him in the stomach.

He grabbed her foot and twisted and she yelped. She twisted with her leg to prevent it from being snapped.

Her palms struck the floor and she pushed away with her strong arms. Driving the foot One held out of his grasp, and she snapped his head back.

Three rolled away as One staggered, shaking his head.

He held up his fists as the two of them circled one another.

She was breathing heavily, her perfect hair slightly lank now with sweat. Her make-up was smudged.

One was breathing heavily too. His eyes locked on Three.

"Ok... I don't know why I'm wasting time fighting you," Three said.

Her hand slipped into her pocket, and she brought out a remote.

One reached out for it, then she pressed a button before he could make it.

He immediately threw his head back and cried out. He grasped his temples and fell onto his knees.

Three smiled again then stepped forward and kneed him in the head.

Me and the others cried out and we ran into the room.

Three stepped back and just watched us as we went to him.

"One, what's wrong?" I asked.

One took his head from his hands blinked rapidly several times.

He seemed to shrink a little. Curling up and shuffling away to get under the nearest console. He hid in the shadows underneath and rocked back and forth.

"No. No. I wasn't supposed to be this way again," he said and his voice was higher.

"One?" I asked.

He shrunk away from my words and looked away from me.

"Joshua?" I asked.

He hugged his knees and turned his back to me.

"What did you do?" I seethed at Three.

She bent over, as if she was going to talk to a small child. "I turned him back into what he really is: a broken, useless boy."

Luciana went for Three, who pivoted to avoid her punch then grabbed the Columbian girl on the back of head and pushed her away. Luciana couldn't stop herself and her head smashed into the screen surrounding the room.

Three grabbed her by her hair then lifted her up. Luciana's face was very bruised and she cried out as Three tugged on her braided hair.

"In case it isn't obvious, I have the same abilities as One. Do you think you could fight him?" she said.

The remains of one of her blades then snapped out of her arm again.

She held it to Luciana's throat.

"Do I need to demonstrate how dangerous I can be?" she shouted.

I looked around the room. The others didn't know what to do. Everything that had happened in the last few minutes had caused us all to panic. It was so much too process. Dr. Ghost's plan all along, the VP, One's mutiny, and now his change?

We backed off not wanting to risk Luciana's life.

"Good," Three said and she threw Luciana to the ground. Moana helped her up.

I looked back at One, but he didn't move, didn't respond.

"Dad?" he cried out.

"You," Three said to Illarion. "Get him out of here. I don't care where."

Illarion looked to the rest of us for confirmation.

"I'll help," I said and I ducked down to speak to One again.

"One, can you come with us?" I asked.

One shook his head.

Illarion joined me. I looked at him and he shrugged, then reached out and grabbed One's arm.

"One, please come with us," the Russian boy said, and tried to gently pull One out from under the console.

One tugged his arm back, and wrenched it out of Illarion's grip.

He didn't want to follow.

"What's happened to him?" Illarion said.

"He had a condition called Rhett Syndrome. Before the Nanite injections, he had the mind of a child. I think she's turned them all off."

"That's right. I did. Now, hurry up," Three said.

I didn't want to drag One out of there, even though he had become who he was before, he still had a super strong body.

"One... er, Joshua," I began and Joshua stopped rocking and turned his head a little towards me. "Do you want to see Nemo?" I tried, hoping that as a child he liked fish.

"Nemo?" Joshua asked and he turned towards me.

It was heartbreaking to see the man I had known for the past few years, who had got us out of so many scrapes, to be speaking like this.

"Yeah, I want to see the fish." Joshua stared off into the distance for a minute.

"Then we could go play some games in the anti-gravity room?" Illarion suggested.

Joshua looked at us with big watery eyes.

"Come on. It will be fun," I said and gestured for him to follow.

He unexpectedly grabbed my hand and I led him out from under the console.

"This way... um... Joshua," Illarion said, and we both ushered him from the room.

"Now that that's dealt with, everyone else, land this ship. You're not going anywhere else," Three reiterated.

I held in my rage as I took One down the corridor heading to the observation room.

"Maiara, what are we going to do?" Illarion asked.

I didn't answer immediately. What we needed was One... That then gave me an idea. "We need to get Two out of her pod. She'll know what to do."

He nodded, "How do we access her room?"

"One knows," I said.

Illarion looked at the docile Joshua who was now holding both our hands, like he was a child and we his parents.

"Erm, Joshua, how do we rouse Two from her sleeping?" I asked.

"Two. Two is here somewhere. I remember her..." he trailed off as his face scrunched up.

"What's the matter?"

"Can't remember her. Can't think. It hurts," One said.

We made it to the observation room and as soon as we entered Joshua's face lit up. "Nemo," he said and he ran for the tank, pulling me and Illarion off our feet as he ran.

When we got close, he let us go and we fell to the ground as he pressed his face against Nemo's tank. He watched the goldfish swim around with childlike wonder on his face.

I bent down next to him and asked. "Joshua, this is important. How do we open Two's room? We need to speak to her."

Joshua frowned. "I don't know. The other me knew. The me my dad gave to me."

"Joshua we need to…"

I stopped when the whole ship rocked suddenly. Out of the corner of my eye, red and orange light danced on the horizon.

I went to the window and looked out. At the edge of the ship, flames were pouring off the flanks of the Ark.

"We've entered the atmosphere," Illarion said.

From here, we couldn't make out where we were heading, but the curve of this planet rose up as the ship descended towards the planet.

We watched as the flames ceased. I think I heard multiple sonic booms as the ship broke through the upper atmosphere.

The curve of the planet disappeared, and the Ark assumed a different angle towards the planet. It was now dropping straight down.

"Illarion, stay with One. I need to see this."

I ran back to the control centre.

Three glanced in my direction as I entered then looked away.

She was staring up at the dome. It was showing the engine firing into a hole in the world where the other ships were similarly parked.

The engines were spewing energy into the hole.

"Won't that destroy the planet?" I asked, astonished by the feat of engineering on display.

"The holes capture the released energy, dissipating it away across the planet. As long as too many ships don't do it at the same time, this planet won't explode like Earth," Three said.

For a moment, I couldn't take my eyes off the dome.

The base of the Ark and numerous thrusters around its flanks were positioning the ship directly over its landing site. The hole was like a mole mound. The edges were raised above the sea. It seemed to go down forever. Around were small, white sandy islands.

The ship settled down in the base with a giant thud.

"Wait, what about the Ammon?"

"We'll deal with them later," Three said.

I heard scraping as something hit the Ark, probably from both sides.

"Erm, Maiara, the engines are powering up," Luciana reported to me.

"You tell me first!" Three said.

"What's causing it?" I asked. "Did we damage the engines?"

"No, I think we're being recharged," Oda said. "Several huge bridges just connected with the Ark's sides. We're also getting an information dump. These aliens are copying our databanks and updating ours with new info, like star charts, system upgrades cosmological information."

"Search for earth like planets," I said.

"That's enough, all of you," Three started and pointed at me. "You open the landing bay. We have guests arriving," and she pointed at the screen.

When I looked where she was pointing, I saw a ship. It was hovering towards the Ark up to our level.

"Let's go greet our saviour," Three said.

•

Three had a bunch of us go with her to the landing bay.

The bay was wide open when we got there, and the ship was just landing.

For a moment, I forgot about the ship as wind hit my face for the first time in nearly two years. It was cold and smelled salty. I also heard the distant rolling of waves, and even a bird squawk. Well, at least I assumed it was bird.

I closed my eyes to feel the wind on my face.

"Guys, wind," Sanna said, as she open her arms to let her clothing billow around her.

"I never realised how still the air is on this ship until now," Koyla said.

We were all snapped back to reality when the ship touched down. It was not like any human vessel we had seen before. It was like a smaller, squatter, version of the Ark surrounded by wings.

As soon as it landed, a ramp lowered itself down and stepping out of it came humans.

The VP was out first. He was dressed in a suit, ironed to perfection, with a crisp red tie. Following him came several others. One man wore jeans and t-shirt, with a baseball cap sporting the logo of one of Earth's major online retailers, I forget which one. A women exited, and she wore a small tiara and jewels. She looked like a princess, but not the nice sweet kind of princess. A second man followed wearing a Thawb, I turned to Sanna. She gasped when she saw the man.

"Who is that, Sanna?" I asked.

"I don't know who exactly, but he's from the house of Saud."

Following these people were a bunch of other humans, all wearing designer gear and expensive jewels or watches.

One of them—a tech billionaire, I think—got out a phone and started taking pictures of the docking bay.

The group moved with the VP, who walked up to Three to embrace her.

"Welcome, daughter. So glad to see you after so long,"

After releasing her he turned his attention to us and strolled over.

"Welcome to the Larceny homeworld. Together we will ensure Humanity's legacy in this galaxy. I'm sure you're all keen to get started," the VP said.

Before I could answer he wandered off out of the bay and into the corridors.

"Let's take a good look around," he said. "Plus, we need to go to the cargo bay."

I jogged a little to catch up to him and said, "Erm, Mr. Vice President, my name is Maiara Jones. I was chosen to represent the USA on the Ark."

"Ah yes, Maiara. Of course. I believe we met once at the White House?"

"No, sir. At the launch of the Ark into space," I replied.

"Oh, right. Sorry. I met so many people while trying to keep everyone together."

"Why are you here?" I asked.

"I wanted to meet the crew of the Ark and be the first friendly face you see on this world. The Larceny are very alien, and since you haven't met one yet I thought..."

"Actually, we have met an alien," Maiara said. "It killed one of our crew."

The VP cleared his throat, "As I was saying, meeting the Larceny for the first time can be a surprise. This way me and my friends can ease this transition."

I turned back to the group of humans following us as we strode deeper into the bowels of the Ark. The VP was heading straight for the Cargo Bay.

"Who are these people?" I asked.

"The best of the best, Maiara. Titans of industry. Those who started with nothing and rose to prominence on our world. Those best suited to start our race again. They have been looking forward to meeting the crew of the Ark."

"They have?" I said.

"Oh yes. They have so many ideas and plans, and now that your crew is here we can accomplish them."

I went to speak again, but the VP raised his hand. "Hang on, Maiara, I have been waiting for this for a long time."

We had reached the cargo bay currently sealed.

"You there, can we get this open?" he said to Koyla and Sanna.

"The buttons are right there," Koyla said to the VP.

The VP frowned, sighed, then went to the controls. The cargo bay door turned and opened. There was a slight rush of air and then lights came on automatically.

The VP opened his hands wide. "Here we are," he said as he crossed the threshold, and went immediately to the crates at the entrance that held all the artefacts from our homeworld.

He opened the first he came to, belonging to Abubakar from Egypt. He lifted the lid off and pulled out the mask of Tutankhamun. "This will do nicely. Have a look everyone." He gestured of the other well-to-do people to start inspecting crates.

I watched as the VP's friends inspected other crates, including mine. A former film star rummaged in my crate and pulled out the bow inside. That's when I stepped forward.

"Don't touch that. It's delicate," I said to him.

He raised the bow up. "Don't worry, girl. I'm here to take very good care of it. We're going to put all this in a museum, you know—put it on display."

The VP went around admiring the artefacts. Me, Sanna, and Koyla then stepped back in alarm. His arm sort of broke apart... into several tendrils.

"What is that?" Koyla said pointing at the arm.

"Don't worry. These are cybernetics. A gift from the Larceny."

A thin beam of light was projected out from the ends of the tendrils, which scanned the shelves beyond the entrance.

"Ah yes. Here we are. Excellent," the VP said to himself.

"What are you looking for?" Sanna asked.

"Unfortunately, when those the Larceny could save boarded the Destroyer, we couldn't take some of our most important valuables. Most had already been put on the Ark by Dr. Ghost to preserve Humanity's past.

"We will of course be taking some of these things, and have them moved to our quarters on the planet."

"You're just going to take them?" Koyla asked.

The VP looked over his shoulder, "We..." He began gesturing to the humans around them. "...paid to get them here, son. It was taxes from the wealth we created that made sure the Ark could be completed on time for you. Besides, you don't need these things now."

The man wearing the baseball cap went up to the VP. "May I have the PC equipment and the motor vehicles. I used to have this wonderful collection on Earth of vintage motorcycles and cars."

"We can keep some for our own use, however, several of the Larceny Greatlords have requested their own. Greatlord Vendak would personally like some of these motor vehicles."

The VP then turned to me and the others.

"He was the Greatlord whose personal Destroyer landed on Earth. Turns out he took a fancy to some of Earth's vehicles. The Larceny never built such things and he finds them fascinating."

The VP turned back to the other man, "Take the electric cars. Vendak will get the gas-powered ones. I suspect he'll put them on his ship."

"Thank you," the man in the baseball cap said. "Those cars are an engineering marvel that I created for my company."

"Didn't you buy the company off someone else?" I asked.

The man faltered. "Yes. I did with my own money. Then built it up from scratch," he boosted.

"Didn't your father have a ruby mine?" Koyla asked.

"Where are the cars?" the man asked the VP, ignoring us completely.

When the VP told him where, he wandered off.

"From now on children, I suggest that you refrain from speaking about things you aren't sure of," the VP said as his hand reformed into a normal human looking one.

"Mr. Vice President, how did you get here and why did you ally yourself with those who destroyed our planet?" I asked.

The VP put his hands behind his back, then started walking around us. "I don't expect you to understand this, children..."

"We're teenagers," Sanna said.

"—who didn't get a chance to grow up and understand how things work," the VP snapped.

"You see, the Larceny came to our world to destroy, that much I admit. However, after I got in contact with the Greatlord on that Destroyer, things changed. You see, the Larceny have been somewhat lonely for many decades. They are unlike other alien species in the galaxy, but they found kindred spirits in us, humanity. By using hard won business and political skills, I convinced them humanity was worth saving."

"So, why didn't they switch the Destroyer off?" I asked.

"Well, it's a valuable vessel, and they couldn't just leave it on Earth. I understood that. The Larceny needed that vessel. It had to leave Earth and that meant the Earth would be destroyed. But at least the Larceny agreed to take me and my friends...those who truly deserved to survive... with them."

"Why them?" Sanna asked.

The VP crossed his arms and his brow wrinkled.

"Look around you, Sanna. These are the ones who truly made Earth what it is.

"Here, you have the owner of the biggest retailer on Earth, making sure all of humanity got what they wanted when they wanted. Over there, her family ruled for centuries leading their people to greatness. And me... an entrepreneur, inventor, and cunning political animal. We're the perfect ones to ensure humanity's legacy. For the crew of this ship, we will show you a brighter future for our race.

"We'll never want for anything again. We'll always have. I have chosen an ally for humanity that will keep us strong forever. Other alien races out there just don't understand how to progress, but the Larceny do."

"You let billions die on Earth," I said through gritted teeth.

"We couldn't take them with us Maiara. Also would it be better if they were here? Billions of humans still polluting, wasting time on frivolous purchases and pursuits... electing corrupt politicians. They could not be saved. There was no way. At least they are not here mucking it all up. Unlike us, they didn't have a vision for the future."

I had to put my hands behind my back because I felt my fists bunching up.

I almost couldn't believe what I was hearing.

I forced myself to relax, and I calmed myself. All that mattered was getting off this world, and away from these people and the Larceny.

The Arkonauts deserved better than the future the VP had in mind.

8
THE OVERLORD

Three took us out of the cargo bay on the orders of her father. We had to leave the great and the good there, pouring over artefacts, deciding which ones would look right in their Larceny homes. She led us without speaking a word... until we reached the control centre.

"Right, soon we will leave to formally meet the Larceny. You, here in the control centre are responsible for getting this crew to the landing bay. We're taking this ship's shuttle. I'll go grab some of my things and meet you all there."

She turned on her heels and strode out of the control centre.

Oda went to the door and peered out after her.

After a short while, he turned back to me and said, "I think she's far enough away that she can't hear us."

"Maiara, what do we do?" Luciana asked.

I licked my lips, One was incapacitated. Two was hidden away. I needed to think like One, to assess my options.

"We need to get away," I said. "Leave this planet. That's our goal. We can't live here."

"But we don't have the power to get away," Oda said.

"Wait. This ship is being recharged. How long to full capacity?" I asked.

Luciana checked her readouts. "We'll be back to full power in a four or five hours."

"Is full power a lot more power than when we left Earth?" Oda asked.

"I remember being in here on our first day since leaving Earth, the power levels were at 15%, I think," I replied.

"Then we fly away. Even after an hour we would have more than enough power to fire the engines multiple times," Sanna said. "That should get us to another planet."

"We need to stall for three or four hours at least," I said.

"It's not that simple. The Ark has been clamped in place," Luciana said.

"Surely if a ship this size fires its engines, we'll tear loose," Oda speculated.

"Yes, but will we tear the clamps from the planet, or will the clamps tear the hull from the ship?" Sanna said.

"We need to get them to unlock the Ark," Sanna said.

"How do we do that?" Luciana asked.

"We have to play along," Oda said.

"What?" I asked.

"We play along. Pretend we're with them now. Pretend that we want to join the Larceny. Then, when the time is right, we get back aboard, unlock the ship and fly away. If it takes a few days, then all the better. The ship will be fully charged. We could get further away," he explained.

"What do you think, Maiara?" Sanna asked.

"I think it's our only option. Go gather the crew and explain what's happening. Three is not to know."

They nodded.

"I'll check on One. Maybe there is a way to reactivate his nanites. Meet in the docking bay."

They left me standing in the control centre.

I felt a headache forming.

We had landed. We had completed the mission.

We had reached a new homeworld.

But everything had gone wrong.

Everything was a mess.

Now, we were in the hands of the race who destroyed our world, and the humans who had turned traitor and joined them.

I shook my head and went back to the observation deck.

For a second, I paused and waited, hoping that through some miracle Future Callum would do something, would reach back through time like he did before.

There was nothing.

The Arkonauts were alone now.

9
THREATENED

Me and Illarion brought Joshua to the Docking Bay.

Before we went in I paused.

"I don't think this is a good idea," I said. "We can't let them see him like this."

"What else can we do?" Illarion said. "We can't leave him here."

"Maiara, what's happening? Should I be doing something? I remember my dad, my dad asked me to do something?" Joshua said.

"It's okay, Josh. We're just taking a flight. Do you like flying?" I said.

"I do."

"Good," I said.

"Come on, Maiara," Illarion said.

I breathed in and straightened up, and then led Joshua into the docking bay.

Everyone was there, and when they saw One—slightly hunched over, scared and docile—there were gasps and expressions of pity spread across the crowd.

The Arkonauts moved forward.

"Is he ok?" Waris asked.

"Physically fine. He's just had his nanite mind taken away," I said.

Joshua made a whining sound then hid behind Illarion.

"Why are they all looking at me?" Joshua asked.

My heart broke to hear our former leader speak like this. He who had led us through so much.

"It's okay. Don't you recognise them? They are your crew," I said.

"Astronauts?" he said.

"No, Arkonauts... Arkonauts," I emphasized.

Joshua avoided my gaze, staring down at the ground. He truly had regressed back to his childhood.

"Maiara, what are we going to do?" Darma said.

I let go of Joshua, patting his hand. He stood quietly next to Illarion, using the boy to hide from all the attention he was getting.

"Oda, Luciana, check the hallway," I said.

They went and looked and then gave me the thumbs up.

"Here's our plan. We're going with Three. We have no choice. Once we're trusted by these Larceny. We're going to escape. We just need to unlock the Ark from this landing base. Once that's done, we'll fly away with a fully powered ship."

"How are we going to do that?" Darma asked.

I paused. I hadn't thought that far ahead yet.

"We have our stuff on this ship, lots of artefacts and equipment," Moana began. "All we have to do is convince these aliens that we need to get back aboard for these things. Once we're here, we take back control of this ship and fly away."

"How do we figure out how to unlock the ship? Is there a control centre somewhere?" Koyla asked.

"That's what we have to find out," I said. "Listen, we don't have One. We don't have Two. And Three is the enemy. I know you're all scared. I am too. But just like every other problem we faced we're going to overcome it, together."

"Together," Moana repeated.

"Together," said Sanna.

"Together," everyone else said.

"How many people are wearing the hoodies Two gave us?" I asked.

I could see a smattering of hands go up. "These all have communicators in them. We don't know the range, and they're supposed to be gimmicks for this sort of clothing, but we're going to use them to communicate and figure this all out. Don't talk around

Three, or any other human we meet on this planet. They can't be trusted."

People nodded.

"Psst," Oda said from the door.

"Relax everyone. This will be fine. Just do as Three says," I said, louder than I needed to. I also winked at everyone I could see.

I turned around to face the door as Oda and Luciana came back to join the rest of us.

"I can hear something," Oda said.

"Sounds like wheels," Luciana added.

Three strolled into the docking bay, and following her came several robots from the storage bay above us. They rolled in, and circled us and the shuttle parked nearby.

They were all gun drones. Tall tubes on sets of wheels that had arms loaded with weaponry.

Once we were encircled, the guns tracked us all as we moved.

Three stopped in front of us. She smirked at Joshua hiding behind Illarion. "You would have done better against me if Ghost hadn't chosen a useless boy," she said to him, then turned back to us.

"I'm sure a gossip tree has spread around what's happening. Well, here's the official word. Everything you were told about this mission is no longer relevant. The fake story Dr. Ghost told you that you will restart the human race, irrelevant. Ghost's attempt to turn this ship into a missile to deal vengeance against the Larceny, irrelevant.

"You are not here to start farms, build new houses, and maintain whatever legacy you thought you were preserving. You're here to join the rest of humanity that was actually worth saving, and become like them. Hardworking, productive people. There is no way out of this situation. This is the future for humanity. We have found a true friend out amongst the stars."

As soon as she finished her monologue, the VP entered the bay. Some of his friends were carrying artwork from our crates. His friends immediately started heading for their ship walking by the Arkonauts, without a word.

The VP walked up to us and said, "Now, children, get aboard your shuttle. We have a short journey to make. Then you will meet the

Larceny. Please be kind and courteous. They are, after all, giving us a new home."

The gun drones rolled forward a little and the Arkonauts huddled together.

Some heads turned towards me. They were looking for me to lead now. I wasn't sure I was up to it, though. We had a plan, but I wasn't sure we could pull it off.

That's when I had a thought; we needed to seem like we were docile and compliant. We had to make the VP think we were nearly onboard with their plan. If we were to rebel later, it couldn't be by being adversarial. The VP still thought we were children, even though we had grown up a lot since leaving Earth. Maybe we could use that.

I stepped away from the group towards Three.

I turned back briefly and gave the Arkonauts a wink.

"Three, can I ask something? Are we going to get food?"

Three looked at me with a raised eyebrow. "Of course. We want you alive."

"So, we're still going to have rooms right? Can I bring my clothes, my make-up, with me?" I said.

Three smiled. "Yeah, eventually."

"Can I get my computer games?" Koyla said.

The Arkonauts picked up on the idea. And started asking other questions one after the other.

"I want my shoes."

"Can we use our phones again?"

"Is there any social media on this planet?"

"Where do we hang out?"

Three raised her hand, and we went silent.

"There'll be time for these childish pursuits later. We'll give you what you crave if it will keep you quiet. Get onboard."

I turned back to the Arkonauts and they followed me onto the shuttle.

The groundwork had been laid. Now we just had to build upon it and convince these humans that we were on their side, gain some trust.

We got onto the shuttle and the Arkonauts took their places. Joshua was helped into a seat, and strapped in, and he stared out of the window he had been given. I tried to find a seat, but Three grabbed my collar. "Not you. You're going to fly us there."

She pushed me forward, and I went to the bridge of the shuttle. "I know you were given details on how to fly the ship."

I took a seat in the pilot's chair, while Three took another seat, and strapped herself in.

For a moment, I wished this ship had ejector seat. Oh, well.

I powered up the ship while I watched the VP's vessel take off and head away from the Ark without us. Once activated, I flew the shuttle out of the docking bay.

I banked it around the flanks of the Ark, both because Three hadn't given me any directions yet, and also to see the Ark in a way I hadn't seen it before. The giant vessel parked in its landing shaft was a sight to see. I saw the four giant bridges attached to the sides of the Ark, feeding it power. We would have to remove them somehow. I allowed myself a little smile. I was gaining info to use later, and Three didn't know.

The Ammon vessel was impressive to see in this light too. I wished there was a way to get them active. They may have been able to help. Doc, their current leader, could have been useful. However, reactivating the Ammon was not something I knew how to do. Only One would know.

"Enough sightseeing. Fly us in this direction," Three said and she tapped at her console, sending me a flight path.

I steered the ship away from the Ark, and out over an ocean.

Soon, a continent neared, and a heavily built up coastline city became visible.

The coastline was intersected by a large river and island in the centre. Three large towers connected by walkways were the sole structures on the island.

I'm no expert at describing buildings. In many ways, this city looked like an Earth city. I suppose some rules of architecture were universal. There was a large square in the centre, and behind it, a huge building was undergoing construction, surrounded by a dozen smaller towers.

Looming over all of this was a *Destroyer*-class vessel. It was parked out to sea, miles from the city, but its size dominated the horizon.

I wondered if it was the one that had destroyed my world. There was no way to tell, though.

I kept following the flight path, and slowed down as I neared the landing site... a raised platform that overlooked the square.

That was when I saw these Larceny for the first time.

Several of them were gathered at the edge of the dais.

I gasped, and didn't do anything with the ship as I saw them in the flesh. Just like the pictures Three had shown me, they were squids and octopuses using their tentacles as legs to 'stand' upright. They had circuitry in their limbs and 'faces', as well as mechanical body parts.

I then thought back to Three, how she had blades in her arms. She had already been modified by these creatures, probably when her father had met the Larceny on the Destroyer back on Earth.

"Land," Three snapped.

I blinked and put the ship down.

"What now?"

"Follow me," She said.

"Get your seat belts off," she yelled at the crew as she passed through the central aisle.

From the command centre, I opened the ramp and followed Three.

The Arkonauts followed me out and we trailed after Three as she walked across the raised platform.

The Larceny closed in and formed a sort of honour guard for us.

The Arkonauts were fascinated by their appearance. Some waved, but these mollusks didn't wave back. They almost all had three eyes rotating around on their faces.

"These Larceny were not what I was expecting," Moana whispered to me.

"Me neither," I said.

"Whatever you do, don't ask for calamari at their restaurants," Koyla joked, and there was a smattering of laughter. That seemed to calm everybody down a bit. That's what we need to do: stay calm, figure things out, then get off this planet and free humanity from this alien race as soon as possible.

More Larceny came in and lined a pathway, nearly reaching to the front of the building under construction.

Three stopped, and we stopped behind her.

More Larceny marched in. Normal tentacles and mechanical ones slapping at the marble covered square as they strode over in huge numbers.

I expected some sort of fanfare to play out, but instead, what was on display was a conformity in this race. Each Larceny was well spaced and never deviated.

The square was filled with them and they all halted in unison.

When that was done, each alien erupted in a repeating mantra of words I had no idea how to translate.

It sounded like they were summoning something.

After a minute of this chanting, they all stopped in sync. From the building under construction, a procession started walking out.

The octopus who came out first was nearly completely covered in cybernetics. Unlike the other Larceny, its 'head' was a skull with its tentacles beneath it. Large pulsating funnels drew in air. It had two putrid yellow eyes, sunken into the skull.

To its side were two smaller versions of itself, and beside them, humans.

The procession walked together, their eyes locked on us. Never glancing to the side.

The humans had changed. They were now wearing the most extravagant clothing I had ever seen. Nothing about it was casual or, in my opinion, practical. There were layers of robes, dangling jewelry, and fancy shoes you definitely couldn't run in.

These people didn't look like they worked hard for a living.

These humans, a larger number than those who had come to the Ark, looked healthy, and some of them had minor cybernetics. They were from all over the world. Some I recognised. Billionaires, celebrities, former world leaders, and old royalty.

Three was going to fit right in with this crowd.

The procession stopped not far from us, and stepping out came the Vice President. My parents had voted for him. As I looked through the crowd of humans, I didn't see the President. He must have been left to die on Earth.

The Vice President was wearing a different suit—pressed and creased—with a red tie, perfectly symmetrical and tailored.

I didn't understand why he was wearing it. Although it would have been strange to see him without one.

He embraced Three, and she hugged him back warmly.

"Well done, daughter, for bringing our fellow humans to us," he said and held her hands.

"Just so glad to finally be here," she replied, "I need a bath. Babysitting these children for five weeks was... dirtying."

"Five weeks? You were meant to wake up two days..."

"Yes, but they figured out a way to get scans of the planet earlier."

The VP finally looked at us, and he smiled a smile that looked like it should have warmth behind it, but instead there was a cold façade. The one nearly every politician wore.

His daughter stepped back, and he approached us.

"Fellow humans... I know it seems weird for me to call you that, doesn't it? We didn't used to do that did we? We never thought of ourselves as one race because we all looked different, and we all had different cultures. Well, now it means something.

"You... Us... *We* are what's left, and we have a place on this planet with the Larceny.

"I am so glad you have joined us. For now, a new future can begin. Please meet our friends. While they look different, they think so much like us."

The VP stepped aside and held a hand out to the leader of these aliens.

The giant octopus 'stepped forward'.

Me and the Arkonauts stepped back a little.

"No need to be afraid," it said, in a voice like someone squelching in mud.

I held out my hands either side of me, palms open, and the Arkonauts paused.

"I am the Overlord of the Larceny. I speak for all my kind when I welcome you to this world. You will join us, just as these other humans joined us from your world.

"Now that you are here, we will embark on a new path forward. My race has been a lonely one for centuries. We have discovered many other races, and all of them were not worthy of a place by our sides. Species that couldn't help themselves. Races that failed to have vision. People that looked backward not forward. Aliens squandering their resources and wealth on the unworthy.

"Then, we found humanity—a species that understood our struggles. A race of the refined, of those who knew the real path forward... the real path towards success. A race who fought to make their voices heard, and rise to the top. Often sacrificing much, but becoming stronger because of it.

"Lesser races did not understand this, for they have never struggled because they lacked what you have. The drive to make something of yourselves, rather than be content with paltry earnings and creations." The Overlord opened its tentacles outwards. "We embrace you, and you will help us ensure our survival in this hostile galaxy, and hostile universe."

There was silence when the alien finished.

I looked at the others, unsure of whether or not to clap.

The Overlord did not seem to expect such a reaction, though, as it dropped its tentacles and stepped back.

The VP turned to us again, his cold eyes appraising us. Could he see that we were unsure? Or that we were planning to run as soon as possible?

He then turned to Three.

"Are they ready for this future?" he asked.

Three looked at us, then shook her head.

The VP sighed like a teacher who had just heard a student give the wrong answer to an easy maths problem.

"Don't worry, crew of the Ark, you will see that our way has always been the best way for humanity—that we have always known what is best—because we built the world for you."

He stepped back, and from the ground shot up several poles glowing red.

Before we could react, a curtain of red light cut around us, connecting each pole, and we were encircled.

Three handed the VP the device she had pointed at Joshua on the Ark. He pressed a button, and the Arkonauts around me grabbed their heads in pain. I winced as something like an electric shock passed through my head.

It lasted only a second.

"You no longer need the ideas of my old shortsighted friend Dr. Ghost. In time, I will give you new ideas—ideas that were repressed by human society, thought dangerous—and you will change for the better. I have so much to teach you. We—" and he gestured to the trust fund billionaires, royalty, and political dynasties in the crowd. "We who started with so little, but built so much. Today, we are just a few humans, but we will repeat our successes tenfold.

"Wait here, children. Soon we will show you."

The VP turned away from us. The Larceny and Overlord marched away, leaving just a few guards.

We were trapped inside this shield awaiting a fate we had no control over.

10
THE WELCOME MAT

"Maiara, what do we do now?" asked Moana.

I paced for a bit along the shield.

They were all looking at me for answers. I had none. I was no longer sure that we could get our plan off the ground. The VP had control over our nanites. Could he give us others? Could we fight back against that?

I moved through the crowd, which parted for me.

I found Joshua on the floor hugging his knees and rocking again.

I kneeled down beside him.

"One, we need you. Can you help us?"

"One? One was my new name, but my name is Joshua," he said.

"Please, One, you have to help us," I said.

Joshua shook his head. "Where is daddy? I want daddy."

"Your daddy wants you to help us. Please, help us," I said.

Joshua shuffled backwards. Then he grabbed his head. "I should help, but I'm not..." and he trailed off and started rubbing his forehead. "Can't think."

"Maiara, we need a new plan. Goodness knows what they are going to do with us," Oda said.

"They're going to inject us with new nanites. He's already turned off the old ones," Koyla said.

"Why don't we just stay," a voice said in the crowd.

Silence fell on the group. There had been so much murmuring I didn't know who had voiced that thought.

"What?" Illarion bellowed over the crowd.

No reply.

"I think..." several Arkonauts said at once. Then they paused as they received stares.

It wasn't just one, lone person.

"Arkonauts, we can't think like that," I said.

"Maybe we have to, Maiara," Moana managed to say.

"Moana?"

"Look, I'm not sure what I'm thinking, but maybe we do have to think further ahead than just a few days. We may be here a while."

"These are the aliens who destroyed our planet."

There was murmuring again in the crowd.

"Maybe it was a mistake. Maybe Three was telling the truth?" said a voice whose identity was lost in the noise.

I covered my hands with my face then ran my fingers through my hair in frustration.

I was confused. I realised that some of the nanites in my mind were not working anymore. Thoughts and feelings borrowed from others that had once given clarity were gone.

Everything I had believed about my place on the Ark was all gone. We had been brought here and the purpose we had for ourselves, for the mission, was no more... and One was not here to do anything, either.

I was starting to think the others were right. There was a pain in my head, and anxiousness in my heart that was beating faster.

I had not felt like this since teleporting onto the Ark. It felt like decades ago now. I was the child I always was, again.

"We can't just give in," I mumbled.

"We're not giving in, Maiara, but what else is there? Why flee on the Ark when they could chase us down," Moana said her eyes filling with tears.

I looked around and saw they were all similarly distraught.

Everything was falling apart.

"Stop. Stop shouting," One said, and he was banging his head.

I bent down again, grabbed his arm, and tried to stop him, but it was like pulling on the arm of a gorilla. One was too strong.

"Joshua, please stop," I said to him, and I sniffed and wiped my eyes of tears.

He stopped and observed me with the face of a young boy, curious about something new.

"You're crying," he said, blinking rapidly, looking left and right quickly.

"One, everything we were brought here for has fallen apart. Of course, I'm crying and I..." the dam broke and I wept into my hands.

I could no longer stay strong, I had to cry. I had to let out the fact that there was nothing we could do. This whole mission had been a failure... and it was always meant to fail.

"I, I," he muttered and tears formed in his own eyes.

"Oh, Joshua. Sorry, sorry," I said.

"No, no you're not supposed to cry," he said.

I wiped my face and tried to compose myself.

"There's no shame in it," I said.

One cocked his head to the side. "You're right, there is no shame, but you should not be crying," he said. "Daddy wanted me to make sure you never cried again. He said no weeping or crying for those days were behind us. I was supposed to help with that."

"Joshua, don't worry. We'll figure this out. We'll look after you," I said.

"No!" he shouted, and he stood up quickly, pushing us back easily with his strength.

"Joshua, what are you doing?"

"I'm, I'm supposed to fix this. I remember daddy wanted me to fix this."

"Joshua, please just sit down," Illarion said.

"Please, Josh," Koyla said.

One marched forward towards the shield.

I didn't know if he understood he couldn't go through it, so I grabbed his arm.

"Don't. It will hurt," I said.

He turned back to me.

"Maiara, this is what I have to do. I may be young, but this is what I'm for... Wait." He dug around in a pocket on his right shoulder. It was a slip of paper, neatly folded. The one he had showed me before. "I, I don't know what will happen next, but I have to try. I have to do what my father sent me to do. Take this."

One passed me the slip of paper and I opened it. The note had a set of calculations on it, but I didn't understand them. Only one sentence was in English. It said *'are they stacked together?'*

"What is it?" I said.

One tapped his head and looked frustrated. "Just, just, erm... I think, I... just something future Callum might need to know," he managed to get out. He turned around, bunched up his legs, and leapt over the security fence.

He landed on the other side, and the guards held up weapons.

"Don't shoot. He needs to talk to the VP," I said.

The guards looked at me.

"Please, don't shoot. He's no harm. He's going to tell the VP and that Overlord that we surrender," I said, blurting out anything I could so they wouldn't shoot him.

I was surprised to see one of the squids shrug. Then they let One go. He walked forward, his chest puffed out and his back straight.

"I'm going to help," he said back to me. "Don't worry. Dad would want me to do this."

We all watch him go, unable to stop him.

"Maiara, what will happen to him?" Moana asked.

"I don't know. I don't know, anymore."

We both hugged each other. I wondered if it was the only source of comfort I would feel again on this strange planet.

Me and the Arkonauts watched One walk into the building and I hoped he would come back.

THE FUTURE

THE BEST OF HUMANITY

I sat alone on the bridge of the *Vengeance*, watching the swirling light inside of the wormhole as we made our way back to Ramothia. I flew the ship side-by-side with the Ark we had stolen.

From a connecting wormhole, a giant squid like organism emerged into ours, and headed right for us.

I reached over and fired a warning shot from the weapons, and it backed off.

The *Vengeance* and Ark vessel exited the wormhole, and space stopped swirling, and I saw the Ramothian star system.

I plotted the course to the planet, which we would reach in an hour with the *Vengeance*'s engines.

I wondered what I should do for the next hour. Ogwambi was in our prison stewing. Maybe I could go talk to him, but what was I going to say to him? It wasn't that long ago that I had stabbed him in the gut. I had tried to kill him. Should I kill him now? That was the goal of this whole thing, to stop the Larceny. Was there even a way back for my friends?

Former friends, I corrected myself.

Ada then strolled onto the bridge and sat down.

She had a scar across her cheek and up above her left eye. Not exactly like mine, but close. She had managed to repair her face after tearing off a bit of her skin during our last encounter with the

Larceny. The edges were rough and black. She had had to melt the pieces back on. Her skin was not real skin, after all.

She caught me staring, and I turned away quickly.

She smiled. "I'm no longer pretty," she commented.

"You look great. No need to worry. After all, we're scar buddies now," I said.

She rolled her eyes at my lame reply. I guess it wasn't a great club to be a part of.

"Wait, are you saying I'm not pretty either?" I said, tracing my own scar.

"Barely noticeable," she said. "Mine won't fade as well."

"I don't think other robots will mind," I said.

She looked at me incredulously.

"You think I'm looking to date other robots?" she asked.

"Well, ones with enough intelligence. I'm not expecting you to date a toaster," I said. "Don't you have feelings? You seem like an independent person."

"I am an independent person. My programming is complete and I am free."

I laid back as comfortably as I could and sighed.

"That's good. Also, you should find another robot like you. Hook up and make robot babies."

"Callum, what are you talking about?"

"You're best the thing humanity has ever made. You'll be the only legacy that matters when we're finally...gone." I gritted my teeth at the thought, of the human race finally ending. "I hope you live forever."

"That's a nice thing to say," she said.

"Do you know what past Callum thought about you? I have his memories... He thought you were the soul of the crew, and that you kept us going in a dark time of his own making."

She stared through the viewscreen, out into the stars.

"I was created. I know that for sure. Fulfilling my purpose was my only joy," she said.

"When this is all over, you'll have a chance to craft your own future," I said.

"I wonder what I'll do?" she said wistfully.

"Anything you want," I said.

"Well, I think he's secure," the Mouth said, waddling into the room holding a tablet. He plonked himself down in a chair which swayed with his weight and creaked.

"Who?" I asked.

"The other human, Ogwambi, I believe, is the sound you use to identify him," the Mouth replied.

"I still don't understand how your species never developed names?" I said to him.

"Taste is a much better way. Everyone tastes different, and unlike your species, there is no repetition."

"Even I, an artificial lifeform, still find it strange that your species identifies each other by taste."

The Mouth shrugged, "Made sense to us."

I swiveled in my seat to face him. "Wait what do I taste like?"

"Mud," he answered, "which makes sense. Your species called their planet Earth after all, like dirt."

"And me?" Ada said.

The Mouth opened his mouth and smacked his lips together. "Metal."

"Makes sense," she replied.

"Antumbra?"

"She would fry my tongue," he said.

I laughed, wondering what that would be like.

"Earlier, you said you thought Ogwambi was secure. What do you mean by that?" Ada asked.

"A lot of his cybernetic implants are crucial to his life continuing, such as it is. I can't turn them all off."

"Nothing that would cause a security breach?" I asked.

"No, I don't think so. However, he is currently communicating with the Larceny."

"That sounds like a hefty security breach," I said. Sitting up, my hand going to my gun.

"Not really. He's in a chamber that I rigged with Ramothian stealth tech, but I've reversed the field. Rather than hiding what's inside, it's hiding what's outside. He can tell the Larceny things, but only what the inside of his prison cell looks like, so it's not very useful. He has a connection... just nothing to report, not unless we let him join strategy meetings. Which is something I don't suggest we do."

"Anything else?" I asked.

"There is a small independent power reading from his body. I can't tell what it is or what it's powering?"

"Is it a concern?" I asked.

"I don't see how. It's too small to be a bomb or a weapon, and I don't think that any device with this small power reading could do anything."

"Maybe it's his watch," Ada said with a smile.

I relaxed and sat back in the chair.

"That's good," I said.

The deck plates then rumbled and I turned to greet Hippo, who was thundering into the control centre. He parked himself in a special chair made just for him and his bulk.

"I've realised something," he said.

"Do tell," the Mouth asked.

"I thought the Larceny kept others from getting through the wormholes to their homeworld?" Hippo began. "How does having our own wormhole generator get us close to their world?"

"They do, but only the wormholes they create. If we create our own then they can't stop them," the Mouth said with a big smile on his massive lips.

I sat up in my chair, "Why didn't we use the wormhole generator on the Ark?" I asked Ada.

She put her head to one side and her eyes buzzed back and forth, "The Ark didn't have the power to use its own wormhole drive," she said.

"Plus, you didn't have coordinates to send the exit aperture to. No way to know where your ship would have ended up," the Mouth said.

"Callum, I'm sure Dr. Ghost, and whoever organised the Ark, knew that it wouldn't work," Ada said.

I nodded, halfheartedly. "Something else is bothering me. The Larceny can open up wormholes anywhere where they know the exit aperture is, why aren't they placing them closer to planets?

"Safety. Yes, they could open a wormhole inside a system, however they need precise coordinates otherwise the exit could be inside a sun or if they are unlucky a black hole. Having their wormhole exits on the edge of solar systems mean that it is very unlikely there will be a space thingy that could come back to bite them on the tentacles."

"Space thingy?" Hippo bellowed with laughter. "Technical term, is that?"

"I'm not sure what the correct term is," the Mouth replied.

"Wait, couldn't Ogwambi tell them the precise coordinates, if he's communicating with them now?" Ada said.

"The stealth tech is locking him out of that data too. The Larceny don't know if he's in space or on a planet."

"So, they don't know where to fling a wormhole exit?" I asked.

"Yes, and they won't just try their luck. For all they know, we've put Ogwambi next to a black hole. They open a wormhole and suddenly their solar system has a front row seat to the biggest nightmare in the galaxy," the Mouth explained. "Hey, maybe we should do just that—link the wormhole generator to a black hole somewhere in the galaxy."

"That would give them a chance to escape their homeworld?" Hippo said. "It's not instant destruction."

"Then... closer," the Mouth suggested.

"Then we run the risk of something going wrong for us," Ada said.

"Let's stick with the plan," I said.

"Use the generator to attack their planet," Ada added.

I then heard a gentle purring, and some static discharges.

"Hello, Lyger and Antumbra. Sit down. We're just trying to decide how best to use our new ship to destroy the Larceny," I said.

"A productive activity," Antumbra said.

She took a seat, as did Lyger.

"Can we use their ship? Do we know how to work it?" Lyger asked inspecting her nails as she sat down, her various trinkets rattling as they jangled about.

"It's simple enough. It's how to use it that's the issue," Antumbra said.

Entering the bridge next came Mantis, the energy playing around his skeletal limbs casting a pleasing orange glow over the bulkheads.

"Mantis, how would you use our new ship to destroy the Larceny?" Ada asked him.

He looked up and tapped his lower chin with a scythe.

Then he made a circle, then a smaller circle next to it. Then he drew another circle and motioned one of his scythes through the smaller circle from one circle to another.

"What's that circle?" I asked pointing at the bigger one.

Mantis mimicked being blinded by a light.

"Light source... A star?" Antumbra asked.

He nodded.

"The smaller circle is a wormhole"

Another nod.

"The other circle was a planet?" Lyger asked.

Another nod.

"I think you want us to open a wormhole near a star. The wormhole would suck star matter through. It would then be blasted out the other end, and I guess we aim that other end at the Larceny homeworld?" I concluded.

One final enthusiastic nod from Mantis.

"I love it. A giant space gun," the Mouth said.

"Can it work?" I asked.

"Doesn't matter. I think the Ramothians will still favour an invasion plan?" Antumbra said.

"Why?"

"Some of their allies want real revenge. They want to fight. They also want to make sure none of the Larceny escape."

"Does that mean we're going to completely wipe them out, like what if we capture a bunch... are we just going to execute them?" Ada asked. "I'm not comfortable with that,"

"You're not?" Antumbra asked.

"Genocide may be in the Larceny's repertoire, but it's not in mine and I don't think it should be ours. I mean, aren't there children on the Larceny homeworld, commoners, people who don't agree with them and their tactics?"

"They don't tell us," Lyger said. "After genociding hundreds of species, maybe trying to find innocent Larceny is a quest without an end."

"I think that even if there were some left that could be considered innocent, the Ramothians would be fine letting them live under supervision, and with less tech, of course," Antumbra said.

"I don't mind if humanity goes with the Larceny," I found myself uttering.

"Your own species?" Hippo asked.

"What's left is clearly the worst of them. The best were killed a long time ago."

"Will you execute them then, Callum?" Ada asked.

I didn't reply because I hadn't thought that far ahead. Plus, I don't think I could even justify it. Deep down, I think I hoped it wouldn't come to that.

She had done it again. The soul of the crew had caught me out. I was not really a killer of my own kind. Maybe I could let the others do it, but that felt cowardly.

The question that remained was if I could bear the knowledge that I had killed my own kind.

When I died, could I face the consequences of that choice?

I sank into my chair, mulling that over, as the *Vengeance* entered orbit of Ramothia.

HISTORY

Lyger landed the *Vengeance* next to a Ramothian security control hub.

I was sitting in the control centre, staring out the window, lost in my thoughts, trying to come up with a strategy to use the Ark vessel we had acquired to get to the Larceny.

As the ship bounced on its landing struts, the jolt brought me back to the world.

"Where did you go?" Lyger asked as she stood up from her chair. She moved with an easy grace with her tail fluttering behind her.

"Just thinking how best to use our new asset," I said, and I looked up into the sky where the Ark now hung.

Lyger bent down and looked out at the ship too.

"At least this one can't communicate with the Larceny on any level. We won't have a repeat of the last time we brought a Larceny ship into orbit of Ramothia."

I smiled and stood up. "Yeah we don't want to make that mistake again. How have you been, Lyger?"

She looked at me with a playful smile. "What do you mean?"

"I've realised that throughout our adventures I've never asked you how you've been. You're alone in the universe as much as any of us."

Her tail moved up and took my hand. Her delicate fur was soft against my skin.

"I'm doing fine, Callum, and I'm not alone. I have you, Mouth, Hippo, Mantis, Antumbra, and Ada. You're all I need right now."

She walked out of the control centre and I followed.

"I should feel alone, being the only one of my kind on this planet, maybe in the whole universe, but, we're all the same—the last of our kind—except for you..."

"Believe me, I am the last of my kind as far as I'm concerned," I interrupted.

"I agree. I was going to say that although you may have other members of your species still alive, your home is with us now."

"Thanks, Lyger. That means a lot."

"I am good, but I'll feel much better when the Larceny are behind us," she added.

"We all will. I genuinely feel as if we have a chance now. Once we learn how to create wormholes, then we can attack them."

We both left the ship, along with the other Ramothians, and the refugee aliens who were fighting beside us.

"That will please a lot of people here. The Larceny's presence has hung over this galaxy like a knife over a throat. It also seems that when the humans joined them decades ago, they stepped up their torment of the other species."

I ground my teeth at what she was referring to. I had taken it upon myself to learn some history of the galaxy over the last few months, to understand how my species allied with the Larceny—what had happened after I was interred in that pod One put me in. That was where the timelines had diverged.

What I know is this. For centuries, the Larceny have been known to the galaxy. They do not take kindly to other races rising up to one day oppose them. They left races alone that had barely made it into space, but when a species starts to form colonies on other planets in their solar system, a Destroyer or Ark is sent in to strip a planet clean of as much water as possible.

The water is gathered to fuel the energy needs of the Larceny. While water is abundant in the galaxy, without needing to destroy a world, the Larceny decided to kill two birds with one stone. The Ark or Destroyer goes in, takes water the Larceny need, and destroys the world, eliminating a potential rival.

Earth was targeted after the Larceny learned of our Mars missions and colonies.

This is when things changed.

Decades ago, possibly thirty years—it's hard to tell since so many races have been destroyed or barely survived, records are fragmented—the VP and his cronies, and then the Ark, arrived on the Larceny homeworld.

The Larceny had found a race they liked, a race that understood them and their ways and that race was humanity.

Things have been different since then. Races were still destroyed—Antumbra's, Hippo's, the Mouth's, Lyger's, Mantis'—all quickly and cleanly eliminated. Plus, that gorgon-like alien I met in the museum. Wow. That felt like ages ago.

But others were not being destroyed.

Some planets held resources humans and Larceny now craved. Those races were, for lack of a better word, enslaved. Humans, it seemed, had taught the Larceny a new way to eliminate threats. And that was through conquest. New refugees spoke of Larceny governments taking over alongside humans, their races' prosperity and interesting technologies sent back to the Larceny homeworld. The Larceny/Human governments also came with new ideas that they taught the populace, trying to convert them to their way of thinking.

There were also hints that these conquests were now a game. Not all Destroyers destroyed a planet the old-fashioned way. Sometimes other methods were used.

Humanity had joined the Larceny in wreaking havoc on the galaxy, deeming the peaceful races weak.

Ramothia was the only known bastion against this.

Yet, the Larceny held the high ground...for now.

"Soon, the Larceny can finally fall and this will all be over," I said.

"And they'll fall at the hand of their own technology," Lyger replied.

"Yes. By their own," I muttered.

"Callum, I have to know... I still don't understand how you were able to choose us over them," Lyger commented.

"How could I abandon my own kind?" I clarified.

"Yes. I don't think I could do it. How could I choose a course of action that would lead to my race and all it ever built, dreamed, and cared about just die? How did you walk away?"

I sighed. I had long debated this in my own mind. When the time had come to turn on the VP and my fellow humans back on the Overlord's flagship, I didn't debate using philosophy or ideology to make my decision. Ultimately, it came down to something much simpler.

"At the time, all I was thinking was just how evil everyone, but you and the other aliens were. They were talking about doing unspeakable things, of conquest and terror justified by their own survival.

"But in my core, in my heart of hearts, I knew that to be wrong. I was always taught—actually all humans were taught—that doing what is right trumps all other concerns.

"I was supposed to do what's right, and what was right was saving you and the others, not my own kind."

"Do you think the ones who have gone ahead of you will judge you for destroying humanity, for erasing their legacy?"

"Humans don't get to judge ourselves after death, Lyger. Besides, what the humans are trying to build alongside the Larceny, is not much of a legacy," I replied, as we strolled across the landing area to the security building.

I turned my head to watch Ogwambi get led out of the *Vengeance* in chains. Ramothians carried several devices, and placed them around him in a circle. It must have been Mouth's stealth tech.

"Our real legacy will not be this history or disaster or evil. That's our legacy right there," and I nodded over Lyger's shoulder.

Lyger turned back to where I was looking. "Ada?" she asked.

"She is the last thing we made, and she's better than anything else we've built. She'll start her own people, and they will do better than us."

"That's nice, Callum," Lyger said.

"Thank you. It's why I need you to help me with something."

"What's that?"

"Ada needs to be kept out of the fighting. When the time comes, help me convince her to stay on Ramothia. Help me convince her to find her own way. That's what she wanted when she first came to the planet—to go out there find other artificial lifeforms and start again.

She needs to be kept out of danger so she can achieve that. She needs to walk away from me and the rest of mankind. She owes us nothing."

Lyger smiled, "I'll do my best."

"Thank you. She is the only thing from our world worth saving now."

"What about you?" Lyger asked.

"Me?"

"Aren't you worth saving?"

"I don't matter. Soon I'll be the only human left and then that will be that."

WAR COUNCIL

At the Ramothian security centre, Ogwambi was taken deep underground to be secured in a prison in the lower levels.

He scowled at me whenever he had the opportunity. I ignored him. We had nothing to say to one another.

After a brief rest and some food, we all met in a command and control centre. It was a large room with a domed roof, large screen on the wall and a circular table in the middle. The table was surrounded by Ramothian defence officers and members of refugee aliens the Ramothians had sided with.

Me and my alien friends stood off to one side. On the largest screen was a picture of the Ark we had captured.

The Ramothian president Abathlia was present and he stood up from his prominent place at the table to speak.

"Various species, thanks to the mission spearheaded by our newest friends..." And he gestured to us. "...we have captured a vessel of the Larceny equipped with a fully functioning wormhole drive. The ship is disabled in every other way so it will not be a threat to us, and just in case, we have locked a black hole cannon onto it. We are in control."

I saw the aliens relax at this news. The last time a Larceny vessel had been in orbit of Ramothia, it had used its giant engines to nearly obliterate the planet. That wouldn't happen this time.

"Now that we have access to the technology, it's only a matter of time before we understand how the Larceny create these wormholes and we can duplicate it. We will finally be able to attack their homeworld."

A cheer went up in the room. I wanted to join in with the cheer, yet I was reminded that an attack on the Larceny was an attack on humans as well. I didn't think I should cheer, even though I backed such thinking.

I stiffened and stared directly ahead, trying to appear as neutral as possible. Some of the other aliens were giving me glances. They probably wondered what I was thinking. Could they trust me?

I hoped that by showing no emotion they would see that this was no problem for me.

That stung though. Had I really abandoned all hope of redeeming humanity? Then I remembered that Ogwambi had been on his way to destroy another planet.

I realised then and there why I would always be able to aid in their destruction. Humanity was a big let-down. Here on Ramothia, the indigenous race had opened their arms to immigrants and refugees. They had power, but had not sought more, or had any will to dominate.

Humanity had let me down. We had no true glorious past to cling to and certainly no righteous future.

I hated my own species for that.

Yet in the back of my mind there was this sliver of compassion, a tiny bit of hope that wanted them to be more. Otherwise what was I but another member of a failed race?

The president spoke again. "We need to discuss a plan of attack. General."

Another Ramothian stood up and walked to one of the giant screens. "The Larceny homeworld is as well defended as Ramothia. However, the Larceny are complacent, believing themselves unassailable since no other species has developed the faster-than-light technology to get close to their home. Thanks to data gleaned from their smaller, world-ending vessel, we can tell that their defensive installations don't take tactical considerations into mind. They are scattered equally around the planets with small clusters at the major cities and Overlord's Citadel.

"Our strategy must be developed to take this in mind," the general finished.

I stared at the map on the screen. I was not entirely sure of what this all meant. I had memories from soldiers in my mind, but they gave me small scale tactical knowledge, not the ability to fight a planetary war of this scale.

Antumbra raised her hand and the president gestured for her to speak.

"I have to remind you all," she began, "that the Larceny possess my species' time travel technology. We have seen no indication that they know how to use it yet, however we must assume that they will learn. We must stop them before they can get it working."

"We have a technological race on our hands. We must learn how to use the wormhole drive before they learn to use the Timerod. Thankfully, we have the minds of hundreds of species working on the problem. We will win this race," president Abathlia said.

I listened as the discussions moved to other minor considerations and planning. I watched as the computer simulated battles based on intel. I saw projected explosions over the homeworld of the Larceny. I wondered how many humans might die as a result.

I managed to contribute a little. I told the group to focus on the Destroyer class vessels the Larceny had. Each one was a stronghold for a Greatlord, and if any escaped the planet, then who knew what they would do?

I told the assembled aliens that the best strategy was to prevent escape of the Larceny, so they could be isolated and then dealt with.

Some of the aliens were impressed with my ideas, and some seemed appalled. Maybe I sounded too clinical.

"Is this how humans fight each other?" The Mouth asked me after I suggested, that since the Larceny had cybernetic devices, a worldwide EMP device would be enough to hobble them.

"We consider all possibilities," I replied grimly.

I realised that the aliens were not considering genocide here. The goal was to neuter the Larceny. Destroy their Destroyer class ships and fleet, and prevent the building of more. The Larceny were to become trapped on their homeworld.

I found myself dismayed at their approach. I had not seen any evidence of the Larceny being able to find redemption, much like humanity.

The meeting ended on a high note. A Ramothian scuttled in and reported that the wormhole drive had been successfully powered up. All that was required were a few test runs.

There was another cheer, and the meeting broke up.

I stood with my friends.

"It seems like victory is near," Hippo said.

Mantis tapped its pincers and did some gestures, and some more charades.

"We won't be complacent, but it doesn't hurt to have high morale. Very soon, the Larceny will no longer be a shadow over this galaxy," Antumbra said.

"Just think, soon we will be free. We'll no longer have to bow to their wishes. We can build without worrying about collapse or disaster from above," Lyger added.

"No more Larceny. No more humans..." the Mouth started, then closed his giant maw.

There was some awkward standing around and shuffling of feet.

"Don't worry, Mouth. I'm with you in that regard," I said.

"Callum, given what we heard today, humanity won't be destroyed. The Larceny are going to be defanged, but they will live on. Humanity will too," Two said.

I shrugged. "They can stay on the Larceny homeworld then, and reap what they sow." I then chuckled. "The VP and his cronies are about to lose it all."

The aliens and Ada were staring at me. They must have thought me morbid.

"On my world, the VP and his lot were what we call rich. They only made decisions that kept that wealth with them. That's why he joined the Larceny. The Destroyer was going to take everything from them. They couldn't handle that, so they found a way to survive... and with all the opulence and wealth they thought they deserved.

"It's going to be great when we take it all and leave them as paupers on the Larceny homeworld."

PRAYER

After a few more days of planning and more success with the wormhole generator, Ramothia was in a buzz. Hope seemed to be in the air. Aliens had a spring in their step if they had feet, and seemed at ease.

I felt like I was standing at the edge of a cliff over some water. I wanted to jump to taste the thrill of the fall and the splash of water. Yet it was too soon. It was like when my parents promised me a trip to the amusement park. Every day was so hard to bear. My little child brain kept wishing that today was the day, the day of excitement, yet I had to wait.

I felt a stab of guilt when I thought of my parents. In all this time I had not thought of what they would think of me now. Would they approve of my plans and schemes against my own kind?

Then again they had no advice to offer me. No human had ever been in the same situation I was in.

To take my mind off it, I walked into the control room. I found Mouth at the desk, his head bent over.

"Hello, Mouth," I said. "Let me take over watching the prison cells."

There was no response.

I wondered if he had fallen asleep so I walked around to his left to see if he was snoozing.

Instead, he was mumbling and his hands were closed together. He was praying.

I backed off and let him finish. It had been a long time since I had seen this from anyone. I forgot how common an activity it was for a human to do it. I was momentarily taken aback that he had his hands together. I thought that would be a human-only thing.

He stopped then turned to me.

"Sorry, Callum. Just finishing up some prayers. It takes me twice as long because I have to pray for Pebbles too."

"You pray for him?" I asked.

"Yes. I'm praying his prayers too. My species and his learned to coexist on our old homeworld. As the only two survivors, we kept up our people's traditions. With him gone, in the spirit of our world, I feel I have to keep up his as well as mine."

I took a seat at the controls and studied the screens for a moment. Ogwambi was still in his cell, asleep.

"No need to apologise. Who do you pray to?" I asked.

"Same person you do, I imagine. The one beyond the stars."

"I think we have a different god to you," I replied.

"Probably not. In the end, it's the same infinite all-knowing one," he replied. "Maybe you just know them in another way."

"I haven't talked to them in a while," I said. "What do you say to them?"

"I talked about where I am—what I have plans for. For Pebbles, I say that he has gone on to join them. I ask that I may live on to preserve his and my people's place in their great universe."

"Do you think your people are with them now?"

"Oh, yes. They were embraced by them a long time ago."

"Your god welcomes them all?"

"They do. As long as we want to be embraced."

"And you do, I take it?"

"Of course. I have known joy by their hands. I want more."

"Your race was destroyed. How is that joy?"

The Mouth smiled.

"That did not come from them. Besides where else would joy come from?"

Silence reigned for a moment. "Well, I'm here now. Go have a rest, some food. Antumbra reports that the Ramothians have managed to open a small test wormhole. Hopefully it won't be long now," I told him.

"Good. I hate being a jailer," the Mouth replied.

He got down from his chair and ambled out.

I put my feet up on the desk and focused on the prison.

The Mouth stopped at the doorway. "Callum, considering what your people have done and are doing now, what do you think God will do with your kind?"

I turned my head to him slightly, staring off into the distance. Humanity had fallen so far since I had last met them.

"God will judge us for all we have done. That is what he said he would always do. Only his mercy will keep us from his justice."

"That sounds harsh," Mouth replied.

I sighed. "It is also how it should be—for us anyway."

He left the room, and I turned back to the screen.

ADA'S FUTURE

Ogwambi did nothing in his cell and I grew bored.

I was right on the edge of dozing off before Hippo came to tag in.

After thanking him, I wandered the halls of the building, sort of in a daze, unsure of what to do with myself. I wasn't going to be useful until we attacked the Larceny.

I found the cafeteria, and inside was Ada.

She had a range of delicacies in front of her, and she was sampling them all and various combinations.

"What are you doing?" I asked.

"Taste testing," she said, raising a fork filled with food in a sort of greeting gesture. "Want some?"

I sat down opposite her and picked up a fork.

"Why are you taste testing?"

"I had some time on my hands, so I thought I would try and figure out what I liked."

"Odd thing to do with your time," I said.

"Efficient," she replied. "I am a robot. Once I've finished this task, I'll always know what I like and never have to find out again."

I laughed. "That's not how this works, Ada," I said. "Your tastes will change over time. You'll get bored of what you like and move onto other things."

"I don't think I will," she replied, and she looked off to the side as she chewed her recent mouthful, then nodded and smiled.

"Something you like?" I said.

"I think so," she said.

"How come you can taste if you're artificial?" I asked as cautiously as I could.

"My body may be artificial, but it was originally designed to house a human consciousness. It feels and tastes and smells like a human. In the end it's complicated nanite technology. It even disposes of the food, since I don't technically need it."

"You have your own mind. What was it like when you were switched on? It's not like you had to go through childhood."

"I don't remember a time before being switched on. I awoke in front of Dr. Ghost with a fully formed set of experiences. Then over time I made decisions that more fully rounded out my personality."

"But you were programmed?" I asked.

She smiled. "One of the things about programming is the wording. It turns out, as great as my inventor and Dr. Ghost were at programming me, they were still human, and couldn't account for everything.

"I'm free now because I was able to calculate that my mission was complete."

"I know we talked about this before, back when I thought Ogwambi was a friend and I could still save the Arkonauts. I thought you should still help me. Now, though, I realise you don't have to. So, what is your plan now?"

Ada prodded her food and smiled a big smile and she laughed. "Do you know what's great? I don't know, myself. I literally don't know."

"Why is that good?" I asked.

"Because it means I'm truly free of my programming. I can choose. I get to figure it out. And I have time, I'm not going to age..."

"Lucky," I muttered.

"I've got time, time to enjoy things," she said and put some more food in her mouth and made a disgusted face.

I realised this was my moment.

"You're not immortal, Ada," I said.

"What?"

"You can be destroyed remember."

She frowned at me.

"Try to remember that. We're going to go to war. But you have a future now. Maybe you should sit out what comes next?"

"What are you saying?" she asked again.

"You want a future, right? Then embrace it. Stay on Ramothia when the time comes. There is no need to follow me and the others to end this."

"I can't do that," she said.

"You were going to before," I pointed out.

"Don't throw that in my face, Callum. Things are different now. I can't leave you alone.

"I'm not. I'm truly not," I said loudly and forcefully hoping that I sounded genuine. "I'm not trying to get rid of you, Ada. I'm not trying to tell you what to do. It's just you need to survive this."

"Why?" she said.

"It's what I said before—you are the last thing mankind ever made, and you can do so much more than we ever did. You have to survive. Take no risks."

"What if I want to take risks?" she said, grabbing my hand.

"I remember when you were a teenager—scared and lost. Whether you admit it or not, you're still lost... More like alone."

I dropped my fork and sat back.

"I need you to live Ada. You and your legacy is what I'm fighting for now."

"It doesn't have to be. You have to look past me and think deeper about you and the rest of humanity. They will survive this war. They will need you to get better."

"I—I'm not sure I want that."

"I still don't understand how you can write humanity off," she said. "You still have a chance with them... to not be alone."

"You can't understand, Ada. Who do you think I should admire?"

"What?"

"What about humanity can I look back on in pride?" I said.

"Dr. Ghost, your parents, your brother... Heck, even yourself— who died trying to better himself in the end."

"Dr. Ghost failed the Arkonauts, and the others, well, they're dead. What is there about humanity that I can hold onto? Our legacy is death and destruction. You are not that—perhaps the only thing that remains of us that isn't.

"I don't want you to understand this, Ada. I don't want you to know what I know about humanity, to feel what's like to be a part of such a failed species. Please. There is no need for you to continue with me. Go live this new life."

Ada dropped her fork on the plate and it clattered. She sat back.

"I'm invested in this too, Callum. They were my crew. They were my crew for longer than they were yours."

"You've seen what they have become. Do you want to save them?"

She looked away from me. "Maybe I do. Maybe that's what I want to live for now. I'm allowed to change my mind."

I was about to reply when my communicator sounded off. It was Mouth. He was calling me down to the control centre.

"Just think about what I said. Don't forget, I want you to survive. I want you to endure. At least do it for me, the last Arkonaut left."

I got up and walked away before she could respond. She would be left to think about my final plea.

A SMALL INFILTRATION

"Hello, Mouth. What was it you wanted to tell me?" I said briskly to the alien as I wandered into the security room.

"Do you remember that small power source I detected in your friend Ogwambi's body?"

"He's not my friend, and yes," I replied.

"It's no longer emitting power," he said.

"Fascinating, Mouth. I'm going to go to bed," I said.

"No. This is important," he replied.

"Why?" I asked, turning back from the door and rubbing my eyes.

"Before the power readings disappeared, my more extensive scans showed that the power source was actually multiple smaller power sources clustered together."

I froze.

"I don't think it was Larceny tech. Is there any human technology that would create multiple small power readings."

"How many smaller power readings did you get?" I asked.

"Weirdly, thousands."

"Did they shut down?" I asked.

"They must have. I can no longer detect them inside his body."

"Mouth, scan the whole facility for the power readings," I ordered.

"What? Why?"

"Because if I'm right, we might be in trouble."

The Mouth turned back to the computer and started his scan.

"Found the same readings. I can see a few hundred scattered throughout the building. Also, there appears to be similar power signatures coming from you and the cafeteria."

He showed me this on the screen. The schematic of the Ramothian command centre was reduced to a wire frame of the building. Two spots were glowing very strongly—one was me, the other was Ada. Through the building, leading up from the prison cells, was a line of blue dots. Much of the line was barely perceptible. The line was made of one or two dots following a path that went up and across inside the walls of the building.

"What are these, Callum?" the Mouth asked.

"Show me the technical readouts of the building," I said, ignoring his question.

Over the blue line various other lines were overlaid.

"Are those power cables?" I asked, tracing the line of blue dots with my finger.

"Yes, they are. The trail of tiny energy sources follow it exactly. Look, they cluster here right in the power distribution room. Callum, what are these things?"

"They're nanites," I replied. "We need to stop them."

I made for the exit, and it was then that the lights went out.

THE ESCAPE TUNNEL

A second later, a few lights started to faintly glow.

"Emergency power just came on," Mouth said.

"What does the emergency power... power?"

"Lights, internal sensors, fire suppressing systems. You know, emergency things."

"Ogwambi's jail cell?" I asked.

"Don't worry, Callum. The jail cells don't just open their doors when there is the main power cut."

"Ogwambi would know that, so why cut the power?"

"Are you saying these nanites were in his body, and they left and shut off the power?" Mouth said.

"Yes. They must have... but why?"

"Maybe he really did think the cell would open for him," Mouth said.

"No, there's something else... Mouth, would the emergency power systems still provide energy to the stealth tech?"

The Mouth then froze. "No," he finally answered.

"So, Ogwambi is now capable of communicating with the Larceny, fully?" I said.

"He's in a room, and any scanning he can do with the tech in his body won't penetrate the meters of stone and metal around his cell."

"Maybe he can tell them something else—something far more dangerous?" I said.

The computer flashed red next to us. The Mouth's jaw fell open.

"What is it?" I dared to ask.

"A wormhole is opening in the prison complex."

SABOTAGE

My ears popped. All the air in the room was sucked towards the door.

As quickly as it had happened the air went still. It was like something had taken a giant breath.

"Please tell me the cameras are still working?" I said.

"They are." The Mouth knew where I was going with this, and immediately brought up the cameras in the prison complex.

The communal area in front of Ogwambi's cell was no longer empty. A wormhole occupied the far wall, and it had eaten into the walls, carving them apart. The hole hung there without moving or drifting. People had already come through it. Arkonauts. No, former Arkonauts, were exiting the wormhole and spreading out.

Moana went to Ogwambi's cell and shot the door open.

Illarion then looked up at the camera and shot that too.

"Call guards to that area," I said to Mouth.

"On the way. But why are they here? Why send this many people to rescue that human?" he asked.

"They may not just be here to rescue him. This is a Ramothian command facility. There could be anything here that they want. I'm going to get my weapons."

As I ran for the residence areas of the base, alarms started to sound. Ramothians were already heading for the prison complex and my heart calmed down. This building was well-protected. My former friends weren't going to get far.

As I made it to the residences, the other aliens were already up and leaving their rooms.

"Callum, what's going on?" Antumbra asked.

"Get your weapons. The Larceny have opened up a wormhole inside the base. Former Arkonauts are coming through."

"Arkonauts?" Ada said, reaching the residences from the cafeteria.

I dived into my room, for my gun and sword.

"We have no idea what they're here for. They could attack at—" I called out from my room, but I was interrupted by gunfire coming down the corridor, hitting the walls. Someone cried out in pain. Before I grabbed my shield, I swung around and returned fire, using my doorway as cover.

I flicked on my x-ray gun and used it to look through the walls. Several Arkonauts were advancing and firing, so I started firing through the walls.

My gun fired blasts of x-ray energy that went right through the stone. My shots were wild, though, and the Arkonauts backed off as shots came out of seemingly nowhere to assault them.

I switch to a more conventional weapon and went to the door, firing down the corridor at them again.

They continued to back off, heading away from the residences.

"Everyone all right?" I said.

"Lyger is hit," Antumbra called out from one of the rooms.

"Get her to the nearest medical bay. I'm going after them."

I darted down the corridor, my gun up and ready to fire should someone shoot.

They didn't. Instead a grenade was thrown. A small cylinder was hurtled into the air. I did the only thing I could and kicked it back. The beeping device hit the T junction at the end of the hall, struck the wall, and bounced onto the floor.

There were cries of alarm, and the grenade exploded.

My ears rang at the explosion. The blast wave hit me, knocking the air out of my lungs.

I kept going, and at the end of the corridor, Oda was there coughing and spluttering.

I raised my gun. The Japanese boy, now apparently in his late twenties, spat up blood and crawled for a weapon.

I shot it to pieces.

"Nice to see you again, Oda," I said.

"Go to hell, Callum," he replied.

I looked his body up and down. He didn't appear to be severely injured. His right arm and right leg were now mechanical appendages.

A part of me was sad to see him injured, even by my own hand, yet that was brushed aside by the knowledge that he had just tried to kill me.

I shot his mechanical leg off.

"Stay here," I said.

The aliens joined me at the corridor.

Ada came from the corridor leading to the cafeteria.

The Mouth went up to Oda and opened his mouth right in front of his face, showing him his many teeth. "Why are you here, human?" he asked, pushing Oda's head slowly into his maw.

Oda was sweating and breathing hard. He looked at me, and then at Ada. I just smiled and shook my head, offering him no help.

Ada looked concerned, but said nothing.

"Two?" Oda begged.

Ada went to say something.

I raised a hand and stopped her, then shook my head.

She stepped back.

"You ever eaten human before," I said to the Mouth.

"No," he said.

Oda looked at me, anger mixed with dread.

My smile faltered for a moment. I knew this wasn't the way to behave. A part of me was enjoying it, and I was ashamed.

Oda's anger disappeared and I saw real fear. For a moment, I saw the child that I had once known.

"Come on, Oda. Tell us, please, why are you here?" I said.

Oda swallowed then said, "We're here for the Ark. We have to stop you from gaining its tech."

"The Ark class vessel we stole is in space, not on the ground," Antumbra said.

"But the controls for one of the Ramothian defence systems are right here," Oda spat.

HUMANITY'S LEGACY

"Where is the control centre for the black hole cannons?" I asked.

"Two floors up," Ada replied.

"Quickest way there?" Antumbra asked.

"Follow me," Ada said, and she led the way to a flight of steps to ascend the building. I heard fighting and explosions down the corridors.

My heart was hammering on my rib cage. Every sound drew my attention. The Arkonauts were in the building. They were going for weapons that could destroy our advantage over the Larceny. We were close, and I needed to stop them.

Ada burst through a set of double doors, then grabbed one and pulled it back right as blaster fire struck the door.

She held the door like a shield and we ducked behind it.

Antumbra put an arm round the door and fired.

She then leant out further and kept firing, suppressing anything from returning in kind.

"The door to the control room is just down that corridor. You need to get there," Antumbra said. "It has three ways in. I'll keep your friends locked down. Get in there and defend it."

"Let's use this too," I said and held out a grenade.

I set it off and threw it down the corridor, right to the end where other Arkonauts were holed up. There were cries and an explosion.

Me and Ada ran swiftly down the corridor and ducked into the control room.

The control room was empty of the normally important dignitaries. The only occupant was Three, bent over the controls of a console on the far side. From her arm, little wires sprouted, and the control console was going crazy.

Three snapped around, and had a gun in her free hand. She pointed it straight at Ada, who paused.

I separated from Ada and went around the central table.

Three didn't move her aim from Ada to me like I expected, which would have given me a chance to fire.

"Step away from the console, Three," I yelled across the room.

"I can't do that. I have a job to do," Three said. "Why don't you go fight your crew members and leave me alone?"

I let my eyes glance at the console she was plugged into. It had stopped randomly flashing, and was now showing a black hole cannon on the screen.

Three's eyes glance at the console too. "Oh good. I can fire now."

I moved forward, gun pointed right at her head. "You fire that cannon and you're dead."

Three smiled, showing me her perfect teeth.

"If my father was here he would try to convince you to join me. You, too, robot. In fact, do as I say. Shoot Callum Tasker," Three said to Ada.

Ada didn't do anything.

"Do as I say, robot."

Ada smiled and didn't move.

"Long shot, but worth a try," Three muttered, keeping her gun trained on Ada.

"Give it up, Three," I said.

"You see, I don't care for you, Callum. You should have stayed in that museum. A nice little exhibit—a monument to a failed dream."

"Detach yourself from the computer," I said.

I wanted to shoot her, but while her gun was trained on Ada, I couldn't risk that. She would get a shot off. She was fast.

I needed to buy time. Maybe more people in the room might change things. Maybe Three could be reasoned with.

"That's all you are... A dream, Dr. Ghost's dream. That man had the wrong idea about everything. Choosing random kids from around the world trying to represent everyone. Pointless."

"Don't let the Arkonauts hear you say that," Ada said.

"They have been shown how to be productive—how to contribute."

"They were children when you got your hands on them. I knew them before you. They were perfect. They had grown. You stole away a better life for them," Ada spat at her.

"Oh, robot, that simple life you and that One were trying to give them—that's not what humans are about. We're about progress. We're about opportunity at any cost."

I sighed. "I don't care what you say, Three. You've taken part in genocide."

"No one cares about those races, Callum. And it's not genocide. We taught the Larceny to control the races that don't use their resources properly."

"Quiet, Three. None of that matters now. If you destroy that ship we shoot. Your mission is a failure no matter what you do. Give up. There is a still a chance to escape. So is it death, Three, or a chance to live another day?"

"You can't afford to sacrifice this ship," Three said.

"It was so easy to take off you and the Larceny the first time, we'll get another."

Three bit her bottom lip. Her eyes looked me up and down. I saw her pupils dilate. What had she seen? Did I have a weak point?

Her eyes looked at Ada.

"Do you know what, Callum, I bet you were so desperate to betray your own race again. And you, robot were so desperate to save your kids, that you both forgot to take a shield with you."

She fired.

Me and Ada fired too, a microsecond after. The blasts struck a personal force field Three possessed.

The console bleeped, and on the screen I saw the black hole cannon fire.

I gritted my teeth and fired again, striking the shield once more.

Three smiled and fired again at Ada.

I glanced at Ada and saw the two wounds she had—one on her chest the other on her forehead.

THE BEST IS LOST

Ada fell onto her side. Smoke coiled upwards from the holes in her forehead and in her chest.

Three was suddenly assaulted by weapons fire from the door before she could turn on me. Antumbra was running into the room, firing without stopping.

Three ducked out of the room, her shield absorbing our fire.

As she dashed past the console, I saw the picture of the Ark ship we had grabbed disintegrating.

I screamed after Three like a banshee. The girl then fired off the concussive blast from her wrist, and I dived to one side as the beam smashed the table in the middle of the room into pieces.

When I got up, Three was gone.

I wondered why Antumbra wasn't following. She was standing over Ada, her arms slack. I ran over and went down onto my knees next to Ada and lifted her head.

"Ada, we can fix you, don't worry."

Her eyes were shut. She felt strangely heavier than she had before. I could not feel any movement. No buzz of her heart. I lifted her arm and only heard the click of limbs bereft of energy to move them.

"Go after Three," I said to Antumbra.

She snapped out of her shock and went to the doorway, gun first. There was no fire. Nothing.

I hefted Ada onto my lap. "Ada, come on, wake up."

"They're running back to the wormhole," Antumbra said, sprinting back to me. "Is Ada..?"

"She's shutdown. Don't worry. W—we can reactivate her... fix her," I managed to mumble.

"Callum," Antumbra said, but her voice seemed far away.

"Come on, Ada," I said. My voice was breaking, why was it breaking?

"Callum, she's... she's gone." Antumbra said.

"No, she can be fixed," I shot back.

"Her brain is gone. We can fix her body but Ada is gone," Antumbra said.

I cradled Ada in my arms. There was no blood.

"Ada?" I said to her.

"Ada, switch on. Ada?" I called out to her.

"Callum..." Antumbra said.

"She was the best thing we ever made. A new race. One with a fresh start..."

"Callum, they're getting away," Antumbra said with a viciousness in her voice I had never heard before.

I looked up my eyes filled with tears.

She picked up my sword and gun that I had dropped next to Ada.

For a moment I stared into space, my mind racing. Ada was dead. Three was smiling. The others just didn't care.

I gently laid Ada's body to rest on the ground, and took up my weapons.

Then I chased down my former crew.

KILLER OF HIS OWN KIND

I forgot all concerns a person might have for their own safety.

I turned each corridor on my way to the prison without checking.

It was foolish, I know, but I didn't care. An anger had overcome me—an anger that could only be sated with the satisfaction of inflicting pain onto my enemies.

A rage I had not known before clouded my judgement. It could not be quelled. It tasted so bitter, yet fueled a fire in me that matched the Sun.

I darted around a corner into the communal area in front of the prison cells. The wormhole was floating right next to Ogwambi's former cell.

The Arkonauts were gathered at its event horizon, some already passing through.

They all rounded on me as I entered.

"Three!" I called out.

The blonde girl was right by the wormhole. She turned and blew me a kiss, and then stepped through.

Ogwambi was nearest the door.

"Final chance Callum come wit—"

He had to jump back because my sword nearly cut him in two. Illarion and Luciana caught him as he fell back.

He looked at me in shock. A thin sliver of blood ran across his chest.

"You can't kill us, Callum. You couldn't before—" Koyla said.

"Ada was our last hope and you killed her," I shouted.

"Fine, Callum. No more last chances," Ogwambi said.

The remaining Arkonauts repeated this.

"No more last chances," they all said.

I raised my sword and pointed the tip at all of them, just as Antumbra entered the room behind me.

"No more last chances," I agreed.

Illarion came at me first and I nearly caved his face in with a punch.

I had expected them to be faster, better, than the last time we had fought, but they weren't. I was still stronger. I wondered why this was, then I realised that Three, the VP, and the other elites of Earth couldn't have them being stronger than they were. The Arkonauts would be since they had enhancements like mine, rather than just Larceny tech.

Luciana came in wielding an arm that ended in a gun, and she fired at nearly point blank range. I sidestepped and the blast hit Koyla, who went down screaming.

My sword lopped the gun off the end of her arm, and she seethed and stepped back, cradling the stump.

Ogwambi came in with his own blade, and I let it stab the air, and then broke his arm.

I started yelling. My voice was broken and scratchy, barely coherent.

Some backed off, others went through the wormhole escaping me and Antumbra, who was warding off her own group of Arkonauts.

"Let us kill you, Callum. You've already died once and you should stay dead," Koyla cried out clutching his side.

"Yeah, you're a relic. We barely recognise you," Gerlinde taunted.

"It's time to put you down," Ogwambi said as another blade came from his unbroken arm and he lunged again right into my blade.

But this time I had not stabbed him in his fleshy side. This time, I got his heart.

There was a gasp as I drove the sword in, down to the hilt.

Ogwambi coughed once and fell to the ground... dead.

My chest was heaving where I stood. I watched the blood trickle down the sword.

Ogwambi's eyes were still open, filled with tears, yet still lifeless.

I then looked up into the fearful eyes of my former crewmates, my fellow humans.

No, they weren't humans anymore.

I gave into the rage inside me. I cannot describe the unholy joy I felt as I let it take me and control me. The mind blocks everything out. The rage was in control. The voice in my head could not even tell me I was doing wrong because it felt so right.

Ada was dead. This was my vengeance for her.

The Arkonauts were cursing, screaming, baring teeth as they came at me. It only validated the righteous turmoil within my heart.

I shot Koyla again as he tried to shoot me.

I took off Darma's arm, and it sprayed not blood, but sparks of cybernetics.

Most of the Arkonauts went for the wormhole, escaping me and Antumbra.

In the end, Illarion ran for the wormhole, and I threw the sword through him. He stumbled and fell to the ground.

Antumbra had taken others out, but now it was just me.

I stood around at least four dead Arkonauts, killed by my own hand.

I finally stopped.

I looked around at the bodies of former friends. That's when the anger momentarily abated. I looked into dead faces of former crew and former friends.

"Callum?" Antumbra said from behind me.

I turned slowly to her.

"I've crossed a line, Antumbra" I said.

"One that you had to cross," she said. Yet she didn't seem to mean the words.

It was at that moment the Ramothians must have repaired the power because all the lights came on.

"I can't believe I did that," I said as I stared down at Ogwambi.

"You got justice. These people were not your people any more. They wanted you dead. You owed them nothing."

Ramothians came into the room. They were carrying pieces of equipment with them.

"We need to close that wormhole before they throw a bomb in or something," they said.

The equipment they brought in projected beams of energy onto the wormhole's surface, and it started to close.

"I can't go back," I said.

"No, you can't."

"I have no choice now. Before I could still convince myself that maybe there was a way back for them, but now there is no way back. Not for them. Not for me."

"We still have a war to win," Antumbra said. "Callum, I'm sorry about Ada."

I sniffed.

"She was the last good thing my people made, and now she's gone forever.

"Let's mourn her. Then we make a new plan to defeat the humans and the Larceny."

I nodded.

That's when several mechanical tentacles passed through the closing wormhole and wrapped around me, pinning my arms to my sides.

I locked eyes with Antumbra, just as the tentacles pulled me in.

THE VP

Once on the other side of the Wormhole, I was restrained. Cybernetic tentacles bound my wrists and legs.

I was in a staging area where Arkonauts and Larceny troops faced the wormhole behind me.

Moana snarled and moved forward, her blade sweeping up.

"No," Three called out, and Moana paused.

She glared at me and I barred my teeth back at her.

Then she stepped back.

"Our leader wants to talk to him, you'll get your chance for revenge against this traitor," Three said.

The Arkonauts, stepped back slowly.

"Take him to the dais," Three said.

Larceny guards took me away. I was led down dark corridors. My enhanced eyes gave everything a green tinge, like night vision goggles.

My rage was now giving way to fear. I was int eh hands of my enemy once more. I had no friends no way out my weapons had been taken from me.

Soon I had no doubt that I would be executed or torture. I shivered at the thought. I didn't want to die and definitely didn't want to go in pain.

I also didn't want to go, I had unfinished business.

So, I steeled myself. I was not going to go meekly.

The corridor opened out into large space with next to no illumination whatsoever. I could make out a figure in the gloom, but in this low light, there was no chance of picking out details.

The chains on my wrists were shackled to hoops on the floor. The Larceny guards left me, in what I presumed, was the centre of this room.

A few seconds later the lights slammed on.

I grimaced away for them as my eyes frantically tried to compensate. They stung for a second or two, then adapted.

Standing before me was the VP of the former U.S.

He was in his suit—a new one since the last time I had seen him on the Overlord's capital ship, when I had used it to destroy a destroyer.

I didn't say anything. There was nothing to say. He was not my VP. I had looked up to him back on Earth, back when I thought he had worked until the end making sure the Ark project continued. I thought he had died along with Dr. Ghost. Instead of saving himself.

I now realise that that had just been clever propaganda.

The man shook his head at me, then opened his mouth to speak but I spoke first. "Did you wait in this dark room just to surprise me like that? Because if you did, that's lame."

He had to pause and regather himself.

"You could have had everything you ever desired," he finally said.

I said nothing.

"No, really. Anything. I still don't understand why you threw it all away."

I shrugged.

The VP clenched his teeth.

"Tell me why," he commanded.

I shrugged again.

He stepped forward, looming over me. He was a tall, powerfully-built man. He hadn't looked that way on Earth. Enhancements had given him this new appearance, not a personal trainer.

"Tell me," he said again.

I admired my nails.

I was expecting him to punch me, but instead he sighed and started walking around me.

"You're going to die soon. You have no chance now. You did before, and you decided to throw your lot in with these other aliens. I can't figure out why."

I said nothing.

"I worked my entire life. I started out with very little," he started to pontificate.

I thought back to the VP biography. He was the son of an executive for a bio-tech company.

"Struggled all my life to make improvements to the world."

I wanted to point out that the world was destroyed because he let it be destroyed, but I stayed silent.

"I pushed my government to give people more opportunities, to give them the chance to rise as I did. I opened the door to entrepreneurs like myself, gave them breaks no one else would so they could make something of themselves—they just had to work hard. Then I became VP, my stepping stone to being the actual president, where I could finally make my country a great place for all Americans born and raised in my country.

"I built so much, and then the Ark came and the Destroyer arrived, and I thought I would lose everything."

"Then I made contact with Larceny onboard that Destroyer. I taught them all about humanity, and found an ally. A race who appreciates that hard work, suffering, and struggles are what are needed for a race to survive.

"I was so relieved that I was offered a chance to survive. I would not have to lose everything I had worked for."

I wished he would shut up. It all sounded so pathetic.

I couldn't believe I was having to listen to the desperate words of someone I hoped humanity had left behind forever. The kind of person who never saw the truth of their fabulous opportunities and status. The VP was like the stone on top of a pyramid thinking he was the best part, the only part worth seeing. Forgetting that beneath him was a foundation of thousands more stones, carrying more weight on their shoulders than he had ever imagined. Or maybe was too frightened to.

I didn't say anything.

"You don't understand, Callum. You got here by genetics you hadn't earned. You got to survive even though you and your family hadn't made and contributed the way I had. Yet you were about to be given a position of authority over the galaxy.

"You see, I taught the Larceny that destroying races was not always necessary. You only have to prove yourself better than these lesser races and they'll fall in line. America was doing that for the world, stepping in when necessary to make sure resources were used properly... Yet you cast that all that aside."

As he finished walking around me, he put his face next to mine, and I looked up at him.

"Why did you throw it away, how could you?"

I still didn't answer.

"I couldn't do that. How could you?"

I pulled my chains tight and straightened up. He backed away a little.

"What is truly valuable?" I asked, relaxing, and then I looked down at the ground.

The VP's hand clenched. I waited for a punch or a stab, but it never came.

"You're afraid. You've been afraid your whole life. Scared of having less, scared not having everything. So scared that you never knew the value of what you did have."

I clammed up after those words. There was nothing else to say. I didn't believe for a moment that he would understand what I was talking about.

The VP relaxed, rotated his head, and played with his collar.

"You will be executed soon, and good riddance. Humanity doesn't need someone like you. You'll just hold us back. And you don't have anything of value to offer."

He walked past me and I heard a door slam.

Then the lights went out.

I was left to dwell on my impending death in dark and silence.

PARADED

I had no idea how long I waited there. The door opened again and I heard footsteps all around. My eyes adjusted, and I saw indistinct shapes moving and positioning around me. Even with my enhanced eyes, I could not make out details.

When the lights came back on, I was surrounded by humans. The first circle was populated by people in fine human clothes, suits and gowns. They were a mixture of people from across my former homeworld. A few of them I recognised. I saw the former CEO of a large tech company, another who owned a packaging and delivery company. Some were prominent government officials. Some were Royalty.

They stared at me with contempt. Their eyes were narrow and they scowled.

Behind them were rings of former Arkonauts. Gerlinde, Sanna... I recognised other faces despite the cybernetics all of them had. Oda was there, his scalp now metal. Darma had made it back through. Her hair was now fibre optic wire, her distinct hairstyle glowing and more pronounced.

The floor then resounded with the footsteps of something large. Something with many legs.

I looked over my shoulder, and the Overlord of the Larceny walked into the room accompanied by the VP and his daughter.

I looked away from them, keeping my gaze at the floor.

The Overlord stood at my left and the VP at my right.

The Overlord opened its mouth to speak.

"Could you loosen these chains? They hurt something awful," I asked it, this ruler of a whole species.

I saw the jaws clench of all the humans present.

The Overlord ignored me and gestured with a mechanical tentacle.

A line of daylight appeared. The walls and ceiling retracted, exposing the room to the outside. The room turned into a platform, rising up above a large square in the middle of a Larceny city.

I looked over my shoulder.

The VP's daughter—Three—smiled at me. I ignored her, looking past at the building behind me. It was a wide, tall structure surrounded by a dozen or so smaller towers.

From the plateau, a wide road cut through the city. Streaming down it were Larceny, all coming forward to fill up the area just in front of the platform. Beyond that was the skyline, and a Destroyer-class vessel, overlooking the whole city.

I had to admit it was impressive.

I was not going to say that though. Instead, I said, "You guys are such dorks. You're putting me on display. You all waited in the dark..."

"Silence, Callum. Unless you want to lose your eyes," the VP hissed.

I decided to shut up. If I was to escape I would probably need those. I also had no doubt the VP would do it.

I would have to temper my comments and be smarter.

The Larceny were gathering before the platform, hundreds of thousands of them.

When they were settled into a big crowd, the Overlord stepped forward to speak. His voice was amplified over the whole plateau.

"Fellow Larceny, before us stand our human allies, but one has betrayed his kind and their dedication to us.

"He stands apart from those we call friends. He is by their own words a traitor!"

"Traitor," the great and good, and the Arkonauts around me echoed.

I straightened my back and held my head high despite the chains trying to hold me down.

I wasn't the traitor here.

"They stand before you now to show their disdain and rejection of the one who killed Larceny—who turned his back on his own kind," the Overlord said.

He gestured for the VP to walk forward.

The VP joined the Overlord at the front of the platform.

"Let this small-minded human stand here for all to see. Come and see, come and mock him for his stupidity and failures. He carries no legacy for mankind. He is alone is his betrayal. Care for him not. Look down on him. He does not stand with us."

The VP then strode towards me. He raised a hand and backhanded me across the face.

I heard my jaw bone break. His hand must had been cybernetic because it felt like he had been hit with a knight's gauntlet.

I screamed, and blood dripped from my mouth onto the ground.

I spat out two teeth from the back of my jaw.

The VP laughed.

The humans present then turned their backs to me, and walked off the platform mingling with the Larceny.

I was left there, my jaw almost shattered, chained down.

The Larceny then started to file past.

I was on display.

I was here to be seen...

To cleanse the humans allied with the Larceny of the taint I represented.

I groaned in pain as the Larceny moved past me to jeer at the one human who would not stand with his own kind.

THE RESCUE

I hated them all.

Every Larceny that passed by, I had a deep loathing for.

I wanted to snap my chains and start fighting them, despite how fruitless that would be.

They filed past looking at me through biological and mechanical eyes. These Larceny were not like the Overlord or Greatlords. They didn't have very expressive features. But I could still detect their hatred for me. I had killed some of their people.

I was also surprised by their collective hatred.

They seemed to value their own people lives, even though they had probably never met the Larceny I had killed.

They took those deaths personally, regardless.

I was also surprised that, when they passed, the other humans gathered nearby were treated with respect.

In my experience, humans only collectively hated other human groups, and even then for the basest of reasons. Like how people will collectively rage against the death of a soldier, until that soldier wasn't the right type of soldier, or came from a different background.

I tried to remain dignified, with my back straight, ignoring the pain in my jaw as the bone reknitted itself quicker than it normally should.

However, I started to slump. Even my body couldn't handle trying to remain dignified. Also, I started to care less what these people thought of me.

The line of Larceny was thinning after five hours of this.

I wondered if I would be killed at the end, after this procession had ended. I tried to pass the time thinking of ways to escape. I wanted to try and gnaw through chains, using my acidic saliva upgrade. Then, I had the thought of gnawing off my hands, which I decided against because then how was I going to escape without hands?

Plus, escape was impossible. I was surrounded.

I held out hope that somehow Antumbra and the others would come out of nowhere to save me. But they had no way to reach the Larceny homeworld.

So, I kneeled there, resigned to a hopefully quick execution.

Maybe they would kill me and my new enhanced biology would keep me alive, then, when they took my body to be cremated, I would escape.

Seemed unlikely.

The last of the Larceny passed by. Behind them came Sanna, Moana, Gerlinde and a few others.

They had returned to the platform and stood in a loose semicircle around me.

"Are you my executioners?" I asked.

They didn't reply.

"Come on. One more conversation for old time's sake, Before the last human dies," I said.

"You're not the last human," Gerlinde said.

"Yes I am. I'm the last one to hope that we can be different... better."

"You think you're special?" Sanna asked, her eyebrow arching over her red lensed eye.

"I am, but not of my own making. My strength, my speed, my soul—all gifts and I've embraced them, while you've swatted what we had been given away, and thrown your lot in with these thieves."

"The Larceny will keep us safe," Gerlinde said.

I looked away from them. "I know. I know you'll be safe. I know that this new race you've become will endure. Shame you cast aside everything you believed in, and what humanity stood for."

Oda scoffed. "What humanity stood for? Callum, humanity has always been this way. We are a species driven to survive, just like the Larceny. The kind of humanity you speak of never existed."

"But it could have. We only had to accept the opportunity given to us." I rose to stand planting a foot down, the chains were strong and didn't budge, but where they were attached to the platform I stood on, the metal bent and buckled.

They all stepped back as I made it to my feet.

"I don't recognise any of you anymore. You've turned your back on what it means to be human."

"Fairy tales, Callum. Made up stories. The history of humanity is survival and we're continuing that. We're more human than you," Moana said.

"Just kill me. Send me onto my family," I spat.

"This life is all that matters, Callum, and we'll live in it forever," Moana replied. "Soon you'll go onto oblivion, and our relationship with the Larceny will be secure. They are just like us."

With that, they all turned away to join the crowd of Arkonauts and other traitorous humans at the edge of the platform.

One final group of Larceny approached me.

With the extra give in my chains, I was able to turn away from them. I took in the city around me.

The main Citadel of the Larceny Overlord was before me. A wide, incredibly tall skyscraper. Beyond, at the end of a huge bridge leading from the Citadel, sat the Overlord's large flagship.

I had to admit, it was a spectacularly constructed city. But I wished I could destroy it all.

"Excuse me," said a slimy Larceny voice from behind me.

I ignored the voice. What did I care that they wanted to see my face?

The creeping realisation that I would soon die came over me. I wondered how they would do it... Laser blast to the chest or head? Maybe I would be tortured first?

That's when I started to think about escaping again. Yeah, I would probably be stuck on this planet, however, I could cause the Larceny a lot of pain. Maybe I could grab one of their Destroyer class vessels again.

"Excuse me," the Larceny behind me said politely.

"What? What is it?" I said over my shoulder.

"Can you swim?" it asked.

I paused, then slowly turned to face this alien.

Behind it were two other Larceny, their mechanical and biological eyes staring at me, but not with cruelty. Having seen thousands of Larceny look at me with cruelty in their eyes for the past few hours, I knew what it looked like.

Were these my executioners? Was I going to be drowned?

"I can swim. Yes. Why?"

"How long can you hold your breath?" it asked.

"Why do you care?"

"Please."

"I don't know… er… Ten minutes now. Used to be one, max."

The Larceny nodded.

One of the Larceny then crouched down. Or it looked like a crouch. The creature was an octopus. I'm not sure how they crouch.

At the end of four of its tentacles, lasers suddenly shot out into the ground.

The Larceny beyond the platform all turned towards the commotion.

The Larceny in front of me then cut through my chains freeing me in an instant.

"What?" I began.

The crouched Larceny then spun around, and the lasers it had sliced a hole in the ground.

The Arkonauts, and their alien friends, started running up the platform.

The third of the Larceny before me ripped up the circular disc his friend had just created in the floor.

I was then pulled down into the hole.

Beneath the platform was a tube. Water was flowing down, out, and away from the platform.

"Wait… What is this?" I cried out.

"A sewage pipe," the Larceny said. I was pushed down into the tube and the flow took me.

The tube was swirling with water, and I took a quick breath as the surge forced me along the tube. I had no clue what was happening as I shot down the tube, in the swirling, slightly green water.

I had no choice. I held my breath as the Larceny piled in behind me and pushed me along the water.

I couldn't hear how the Arkonauts were reacting to this escape.

Clearly, it wasn't part of the execution.

There was a small explosion in the distance.

It vibrated down the sewage pipe as the current swept me away.

SECOND HOME

I was travelling underwater with a breathing device on my face.

There was a desire to escape, but I kind of suppressed it to see where this was going. I had been freed from execution by some Larceny. That was odd. I had been carried from the sewage pipe and into the sea, and now I was being taken across their ocean to who knows where...

I should be struggling, but I had left it too late. If I killed these Larceny and got free, I would be in the middle of their ocean. I probably couldn't swim back to shore. Plus, while I was effectively being dragged through the water I caught glimpse of large sea life. It was not something I wanted to tackle right now.

Eventually through the water a giant shape appeared. It was like a wall in the sea, and it went deep into the darkness beneath me.

I wondered if it was a port, a harbour... Had we reached the other side of this ocean?

The Larceny took me up to the surface. When we broke through, they stopped swimming and we bobbed amid the waves.

It was not a port or harbour.

I wiped my eyes and stared up at a ship I had not seen for an age. The Ark.

THE RESTITUTION

It was not the Ark I knew.

On top of the ship's upper pyramid were the remains of another pyramid that had sort of capped the original. This was the Ammon ship I had been told about by Ogwambi back on Ramothia. However, it was shattered and a wreck. Great gouges had been made in the side of the Ark as well, and its hull was rotting away.

Years ago, the Larceny must have landed it, then abandoned the whole thing entirely.

The Larceny who had dragged me through the water, floated me over to where the Ark rose out of the water. Waves gently caressed the upper pyramid. I was taken to a gap in the hull, which looked like the entrance to a tunnel leading upwards within the Ark towards the peak.

The Larceny beached themselves on the Ark's flanks and let me go.

I strode out of the water like I was walking up a beach, stepping onto the hull of the ship. The last time I had done this was when me, Moana, Ogwambi, Gerlinde, Illarion, and Maiara had to walk across the hull to get back inside the Ark...

No, Wait. That wasn't me. That was my past self. That was only a memory. Technically, I had never done this before—stood on the outside of the ship—but in my mind the other Callum, the one whose memories I had inherited stirred. I remembered walking on this hull when he had accidentally forced everyone out of the ship.

The Larceny gestured for me to follow them to the tunnel.

I was soaked, and my shoes squelched as I followed them.

Then I realised something and stopped.

"Hang on. What is going on here? Why did you help me escape?"

One of the Larceny stepped forward on their robotic tentacles. "We saved you because we are not Larceny. We are the Restitution, a movement dedicated to ending our species' dominance of the galaxy."

"You want to bring down your own people?" I asked.

"Yes, we do. Please come with us. We wish to show you something."

"What is it?"

The leader of this Restitution group paused. "I was told to leave it a surprise."

"Are we safe here?" I asked.

"The Larceny will be looking for you, but they will not look here," the alien said.

"How do you know?"

"They don't know we exist," the Restitution leader said, "They won't know where to start looking."

At the entrance to the tunnel was a platform bobbing gently, but not in the water. Instead, it was floating five centimetres in the air.

I was taken to the platform, and as soon as we were all standing on it, it moved up the tunnel.

We rose upward towards the tip of the pyramid.

I was flustered. Soon I was going to see what remained of the home I had known myself, and also through the life of the other Callum whose memories I had. I thought about my room. Was my stuff still there? I thought about the robots. Nemo, was he still alive?

We reached a hanger. In the corner was the spaceship, a front landing strut had caved in, and the nose of the ship was resting on the ground. It looked like a beached whale.

The hanger led to the corridors in the residential area.

The Restitution walked across the threshold of the hanger.

I stopped. I stared down the corridor. Memories in my enhanced mind gave me rich and detailed echoes of this corridor. It led all the way to the command centre. A few hundred feet to the right was the living quarters. I felt drawn there, to clothes which might be familiar, to pictures of my parents and brother. To things I hadn't seen for, well from my perspective, months. But in actual fact it had been decades. I craved the familiar, an instance of home.

I started breathing more deeply. I took a step back. This was so overwhelming. There were a hundred things I wanted to see and experience. To repeat my memories here, and the memories of the Callum who did more than I did after I changed time.

Yet everything on this ship carried a memory of my fellow crewmates and how everything that was good about this place was covered in shame and disgraceful, horrible acts.

"Come on, human," the nearest Restitution said, and it gestured to me with a tentacle

I pushed my feelings of dread and discomfort down and stepped into the home I had once known.

As we walked down the corridor, I saw graffiti.

Ada had spoken of this. The way she had tried to bring the crew together, how they made their mark on the ship that saved humanity... or failed to, really.

The first picture was of a volcano or mountain I recognised, with the northern lights behind it. This was Erikur's painting, something I guessed before I saw his tag next to it. This peak was often used to promote Iceland, Erikur's former home. Something he no longer cared about now that he was with the Larceny.

I saw more. Luciana's picture was of her holding a knife outstretched to the observer of her drawing. She clearly wanted people to remember that life before the Ark had not been rosy.

I then came to mine, or the other Callum's. The red X that Dequan had made to vandalise it was faded. As was the red writing he had put over it to settle the anger between him and the other Callum. It was the oddest feeling in the world to look at this painting knowing a hand just like mine had created it, yet the hand had another mind behind it.

I was taken on, and eventually we came to the Control Centre. The doors hissed open, slowly groaning as the hydraulics inside struggled to perform their duty.

The dome above was cracked and slightly offset. The image of the planet on the screen beneath my feet was weirdly disjointed, like a *Malteser* cracked in two and then badly re-aligned.

Around the room, Restitution stood at the consoles reading data.

"Look, I think it's time you told me why you brought me here." I said.

"We liberated you from the Larceny. Now it's time for you to leave the planet," the Restitution said.

"You're getting me off world? Why are you doing this?"

"We have debts, and we repay them when we can," said one of the Restitution

"You owe no debt to me," I said.

Suddenly the domed screen above me flickered and a face appeared—an old lined face I had not seen for many, many years.

"Hello, Callum," said the face.

"Dr. Ghost?" I gasped.

THE GOOD DOCTOR

Of course, it wasn't Dr. Ghost. He had died years ago. I remembered what this was—an AI based on his thoughts, preserved for One to converse with when he needed guidance.

I looked at the Restitution.

"Why are you showing me this?"

"He wanted to speak to you... to explain the situation."

I turned back to the screen.

"You're just a recording, right?"

"Yes, a remnant of the doctor, drawn from nanite injections that took his key personality and memories—all of them. I suppose I'm more of a copy, really."

"I'm surprised you're still up and running. I'm surprised the Ark is even this intact."

"The Larceny captured the Arkonauts and dumped this unneeded vessel out in this part of their primary ocean. It's been left to rot.."

"Doctor, who are these Restitution? It seems as though they are friendly with you, but you're just a recording."

"A recording of someone they used to know," the doctor said.

I rocked on my feet. These revelations could have only meant one thing.

"These Restitution visited Earth?"

"Yes... On the Destroyer. Let me explain..."

A NEW ALLY

The road my three car convoy was travelling on was incredibly bumpy and pock-marked.

I bounced on the chair at the back of the limo, the papers strewn on my custom desk kept threatening to fall onto the floor, disrupting my filing system.

I didn't complain at the sub-par road. It had only been built ten days before—a quicker route between the launch site of the Ark and the control tower.

The road could only have been built thanks to the fact the Destroyer had sucked up so much water that the coastline had receded already. Unfortunately, the temporary nature of the road and the speed that it had been built, meant it was always fracturing.

A particularly large bump tossed me and my retinue upwards along with my papers, which came crashing down, spreading everywhere.

"Sorry, sir," the driver said from up front.

I groaned as my staff picked up everything. I sat back and looked out the window. The sea was now breaking on a long stretch of sandy beach.

I thought about Joshua, now safely on the Ark, where I had just been. His pod was secured, as well as a backup. Right now it was enhancing his body, and he would be ready for the crew when the time came.

"There you go, sir," a staff member said, placing the paper on the desk.

It was askew, but in the correct order.

"You all are angels," I said. "Thanks for coming with me on this trip."

The staff nodded and returned to their own work.

I closed my eyes, thinking of the hundreds of things left to do.

I chuckled to myself when I realised that this stress was my own doing. I had distributed my nanites to the right people. I had taken charge of this whole project.

Opening my eyes, I looked out at the beach of black sand. Along the edge of Iceland where the Ark was still embedded, the sun was setting, and the sky seemed to be on fire as the light lanced its way through thin clouds.

I looked down the new beach. I wondered if the last time this stretch of land was dry was during the last Ice Age. I marvelled at seeing this. It wouldn't be here for long, of course. The Destroyer was in a static phase for the time being—it wasn't sucking up water—but soon it would resume and this beach would be new land.

As I watched the sun dip below the horizon, I saw three figures emerge from the sea.

I frowned. Were they surfers, wanting to brag about riding the new waves on the new beach?

Then I thought they couldn't be surfers. No one technically lived in Iceland anymore.

The three figures bobbed in the water. As the convoy neared, they started crawling out of the sea and onto the beach.

They appeared to be walking on all fours, which was odd. Then I noticed that the arms and legs writhed about, and there were also lights up and down their limbs.

The convoy was only a few hundred years away now, and the figures ran forward. I saw that their limbs were not arms and legs... but tentacles.

"Driver, speed up. Alert the security. Something is coming at us from the beach," I yelled.

My assistants looked out of the window and screamed when the three figures struck the convoy, each one taking a separate car.

The two four-by-fours that held my security detail were attacked first. The octopus-like creatures slammed into their sides and used their tentacles like carjacks to lift the vehicles off their wheels. The vehicles tumbled over, off the road, and down an embankment, crashing and sending glass everywhere.

My limo driver slammed on the brakes, and the third creature burst through the windscreen headfirst, trailing its tentacles behind it. The snaking limbs unfolded and darted at everyone in the limo, spearing them with blades. I backed up into my chair, heart racing painfully in my chest, as the creature killed the last of my assistants, letting her body drop to the floor.

It turned toward me.

The thing looked like a large octopus that had been cybernetically altered. Some of its tentacles were cables that flexed. Its eyes were lenses, and there appeared to be very little flesh left.

I instantly knew what this thing was. There was only one thing it could be... a creature from the Destroyer. An alien.

The alien loomed over me as best as it could in the cramped limo.

The door then opened and, outside, another stood and beckoned me out.

"Please exit the car, Dr. Ghost," the one inside my limo said calmly, in a digitised voice.

I was frozen, still unable to process what had just happened, and why I was still alive?

"Please," the creature repeated.

I slid along my seat, and out into the cold, Icelandic night.

The three creatures stood over me, various lenses of different sizes scrutinising me.

I looked around and saw carnage. The cars were now wrecks. Bloody corpses lay around, stabbed once in the heart, quickly and efficiently.

I turned to look up into the eyes of the nearest monster who had done this. I glared at him. My old, frail body probably not intimidating it whatsoever.

The creature had no real face I could read. It was obscured by the metal implants. It merely looked down at me, waiting.

"Well then... Kill me," I said.

"We are not here to kill you," one of the aliens replied.

I waved my arms at the dead guards and colleagues around me, "WHY KILL THEM?"

"They were already dead, as you well know. We did not need to talk to them."

I felt like I had been slapped in the face. My mind raced. What were they talking about?

One of them nodded, as if sensing my sudden realisation.

The Ark's computer... I had seen these creatures before. Only me and few others knew this secret. We had discovered who had built the Ark. We knew the name of the species.

Larceny. The mollusk organisms that had sent two means of destruction to our planet.

Three of the Larceny stood before me now.

"I understand," I spat at them. "You're here to stop the Ark. You've come from the Destroyer haven't you... to stop my race from saving a remnant of ourselves? Well then, kill me too."

"As I said, we are not here to kill you," the Larceny continued, in a fairly neutral tone—not at all put out by the venom I laced my words with.

"You sent two ships to my world to destroy us. Why else would you be here?"

"To ask you to help us."

I laughed in their 'faces' at that remark.

"Me help you? Are you insane?"

"We want you to destroy us."

I stepped back, bewildered and confused by their remark.

"What are you talking about?"

"You are correct that we are from the ship you call the Destroyer. But we stand apart from the rest of our species."

"Stand apart?"

"Yes, we... despair... at what our species is doing, how they strip worlds and kill whole species. We wish to see it ended."

"Then do it yourself," I said.

"We cannot. Our group is too small. But you can."

"Me? I can't destroy your ships. How can I stop you? No... This ridiculous," I said and waved them off.

"Please, Dr. Ghost, only you can help us. Only you can stop the genocide."

I paused, their digitised voices actually betrayed some emotion.

"You just killed my fellow humans. You'll get nothing from me."

One of the creatures' tentacles shot up, and from one end a 3D image of a friend was displayed. He was walking forward, arms wide. His hand then came forward and shook the end of a tentacle, leading up to a Larceny with a skull perched on the top of a nest of tentacles.

"Welcome, Mr. Vice President. Thank you for joining the Larceny," the skull with putrid yellow eyes said. "Long have we waited to meet a race like yours."

My eyes widened and my jaw dropped. This had to be fake.

I watched my friend, and people I recognised as the movers and shakers in human society, embrace the aliens who had scoured our world.

"What? What is this?"

"Your Vice President has made alternative survival plans. Our leaders have chosen to save some humans, and he was amongst them. They will board our Destroyer and flee the planet when it dies."

My jaw clenched so tight I almost didn't care that my teeth might shatter under the pressure. My breathing was heavy and I snorted it out through my nostrils. My heart might burst in rage at the betrayal.

I went back to the limo, fished out my phone and started dialing.

Then one of the creatures slapped it away.

"What are you doing?" I asked. "I have to do something."

"You can do nothing," the creature said.

"The hell I can't. I've got to tell the world. I need to stop him so that the plan can happen. He's not getting on that ship with those monsters," I yelled at them.

"Who will believe you?"

I stopped. "I—I will find evidence," I said. "Give me that recording."

"We won't. It will gain you nothing," the creature said.

I glared into the lenses of all three creature standing around me in a loose triangle.

"You've told me this. Why won't you let me do something?

"We need your help to stop the Larceny for good. We represent the Restitution—a sect of our own culture who are deeply ashamed. Our race has become planetary killers and thieves and it must end. The depth of our crimes is deeper than even your small world, and it must end.

"Help us to kill our own kind."

NOT ALONE

I stared into the eyes of the computerised Dr. Ghost. He paused in his story. Was he wondering if I was supposed to figure it out? Where was this revelation going?

What had they asked him to do? Why had he had agreed to it?

"They showed me so much more after that day, until the evidence was overwhelming. I found out the truth with my own investigation. The Vice President and those he selected were joining him on the Destroyer.

"I saw the truth in the Restitution's words. His hard work on the Ark, his speeches, his lies—all to save his own skin and the ones he deemed worthy."

"You didn't stop him?" I asked.

"No. I watched him continue to impress the people with his words of courage and dignity—words soured by the craven lies he hid in his own heart. It was more than I could bear, but bear it I had to so that I could put a new plan in place."

"A new plan? Nothing changed. The Ark took off. We survived in our own way."

"Callum, the Restitution made me see a truth I had not really dared consider. That there was no way for the human race to survive the Destroyer."

"What?"

"When the plan for the Ark was first drafted, I didn't know the wormhole was the Larceny's. The Restitution showed me otherwise. Once I knew that, humanity was always lost."

"I don't understand," I said and my head hurt—a headache was forming behind my eyes.

"Once I knew the wormhole only led back to their homeworld, and it couldn't be used to save the crew, I would only be sending you and your fellow Arkonauts into the arms of our enemy.

"I also couldn't just send the Ark out into space to find a new home. It didn't have the means to do that; not enough power. It might have limped to the Alpha-Centauri system, but there're no planets there to support human life. With the wormhole option gone and the Ark a useless life raft, all was lost for saving a remnant of mankind."

"So, you let the VP go onto the Destroyer? You let him save his worthless behind."

"Indeed. Because me and the Restitution devised a new plan. The VP didn't care about the Ark Project's original goal. He saw it as a way to preserve the things he wanted to have when he joined the Larceny. It became a giant shipment of everything he had grown accustomed to on Earth. Even though he was going onto the Destroyer, he let me prepare the Ark and even placed his daughter on it too—something my original self didn't know. Just to make sure it arrived and dropped off the luxuries of Earth he wanted.

"But what he didn't know was that I gave the Ark a new mission. I turned it into the ultimate sacrifice."

"Sacrifice?" I asked.

"Yes. It would no longer take humans to a new world, a doomed and hopeless endeavour, as it turned out. Instead, the crew would guide the Ark back to the Larceny homeworld, so it could be used as a weapon."

"What?" I shot back, but the answer was already in my head. I knew what it meant.

"The crew of the Ark would go through the wormhole, enter the system of the Larceny and arrive in orbit of their world, just as the VP hoped. Me and Restitution assumed the VP and the Larceny would greet it, which they did. It turns out the VP had plans for the Arkonauts when they arrived, a new class of servants it seemed.

"But what he didn't know was that I had put myself into the computer of the Ark, to take control at the pivotal moment and plunge this ship down onto the Larceny planet."

Next to the doctor's head on the screen a rendering of the expected impact was displayed to me.

"Me and Restitution predicted that the Ark striking a Destroyer class ship on the surface—or even another Ark like vessel—would destroy this whole planet, and the Larceny."

Unconsciously, my fist closed and I started shaking.

"I'm sorry, Callum. I'm sorry for lying to you. The original plan was to save you and the Arkonauts, but when that was no longer possible, there was one option left. Turn the Ark into a bullet and shoot straight into the heart of our enemy.

"You failed," I spat back at him.

"Indeed I did. The plan didn't work. The VP was more prepared than I thought he would be. He and the Larceny stopped the Ark from completing its final mission."

"So, it was all for nothing. You mind-controlled millions to get the Ark off the Earth to save us. You sacrificed people without their knowledge for your grand plan. And it failed. The Arkonauts bonded and became a family and hoped for the future, and yet they didn't know it had been taken from them before they even stepped foot on the Ark!"

Dr. Ghost hung his head.

"Yes. I dare say when the Arkonauts found out it might have been the catalyst for them to embrace the VP as a saviour in the end," he uttered.

"All for nothing. Except for this ship, disposed of, to fall apart in their ocean—a monument to your failure," I shouted at him. The Restitution around the room turned from their computers to look at me.

"And now I am left alone to shoulder the mistakes of my people, and like these aliens, wish my own kind had died on Earth with something close to honour."

I glared at the recording of a dead man, a failure in every way. The recording didn't look up.

"I'm all alone, Dr. Ghost. I turned my back on my people... a species that doesn't deserve to live. You and the VP took the few humans who had been shown how to be righteous, accepted it, and brought them down into the dirt. I'm not like those former

Arkonauts. I'm not like them... I'm the last human who believed in more for our species."

I felt the edge of a panic attack on the horizon. My body and my emotions seemed spent.

I teared up. I had no one to turn to, not for comfort, or kind words.

My chest was tightening and I felt like I was floating in a void of darkness, forever alone.

A tentacle rested on my shoulders.

"You're not alone, human."

"You think you know how I feel?" I said to it through gritted teeth.

The door on the other side of the room hissed as its old hydraulics pulled it apart.

I wiped my teary eyes and let them focus on the blurred figure standing the doorway.

She smiled at me, and memories that were not mine rose from the depths of my mind. They were memories of kisses or hands intertwined, of late night chats and the feel of soft skin.

"Hello, Callum," Maiara said.

PAST LOVE

How to describe this sensation?

Seeing the boy, now a man, that I loved—still loved... someone I had waited for... someone I went to the edge of time for.

I strolled forward gazing at the face that still bore the hallmarks of the person I knew. The scar had faded, but the eyes were as bright as ever. I raised a finger to trace the scar from forehead to cheek across his eye, just to make sure it was the one I knew.

I wanted to kiss him, it had been so long—and how many even get to see their loved ones again? I think I was the only one.

We were equal height. The same bio engineering that had been done to him had been done to me, and given us the same set of abilities.

He stared at me as if I was someone he knew. Yet he wanted to stay away from.

Why was that?

He finally blinked and took a step back.

"It is... so good to see you," I said.

His lips rose in a smile. He visibly relaxed, like a weight had left his shoulders and he stood straighter.

"It is good to see you, too," he said. "I remember you."

"Of course you do. Remember when we were prisoners of the General?" I breathed and steeled myself. That was the last time he had known me, when this Callum had separated from me forever.

"I remember more than that," he said.

I couldn't stop myself and I reached for his cheek. I wanted to pull him towards me.

He stepped back again and shook his head.

"But those memories are not mine," he said.

"What memories?" I asked.

"The ones I have of the other Callum—the one who died—I remember his dates with you. I remember your laugh. I remember his... his death. His longing for you..."

My smiled faded. I wondered how he had got his other self's memories.

"Sorry, Maiara. I'm not your... I'm not him."

I sighed.

"You told me once why you wanted to date me. When was it?"

He stared into my eyes.

"Forget the extra memories you have, the moment you decided to ask me out will be the same."

"I—I saw you stand up to the General, fearfully. But fear held back by courage. I knew I wanted to know you more. You were spectacular then."

"Then you are my Callum. You're the same man."

I stepped forward, eyes darting to his lips.

He looked at mine and leaned forward. That was it. All we both need.

He smiled.

I smiled.

And we kissed.

We embraced each other and kept kissing. I was dimly aware of the Restitution around me watching, probably confused since they didn't have lips. Who knew how they showed passion?

I ignored my alien friends for now was the time to enjoy this moment, feelings I thought I might never experience again.

We broke apart and stared into each other's eyes.

"I'm not alone," we said together.

CALLUM

FUTURE LOVE

The Restitution left us alone for a while as we walked the old corridors of the Ark—once our home, now a decrepit mess.

"How—how are you here? Not that I'm complaining," I asked Maiara.

"Same way you are. There is a pod on this ship that can turn one human into another One. I had the Restitution put me in it over a couple of decades ago... to wait for you."

"Wait for me?"

"Well, yeah. Our timelines have blended together. I knew you were in the future somewhere—the one who changed time with that piece of your t-shirt years ago. I wanted to sleep in the pod until I could meet you again. You're the only one who had escaped the fate of the other Arkonauts."

"You've seen what they become?" I practically spat.

"Yes," she replied, her voice almost breaking. "They suffered so much. It is no surprise."

"They have sunk to the worst depths humanity have ever reached."

"Let's not talk about them."

"Fine," I replied.

We walked in silence, and reached the observation room. The window was gone, and beyond was the sea churning. High winds swept into the room and gave me chills.

The remains of a pedestal sat near the shattered, meter-thick glass.

"What happened to Nemo?"

"It's been decades, Callum. He died, I'm afraid. I burnt him and spread his ashes on the wind before I got in the pod."

"What about the robots you picked up? Where are they?"

"The VP destroyed them... set their extra pieces of our ship adrift into the sun. I couldn't wake Doc up in time to get the Ammon to reactivate. Maybe if I had, those robots could have helped us fight back."

"What about our robots?" I asked.

"Destroyed. The Larceny don't need them."

"So, they just took the Arkonauts off the ship and dumped it here?"

"Yep."

We kept walking. We passed by rooms filled with cultural junk. The cafeteria stank of rotting food. The anti-gravity room was useless.

Maiara took me to her room.

It was cluttered and filled with preserved items from around the ship—Nemo's bowl, Heston's shell, and some artefacts.

"So, you escaped from the VP and Larceny years ago, when the Ark reached this world?"

"The Restitution helped. I hid with them here on the Ark for a while trying to think of a plan. They worked out ways to get me off this planet, although I had no idea what to do. For a few years, I tried to get to other Arkonauts and free them, but the VP had already corrupted them. Then it occurred to me all I had to do was wait, and soon you would wake up."

"Me?"

"One figured it all out. In the old timeline, when the bomb was set to destroy the Ark, he knew he would have grabbed an Arkonaut and sent them into the room with the pod to survive. It was you because you went to him first. But when the portal opened, and out came your message, the timeline changed. In yours, you were still in that pod. He told me you would be waking up soon."

"I did... Months ago."

She nodded. "So, try to understand—there were two timelines…" and she extended a finger on each hand and drew them parallel to each other. "One is yours, and one is the timeline you created." She then brought her fingers together. "Then they combined pretty much as soon as you changed time… when you were on the Destroyer you stole heading for Ramothia. The Restitution didn't wake me. There was no point. I wish they had. I would have left to come and find you much earlier. But now is the right time. I have found you again and I am no longer the last true Arkonaut."

I walked to her bed and sat down. "What now?" I said.

"We're safe here. The Restitution have kept their presence hidden very well. We can get off this planet at last. We can go anywhere we want. I wish we could save the Arkonauts, but we need more time more resources. Thankfully, you've made new friends so that will be easier."

"Save the Arkonauts? There's no point, Maiara. They're gone."

"What do you mean?"

"I'm not going to save the Arkonauts, I'm going to help the Ramothians and every other alien in this universe to destroy them, and end the tyranny of humankind forever."

"No. Wait. We can save them."

"There is no saving them."

"Of course there is!"

"They have done terrible things, and they're not mind controlled. They're doing this themselves. Humanity has fallen, Maiara. We have to take them down."

"I—I can't be a part of that," she said turning her back on me and walked to the door.

"I need your help, Maiara. We can find a way to destroy this planet, these Larceny, and mankind for good. It will just be us afterwards, but it doesn't matter. We can't restart the human race. But we will do one final righteous act of justice, and end our corruption on this universe."

"Who told you it had to be this way?" she said.

"I did. It became clear to me long ago."

"No. There has—"

A Restitution appeared in the doorway.

"Human Maiara, human Callum, please come with us... Something has happened."

The Restitution headed off and we followed. Our argument put on hold, for now.

We followed it to the control centre. Inside, the screen was showing us a live feed from a room somewhere on the planet. The VP and Larceny Overlord were standing amongst an audience of Greatlords. They were all standing around Antumbra's Timerod, which was interfaced with machinery in the middle of the hall.

"What is this?" I asked.

"It's being broadcast galaxy-wide to all known species. It started with the announcement of a test," a Restitution said.

"What test?" I asked.

The aliens and Maiara didn't respond. They just watched.

A portal opened next to the Timerod, just like Antumbra had done for me.

The VP stepped in and the portal closed.

"Where in time did he go?"

Suddenly, the whole universe shifted. It was like the whole of reality flickered or reset. It reminded me of when my dad used to slap his old TV and the picture would go out, then come back on.

The audience in the room shifted positions, turning towards a door where the VP walked back in.

"It worked," he declared and there was a round of applause.

"My Overlord, we can recharge the rod in roughly twenty minutes. Our weapon is a success," a Larceny said to the room, checking the Timerod.

The VP shook tentacles with the Overlord. There was more cheering.

"What have they done?" I asked.

"They used the rod to go back in time. They figured it out!" Maiara said.

"It's worse than that," a Restitution said.

"Why?" Maiara asked.

"They changed something. Not a lot. There's a power plant on the edge of the capital, and now it's generating more power than it should be. The VP must have gone back altered its settings, creating an alternate timeline five minutes long. But when that timeline caught up with ours, both blended together again just like before. The two universes didn't have large enough differences so they combined."

"Okay, so we knew they might figure out how to use the rod. It doesn't matter. They can't go back further than now. Antumbra, the alien who created the device figured that out."

"They might not know that... But it doesn't matter," the Restitution said.

"Why?" Maiara asked.

"They changed the rod. For some reason, it now ensures the new timeline is the one the old one combines into. They can now make changes to the timestream and ensure those changes become the true reality. They may not be able to go back in time that far, but it doesn't matter... They can alter time however they wish."

"Oh, no," Maiara said.

"Wait... what am I missing?"

"It's over. The Restitution has failed," the alien said.

"What?" I asked.

"If they can change time at will. They are undefeatable," the Restitution said. "We could start a chain reaction that destroys this planet, but it no longer matters because all they have to do is go back in time and stop it... And the reality where they stopped it becomes the true reality. The Larceny cannot be stopped now. They have the ultimate weapon."

The image onscreen changed to the Overlord of the Larceny.

"They are broadcasting a galaxy-wide message to all known species remaining alive... everywhere. It contains information on the test just completed," the nearest Restitution said.

"This is a message for all species in communication with the Ramothians. We have just demonstrated that we, the Larceny, now have control over time itself. There is nothing you can do now to bring us harm. Any advantage will be overturned Any victory will be ours.

"I send this message not to strike fear into your hearts, but to give you perspective. We are this galaxy's mightiest species. We alone will now decide the future of this galaxy.

"Soon, I expect your ambassadors to communicate with us, to offer us your words of understanding regarding our new position.

"Your ways—that have not led to the strength and wealth that we have, not accumulated anything of note—they will be done away with. We, and our human allies, will show you the way forward now.

"Do not move against us. Time is not on your side."

Then, the Overlord disappeared.

The Restitution slumped where they were.

"That's it," their leader said. "We lost."

THEIR BIGGEST WEAKNESS

I wandered with Callum down the steps that once led to the cargo bay.

We didn't speak. There was nothing to say.

The Restitution were not taking this news well. I had known their resistance cell for many years, listened to their attempts to destroy their own kind. Despite what their race had done to mine—to the galaxy—I was not angry with them.

Despite all I had seen, I was not angry at all.

My mind had been focused for years on seeing my ally, the only one I could trust, and the thought of us both freeing our friends. Though it seemed ages away, there had always been the hope of getting the Arkonauts to a new home. The ones that were left, anyway.

However, this latest bit of news was unwelcome. There were so many new obstacles in the way. How on earth was I supposed to get around time travel?

I guess I would have to destroy the rod... if that was possible.

Callum was walking ahead of me and he went into the cargo bay first.

He wouldn't find much. The VP and his cronies had stripped it clean of nearly everything they wanted. Artwork, vehicles, jewels, even some food stuffs they wanted to remind them of Earth. Lots of other stuff had gone to the Greatlords and Overlord.

Callum looked around. I wondered what he was thinking about now that he was back here. Was it the time when One had first protected us? Matthieu's death? Or the boring checks we had made on everything in here?

"The VP took vehicles and the artefacts from our countries. And some luxury food that Dr. Ghost had preserved so we could celebrate, and enjoy some delicious food and drink on our new homeworld."

"All for nothing," Callum muttered.

"I'm surprised you aren't freaking out," I told him. "The VP and Larceny might be preparing to use the Timerod to make sure they can recapture you."

"It wouldn't do them any good," he smiled. "The Timerod can't open a portal to a time before the last time it opened a portal. By running that test, they can't go back in time before that, and the Restitution had already helped me escape. I'm in the clear."

"I guess they will figure that out themselves when they try."

"Why haven't they tried?" Callum asked.

"The whole planet went dark when they used it. I guess they don't want to use it unless it's an emergency. They probably think you're going to try and escape the planet again."

"They'll probably try eventually. They put me on display to be executed. They want me badly."

He kicked a lid off a crate and out spilled a bunch of screws.

"Something we could have used to build a house," I said.

"Emphasis on could have," he muttered.

We went down to the engine room. A part of me didn't want him to go down there. Would fate repeat itself? Would I lose him again?

He seemed lost already though.

The engine was still powered on, but barely. Some Restitution were down here, sitting next to the controls, barely moving.

"They've given up," Maiara said.

Callum held back from going any further. "Can we trust these... Restitution?" he asked.

I nodded towards one of the squids lying by the control console. "That's Stauffen. He's one of the Restitution who helped get me away from the Larceny when we first landed on this planet. That one over there..." I pointed at another who stood over a console, the tips of her tentacles spread out. "...Maier. She's one of the oldest Restitution and managed to assassinate a Greatlord fifty years ago."

"Oh," Callum said.

"They've been working against their species for centuries Callum. And they've never tried to turn me in."

He nodded at my remark. "I understand where they are coming from." He then headed out across the walkways suspended over the engine room.

I looked around the engine room. It was ninety percent submerged in water. The Ark's lower section was completely underwater. As he stepped onto a gang plank, which was a mere ten meters above the sea level, Callum stared out across the empty space at the top of the Ark. In the distance there was a huge gash in the hull, and the ocean stretched onwards.

"This is crazy. It's all gone. Everything I knew is gone," he said and lent down holding the rail of the gangplank. He stared down into the dark water.

"I know. I came down here many times before I entered the pod and slept. I hoped that this whole ship could be repaired and we could leave this planet with the others—that we could start again, like we were always told we could."

He smiled and shook his head. "You still think they can be saved," he uttered. "We know they can't."

I gritted my teeth. "Why do you keep saying that?"

"They're gone, Maiara, all gone. There is nothing we can do, and neither can the other aliens. They will all now be enslaved by the Larceny and humanity."

"We just have to destroy the Timerod. That's possible," I began. "It—it's going to be hard and tiring and take a long time, but we can do it. Then we jus—"

"Give it up, Maiara. It's over," Callum said, and held his head in his hands.

"Why do you talk like that?" I finally said to him, after a pause. "How can you give up on them?"

"What else can I do? Everything has collapsed around me. Please, Maiara. I changed time. I had hope and then when I found the friends I had saved, they were no longer the friends I knew. I did what no human thought we could ever do, and look what happened. It's been made worse.

"Destroying the Timerod will do nothing. If they can use it, they can build another. I can't see a way out of this."

"We can't give up."

"It's over! I'm done!" he yelled at me.

And he turned away.

I turned away from him, crossed my arms, and huffed. But then I felt like a hypocrite. How could I hold this against him? He had already had to kill Ogwambi, just to get free. I had never faced a former Arkonaut before, never had to kill one trying to kill me. I didn't know what he had been through.

I looked out across the water; in the distance I saw a wave build up and head towards us.

Then I smiled.

"Callum, come over here."

"What is it, Maiara?" he asked sighing.

I grabbed his arm and pulled him over and stood with him at the edge of the walkway. "Just wait. You're going to meet an old friend."

"What old fri—"

Kraken's head erupted from the water, and a shower of water fell on us both.

Callum screamed in surprise, like a little boy being hit with water balloons. I held onto him as he tried to back away and the water doused us both, soaking through our clothes. I then opened my arms. Kraken had done this before, and I welcomed it.

"My old friend, you are finally awake," Kraken said, and his snout inched closer to nuzzle me in the chest.

I rubbed his rough scales and said, "Good to see you again... Although for me it's felt like just a few hours."

Callum stood next to me, hunched over, dripping wet, and breathing deeply. The water was cold and no doubt he was in shock.

He then looked into Kraken's eyes as the giant crocodile chuckled in the water, his head rising up to our level.

Callum was terrified for a moment. Then his memories caught up and he seemed to realise that Kraken was not his enemy.

The crocodile leant forwards, put his giant nostrils above Callum, and sniffed.

"He is familiar. Where have I smelt you before?"

Callum did not reply, and I put a hand to my mouth to stifle my laugh.

"Turso... The sub," he finally replied.

Kraken growled at the mention of Turso's name, then his eyes went wide.

"Ah, yes, the boy in the sub. Wait, I thought you were dead!"

Kraken turned to me.

I knelt forward on the rail and stared into one of his eyes.

"Don't you remember? I told you there was a version of Callum in the future. We've finally caught up with him."

Kraken's forked tongue snaked out and licked my face. It was rough and slimy, but I turned my cheek into the tongue. "It has been years since I have seen you," Kraken said. "You have changed and grown."

"You're the same," I said to him. "But what happened to your eye?"

Kraken turned his face. There was a scar where one of his eyes had been.

"I was attacked by one of the creatures that exist in this ocean. It was tasty."

"Sorry, Kraken," I said to him.

"I have five more," the beast said.

"How are you still alive?" Callum asked.

Kraken managed to shrug. "The humans and Larceny never worried about me. What could I do to them?" Kraken answered.

"You've been in their ocean for what, decades?" Callum asked.

"Yes. At least I am alive, and also bigger," the croc said and he started swimming around beneath us.

"Well, it looks like three of the Arkonauts survived," Callum said and laughed.

"Arkonaut?" Kraken said.

"Huh. I never called you that before, but you are one, I guess," I added.

"I'm an Arkonaut?" Kraken asked.

"Yes," I replied.

"Finally," the beast said. "Maiara, do we have a plan to save the others at last?"

I looked away from him.

"I'm afraid things have just got very complicated," I said.

"How come?" he asked, and he stopped circling.

"It's a bit difficult to explain. Unfortunately, the Larceny now have the ability to travel back in time. Attacking them will harder, but not impossible."

"It's impossible," Callum muttered.

"Why does time travel make it impossible?" Kraken asked.

"It doesn't," I said.

"The Larceny can now undo anything we do. We fight them, they'll undo any victory. Nothing will work," Callum said.

"Hmm," Kraken said and then he started circling us again.

"Stop it, Callum," I whispered. "Kraken needs to hear that there is hope."

"Why'd you make friends with this beast? He tried to eat me."

"He tried to eat the other you. Also, he's the only other Arkonaut left... The only other one who still has hope, anyway."

Kraken raised his head up to our level again.

"I have a question," Kraken said.

"What is it, Kraken?" I replied.

"Why is being able to change the past an advantage?"

Callum huffed and rested his head in his hand.

"Kraken, I'm afraid it's science you can't understand. But imagine you were being attacked again by the beast who took your eye. If you knew where it was going to attack, because you sent a message through time to tell you that from the future, you would dodge at the right time and keep your eye."

"So, it's like getting a prediction of the future?" Kraken asked.

"Yes. It helps you to know exactly where to be to avoid something bad," I explained.

Out of the corner of my eye I saw Callum's eyes go wide.

"What is it?" I asked.

Callum stood up eyes still wide. He raised a hand and pointed into space. He traced a picture with his finger, and then smiled.

"What is it, Callum?" I asked.

He turned to me, his smile getting bigger.

"'You know exactly where to be to avoid something bad'," he repeated.

"Yes?" I said.

"Maiara, that's how we win!"

CALLUM

A NEW PLAN

I turned to the Restitution in the engine room.

"Get up, fellas. We have a war to win."

"Human Callum, the war is over. Our resistance is over. The Restitution have failed," the one called Stauffen said.

I crouched down next to it, and grabbed its squid body, and made its eyes look at me. "No, it's not over. We've got them," I then let go and wiped the slime off my hands on my trousers.

"Callum, what on earth is your plan?" Maiara asked.

"The Larceny and the VP don't know that you can't go back in time past the point you first travelled. You can't try to undo things twice," I explained and hoped she would realise.

"What does that mean?" She pleaded with me.

I didn't answer.

"Get up, guys. Come on. I need to talk to my friends. Can you get a secret signal out to planet Ramothia?"

"We can, why?" Maier asked.

I was feeling excited and energetic. I was bouncing and their questions were frustrating. So, I slowed down and finally answered.

"The Timerod may be their greatest asset, but it's also their greatest weakness," I said.

"How?" Maiara asked.

"It's like you said. They will know exactly how to dodge an attack. It's like they're predicting the future, when in actual fact, they're getting advanced knowledge.

"So?"

"Let's say I go to punch you right now. I'll hit you because you don't see it coming." I mimed the punch towards her head. "Now, let's say a portal opens and a message comes out saying you're about to get punched... Now you know. What do you do?"

Maiara smiled, "I have the same enhancements and training as you have. I'll deflect it. Then you're open to attack." She mimed the block, and she was right. By forcing my punch up and away from her head, my side was open. She sent her punch in, slowly.

"My punch—if you know it's coming—actually defines your next action, yes?" I asked.

"There are other options, but it's by far the best one..." she trailed off and her eyes went wide. "Oh," she said, slowly.

"What?" one of the Restitution said from the floor and it sat up.

"Oh," Maiara cried out and she smiled. "We don't need to destroy the rod. It works in our favour."

"Explain," Maier said.

"Maier, it's simple. We need to attack the Larceny with a plan that can't fail. But looks like it has a clear flaw," I said.

"Why would we do that? They'll just go back in time and use that flaw against us. They'll change the past, create the new timeline that will become dominant, and our clear victory becomes a loss."

"Not if we know what they're going to do to take advantage of that flaw!" I said and let my idea hang in the air.

Then Stauffen stood up on its tentacles. "If we know what they are going to do to respond to our attack, we can counter it," the alien replied.

"Yes. You're getting it," I almost shouted at them. "And get this... The Timerod can't correct that mistake again. It can't open a portal to a point in time before the last time it was used. If we get a foothold on their world, they'll use the rod to change time, but as soon as they do and we counter them, we'll secure that foothold indefinitely."

"But they can still use the Timerod to counter our tactical decisions. Yes, they'll be sending messages back through time in twenty minute gaps, but that's enough to turn the tide of a war," the Restitution said.

"You saw the city wide power drain after the test. If we can disrupt the power grid as part of our attack, they won't be able to recharge the Timerod fast enough," Maiara pointed out.

The Restitution all stood up. Their tentacles coiled over one another as they appeared to think about it.

"We can attack in such a way that there is a clear escape route for the Larceny to exploit... An exploitation that only works if they use time travel. They'll send a message back through time. They'll do something to prevent our attack, but our past selves will be looking for them to exploit the flaw. A flaw they think will win them the day. Instead, we already know what they are going to do, so we'll stop it."

"It's a trap!" Maier said.

"Yes! They'll never see it coming."

The head Restitution went to the controls.

"Reactivate our cells. Hack the communications network. If we're doing this, then we need the Ramothians too."

Maiara came up to me. "What's the flaw in our plan?" she asked.

"We need a plan of attack first. Can we get control of the wormhole generators, give the Ramothians and others a way to this planet?"

"We can, but that's a difficult task in itself. The generators are onboard the Destroyer-class vessels now. Ever since you managed to steal one, security is extremely tight."

"We can get through it," I said, brushing the concerns away.

"No, you can't Human Callum. The security is an army on every Destroyer. You would need an army of your own," Stauffen replied.

"An army!" Kraken said, who had been listening this whole time and he dipped below the waves and disappeared.

"Maybe we can sneak a Ramothian ship here with enough forces to fight our way onboard the Destroyer. Then we use its generators to bring the whole Ramothian army here," I asked.

"How do we bring a Ramothian ship here?" Maiara asked.

"I don't know," I replied. "Can we build our own wormhole generator?"

"Yes. In twenty years," the nearest Restitution said.

I sighed. "Maybe we should get started? Play the long game?"

"While the Larceny destroy more worlds? How do we even power it without the Larceny knowing?" Maiara asked.

"There must be a way to take a Destroyer... maybe with a smaller force?" I asked.

There was a splash of water beneath me, and I looked down. Kraken had resurfaced.

"You want an army?" he said.

Around him, lots more creatures broke the surface. They had heads of tentacles, and serpentine bodies, their faces angular. They licked the air with forked tongues.

In front of Kraken, a large one broke the surface, bigger than the others around them.

I leaned over the rail.

"I recognise you," I said.

The serpentine alien nodded.

"What is this?" I asked gesturing to the other smaller versions of her.

"My species' plan for revenge," she replied. "When my race learned that our kind was going to be annihilated—when their Destroyer was going to leave our world—we made a plan. I was created, a member or my race able to birth an army. I was purposefully chosen to be the Larceny's trophy in the hope that our plan could be enacted. When you freed me from the prison cell I was finally free to begin our revenge.

"Kraken tells me you need an Army. While not as big as I would like, we are willing to help you. Especially if it means the death of the Larceny."

CALLUM

CONVINCING

I stood with the Restitution, the serpent alien lady, and one of her children. Kraken was bobbing in the water below us and Maiara was by my side.

On one of the engine room screens was Antumbra, a Ramothian, and in the background were my alien friends.

"The connection is secure," a Restitution said. "The Larceny can't track our communication."

"Callum, can we trust these Larceny?" Antumbra said.

"They are not Larceny. They are different. The Restitution is a splinter group and they want to help you invade this planet," Maiara cut in.

Antumbra stared at Maiara, then turned to me.

"We can trust them. They saved me from execution," I said.

The Ramothian looked at Antumbra and whispered something into her ear.

"And the other one?" Antumbra asked, nodding towards Maiara.

"I vouch for her. She is not like the other Arkonauts," I said.

Antumbra seemed satisfied. The Ramothian less so.

"So, what is this plan you have?" the Ramothian said.

"We will infiltrate a Destroyer-class vessel on this planet, one with the ability to create wormholes. We will open multiple access points above the planet. Then what remains of the Ramothian fleet can pour through and attack the planet."

"Our fleet was decimated by our own black hole cannon when those humans invaded. There's not much left," the Ramothian said.

"We have a small army down here to help... and a Kraken," Maiara replied.

"What's a Kraken?" Antumbra asked

"A giant space crocodile," I said.

"What's a croc..." the Ramothian said.

"Never mind. It's a beast the size of a ship," I interrupted. "The point is we'll give you a chance to hit the Larceny where it hurts, and what's more, they won't be expecting it."

"What about the Timerod?" Antumbra asked. "You said that the Larceny have adapted it?"

"Yes. They can travel back to the past and cause two universes to combine the way they want," Maier, the Restitution, said.

"Doesn't that mean that even if we attack, they will just go back in time and stop us?" the Ramothian asked.

"Yes, it does. But that is our advantage, not theirs," I replied.

"How can that be our advantage?" the Ramothian asked.

"Because the Larceny don't know about the restriction on the Timerod. They don't know that you can't travel to a point earlier than the last time they time travelled. Also, a recombined universe will still require the Timerod to be recharged, which takes twenty minutes, and drains their power supply," a Restitution explained.

"I still don't see how this is an advantage. You open up the wormholes, we attack with our fleet. They use the rod to send a message to the past and stop the wormholes from ever being opened in the first place. We lose," The president stated.

"No," Antumbra replied.

I clicked a finger towards Antumbra. "She gets it."

"What do you mean?" the Mouth said, from behind her.

"Even if the Larceny use the Timerod to correct the timeline, we can predict what they'll do to stop us and counter it."

The Ramothian sighed and pinched the bridge of its nose.

"It's like you said, Mr. President. We open the wormhole. The fleet comes through. The Larceny go back in time to stop the wormhole from ever opening—the simplest solution to the problem—

but since we know they're going to do that, we can stop them," Antumbra tried to explain.

"So, we're actually making the Larceny react how we want them to?" he said slowly.

"And worse for them. As soon as they try to stop the wormholes from forming and fail, they can't go back again to stop it. It's locked in. Then it's just up to us to fight them before they can use the Timerod again," Antumbra said.

The Ramothian mused on this information. "It could work," he said tentatively. "But what if they choose a different point in time to change?"

"Then we need to have counters for everyone one of those potentialities, too," I replied. "I'm not saying this will be the simplest operation in the universe, but it is the only way. They have time travel. In all future engagements, they will have the upper hand. This is the last chance we have to crush them, while they don't realise the flaw in their new weapon."

"The Larceny can be defeated," the Restitution said.

"We will fight," the serpentine queen said next to me.

"Me too," Kraken's voice bellowed from below.

"We can do this," I said, staring hard into the eyes of the Ramothian.

He leaned forward. "What if the Larceny time travel, but go further back than this battle? What if they simply decide to play it safe and time travel to a point way before the battle? They could choose any number of moments to time travel to. How do we steer them down the path we want?" the Ramothian asked.

I looked away. The Ramothian had a point. How could I make sure the Larceny would choose the right moment in time?

Maiara tugged on my sleeve.

"I know how," she said.

CALLUM

ALLIES

Maiara's plan was sound, and I knew we could both pull it off. All of us... The Ramothians, other aliens, Restitution, serpents, and Kraken agreed to attack as soon as possible.

I had some time—as arrangements needed to be made—and I had no idea how to arrange them. I felt like chatting with the snake-like woman. I had met her briefly during my first escape attempt from the Larceny.

She was bigger than I remembered. Her long emerald-scaled body writhed beneath her. The smaller versions of herself, although they were still bigger than me, came up to her, got instructions, and then slithered off.

Two slit like eyes turned to me, and the lady moved her head down to my level, as I approached.

"I always wondered what happened to you when we parted company in the museum," I said. "What is your name?"

"Unpronounceable in your language, I'm afraid," she said.

"Then can I call you... Medusa?" I asked.

"Medusa," she said testing the word out. "Yes, that sounds fine where does it come from?"

"A mythological creature on my homeworld. She was wronged by gods and men, and so was given the power to turn them to stone... My name is Callum by the way."

"Thank you for freeing me, Callum. And thank you for creating the means for me to finally take revenge on the Larceny."

"So, you are... the last survivor of your people?" I asked.

"In a way. However, I was meant to be the survivor. The humans on the Destroyer that claimed my world made us pick a survivor. They thought it would be fun for our race to clamour and fight for the opportunity. We used it to get revenge."

"How?"

"I was chosen to survive, and engineered to be a weapon."

"A weapon?"

"These are all my children. As soon as we parted ways in the museum, I started breeding this army. My race will live on through them, but right now, here in the heart of the Larceny empire, we will strike back."

"You're not the first alien race who suffered under the Larceny, and the humans, who had a plan for revenge. A creature I met once was also engineered to fight back. I saw it tear through hundreds of Larceny," I replied.

Medusa smiled and gestured. Slithering forward came a large muscular child. "This is my first born. You need to choose a name for him too."

"How about Euryale," I said, dredging up another name from mythology.

"Euryale it is, then," Medusa said.

I nodded at Euryale, who came forward and towered over me, his fists clenching and unclenching at the sides of his serpentine body.

"Not this one, Euryale," Medusa said.

Euryale backed off.

"He may be only a year old, but he has the memories from my species. Euryale knows to dislike humans."

I smiled at him. "Me too," I said.

Euryale frowned. "You hate your own kind?" he asked, and he slithered around me, inspecting me from all angles.

"My race was supposed to be so much more that what they've become. They have done evil, even in our own culture. We don't deserve our high and exalted position."

Euryale stopped circling around me and went back to his mother.

"Curious," he said.

"He is our ally now, Euryale, and he intends to fight against his own kind," Medusa said.

"Will you see this through?" Euryale practically demanded.

"I will," I replied without hesitation.

CALLUM

THE CHOICE

As the time for battle neared, I walked the remains of the cargo bay and prepared myself for the conflict ahead.

This was it. Before, when the Ramothians had the Ark ship we had captured and were preparing to use its wormhole drive to attack the Larceny, the end of my kind seemed far away. Now it was mere hours. It was nice to be distracted by what remained of our journey.

The cargo bay was a wreck, though. Many shelves had been knocked over, like a drunk forklift driver had been let loose in here.

I remembered the first time I had walked these shelves, the conversations I had had with Ivaylo, Matthieu's dead body, One going *John Wick* on the stowaways. I hadn't really bothered with what had been in all these crates. It was surprising to see it strewn about.

One whole section was tools. Hammers, drills and screwdrivers. All to help us build our new homes.

Another collapsed stack was full of microwaves of various styles. I didn't quite understand Dr. Ghost's reasoning there. Maybe microwaving food was supposed to be our means of cooking on our new homeworld. Maybe he had a lot of microwavable meals in storage, which also made sense since they would keep for a long time.

I kept looking, and everywhere I went were reminders of my home planet.

I found a few of the artefacts that had been preserved. Most of it was gone. I found no paintings from any of the masters, no statues I had seen in the British museum. I found art from Ogwambi's box, from Luciana's crate, and Darma's. But I didn't find anything from mine.

Much of what was here were the resources humanity no longer needed. A lot of it brought back good memories. I found toys. Dr. Ghost must have thought that children born to the Arkonauts would need them. Some I recognised from my own childhood.

I found a cache of old films, and TV's to watch them on. A lot were documentaries. I picked up a disc and smiled when I remembered the softly spoken old man who had narrated this particular one.

Nostalgia flooded back to me as I wandered the valleys of stacked crates.

I dipped into one, and pulled out a phone. The dark screen reflected my aged face. I imagined that the plan was to build a new network on our new planet, so these communication devices could be used again.

It made me think of an old comic strip my mum had once shown me, of the evolution of man from ape to upright Neanderthal, and afterwards an office worker hunched over a phone.

I chuckled, because here I was, one of the last true humans left doing the same.

It was all that remained of Earth now. The Arkonauts were not continuing this legacy. They had started anew.

I was now shorn of this past too. Yes, I had connections to it. However, I knew I would not be picking up this legacy. The battle to come might erase all of this.

I found myself not caring.

What a sensation to feel. Thousands of years of history, philosophy, science, religious belief, progress, and lifetimes and I didn't care. It was both liberating and shaming. I felt ashamed that I was turning my back on my own kind. I imagined, behind me, row after row of humans shouting at me, not wanting to be forgotten. Yet I looked forward and didn't turn around to face them, because to no longer have such a weight on my shoulders was a wonderful feeling.

I was still just a boy in many ways. This wasn't my burden. It shouldn't be. Even better, I was going to do the universe a favour.

When humanity was gone, only Maiara could judge me.

That... was a painful thought.

I heard footsteps amongst the stacks.

Maiara walked towards me, admiring the crates as she went.

"I love this place. Reminds you of home, what could have been. Shame that the VP, his cronies, and the Greatlords plundered most of what was here for their own private collections."

"What could have been..." I repeated. "What can never be now." I threw the phone away and it smashed in the shadow of a pile of crates.

"It can still be, Callum," Maiara said, as she walked around me to look me in the eye. "We can save them."

"How, Maiara? How? They have those implants. Our ship is here, forlorn and forgotten, rotting away," I replied.

"It's not about this ship. It's about them. There are some Arkonauts left."

"Those 'Arkonauts' killed Two, Maiara," I said.

"Two is dead?" She paused, head down. "How?"

"They killed her while we were trying to escape planet Ramothia. They didn't care about her... and she was the best thing humanity had ever made."

Maiara sat down on the edge of a crate.

"Did you know what she was?" Maiara asked.

"Yes, she revealed it to me. How did you know?" I asked.

"I had the run of the computers when I got away from the Larceny and was taken in by the Restitution. I found out everything," she replied.

"I only have... previous Callum's memories of her from your time. She was great. She was going to live a life free of her creators—creators who couldn't stay on the straight and narrow."

"What would she want us to do, now we have a choice to either end the human race or save it?" Maiara asked.

"She was on my side in the end," I replied.

"Really?" she said.

"You weren't there when they destroyed her," I said.

Maiara sighed and put her hands together. "And you weren't there when I saw how they changed the Arkonauts. Those left, they had to see others getting tortured. They had to see them die. They had been forced to take those implants... They were children... Then they became who they are, they had poor mentors."

"They still had a choice. Not long ago, they were on Ramothia. They could have turned to our side. Instead, they did their new master's bidding."

"Callum, have you ever gone through what they did?" she asked.

I paused, because of course I haven't. "No," I replied.

She gave me a pleading look.

"Maiara, they're going to fight us every inch of the way. To stop the Larceny—to free this galaxy of their never-ending crusade to erase any species that might threaten them—we'll need to go through the Arkonauts."

"We just need to give them a way out, that's all," she said.

"A way out. How?"

"I have faith that a chance will reveal itself. They've been under the thumb of the VP and his cronies for a long time. Just as Earth was under his and his cronies' thumbs for years.

"Remember what happened in the dying days of Earth, when all the wealth and privilege of the few was nothing compared to the might of those beneath them, finally realising they have been conned? Remember when the billionaires hoarding food were brought down by the mobs of the starving? When governments like those in Korea, Russia and Britain were turned out and resources used more wisely?

"That's what we need to show the Arkonauts. We need them to see that they have been hurt and tortured and made to believe lies by the few—those hoping to cling onto power and wealth just a little bit longer. We have to show them the exit I know they want to take. We have to show them a door, a way out they can believe in.

"They'll step through it I know it. They just need an option. And this battle will give them that. We will have victory and they will believe in that victory."

I stared back into her eyes, and saw no lie. She really believed in that goal.

I looked away. "I—I don't think I believe," I said.

She rose and placed a hand on my cheek to turn my face back to hers. "Then all I ask is you give me time when the moment arrives," she said.

I gave a small nod.

"Come on. The Restitution are ready. The Ramothians, the other aliens, they are going to war... We're going on a rescue mission."

PLANNING

We gathered with the Ramothians and Restitution in the Ark's control centre. On the cracked dome was a Destroyer class vessel.

"This belongs to the Greatlord Vendak and his family. It's the nearest to the capital city."

"But is it the least guarded?" Callum asked.

"They are all guarded the same way," Stauffen the Restitution replied.

"The proximity to the city is the bonus," I said. "The question is, how do we get in? And how do we get in without the Overlord or the VP knowing? The less they know the less likely they will be to go back in time before that point... They'll figure it out, eventually."

"If we want the Overlord and the VP to use the Timerod when we want them to, we need to limit their options," Callum said. "We need to encourage them to go back in time to when we want them to. That gives us the advantage. A stealthy approach will limit their knowledge. Are there any Restitution within the ship or the family house?"

"We have one."

"So, we have a man on the inside. They could open doors for us?" Callum said.

"Afraid not. Our spy doesn't have access to the door controls. Plus, the second it did anything of the sort he would be identified and killed."

"If we can't get to a wormhole drive, we can't start the attack," Callum pointed out. "I could get captured trying to break into the Destroyer?" Callum suggested. "Maybe they'll take me to the control centre and I fight them off?"

"Won't work. Too many Larceny on the ship. Besides, how will you escape them?" I said.

"This was easier when me, Antumbra and the others stole a Destroyer," Callum said.

"You are a victim of your own success. The Larceny never even considered that there was someone on their planet who could achieve that," the Restitution said. "After that, security was upgraded."

"Maybe we just storm the thing with Medusa's ad-hoc army?" I said.

"How? The Destroyer's armour is hundreds of meters thick." Restitution replied.

"We can't storm it. Our man on the inside can't just open the doors for us," Callum commented. "Medusa's got a large enough army to take it from a hundred Larceny, we just can't get them inside."

"There's no way in from the outside," the Restitution reiterated.

I stared at the display of the Destroyer. "Is this the one that sucked water from my homeworld?" I asked.

"It is, actually. The same one that the VP used to get to the Larceny homeworld ahead of the Ark.".

"I remember when this thing sent out pipes over our world, destroying everything in its path. What I wouldn't give to see it destroyed," I said.

"Wait. Restitution, you said the spy didn't have access to the door controls. But, what do they have access to?" Callum asked.

"They work on the Destroyer's water retrieval systems. They make sure the pipes and chimneys are ready to be deployed once on an alien world."

"Ah, that won't help," Callum said.

I clicked my fingers.

"What?" Callum said.

"I think I have a plan."

CALLUM

THE WORST WATER SLIDE

As I waited in the cold water, I tried to stifle my fear and anxiety. I was not anxious about the plan, which, in a few minutes, was going to get underway. I was actually terrified of the fact that I was underwater, looking into the gloom all around me, wondering when a giant sea monster would appear and eat me.

I never used to think this way about the sea. I think the memories of the other Callum from the past whose memories blended with mine. I remembered that he had met Kraken when he had been a vicious creature. Also, he had almost drowned in the underbelly of the Ark. That must had instilled in him a fear of the sea that I now possessed.

I tried to focus on the fact that I was floating alongside some Restitution and fifty of Medusa's children, including Euryale. At least they could swim far better than I could, and probably be able to sense danger coming.

I got a tap on the shoulder from the Restitution and my arm was taken in their tentacles. The group, as one, swam forward. I breathed in deeply using an artificial gill the Restitution had made for me. It was attached to my face, taking oxygen directly from the water and turning it into air for me to breathe.

It struggled to give me oxygen as I breathed faster and faster.

The murky water grew darker as we neared the face of a wall that stretched left and right in front of us.

It was part of the landing base for the Destroyer we were approaching. We hung in the water again, waiting.

I looked across at Maiara, who had her own breathing device attached to her face.

We looked each other in the eyes.

This was it.

That's when I was grabbed by the more capable swimmers around me, and dragged back though water, bubbles swirling around me.

I heard a huge thud, and then a pressure wave nearly sent me tumbling in the water.

I looked up to see a giant snake enter the sea, its wide mouth was descending towards us.

It was one of the Destroyer's pipes. The Restituion inside the Destroyer had activated them by 'accident'.Now it was in the sea it immediately started sucking in water.

The whole group was pulled upwards.

Everything went dark.

On the Restitutions' faces, lights switched on.

Medusa's children were keeping us together, swimming fast down the pipe.

Then the pipe suddenly pulsated.

The Restitution slammed us into the wall and used their tentacles to pin us inside the pipe.

The water flow ceased, and it drained away. The pipe continued to writhe. It was like I was in one of those old, children's cloth tunnels and the adults were swinging it around.

I heard the sounds of giant mechanical components chugging away to move the pipe, which I was sure was retracting back into the Destroyer.

All I could do was hang there like a criminal snagged by *Spiderman* and wait.

It didn't take long for the pipe to resettle inside the Destroyer.

Once it was still, the Restitution released us from the wall and our special forces team slid down the edges to the base.

I looked up and down the length of the pipe. It was like I had been eaten by a giant serpent.

Maiara pulled out a scanner, and the Restitution started scanning with their own cybernetic parts.

"Status?" I said.

"The pipe network has settled. We're past the primary hull," Maiara reported.

"Where's our exit?" Euryale asked.

"It's an inspection tunnel for the pipe network," the Restitution said, peering around. It then stopped and pointed. "There. That's our way into the ship proper."

The Restitution used their tentacles to clamber across the pipe to a spot on the other side. They planted bombs, and backed off.

There was no explosion, as such. Instead, the bombs completely blew into the wall, melting the metal incredibly quickly and tunneling through. There was a sizzling sound, and the smell of iron in the air, as the bombs did their work. In seconds, they had made a hole, and beyond was the corridor ten feet from the pipe.

Maiara raised her gun and blasted a hole into the tunnel. It was one of many that went around the storage area for the pipes. We never had this on the Ark because we had sent bombs down the Ark's pipe network to explode inside the vessel, wrecking this system entirely.

We now had a way in.

Me and Maiara leaped across to the tunnel without difficulty.

The Restitution climbed over the walls.

Euryale and his people formed themselves into a bridge that reached the tunnel, then they slithered over one another to make the crossing, then pulled those who remained into the tunnel.

"Have we been detected?" I asked.

"No," the Restitution said. "There's no sensors down here. There would be no point."

"When do we show up on their sensors?" I asked.

"Once we reach the main corridors."

"After that, we have to move fast, secure the control room and do what we came to do," Maiara said.

I looked around at the aliens. "This is it. If any of us falls, keep going. Something bigger than us needs to be finished now."

"For our revenge," Euryale said.

"For reclaimed honour," the Restitution said.

"For the future," Maiara declared.

I gritted my teeth, readied the gun that the Restitution had manage to save for me, and flicked out my sword.

"Let's go."

OLD VEHICLES

"Where are we?" I asked the Restitution.

"We're going to come out near the top of the engine room. We will then appear on their internal sensors."

"Nothing else for it: just break out and start fighting," Callum said, and he charged through the corridor and out into the engine room.

Just like the Ark, this engine hung from the ceiling like a giant multicoloured stalagmite or stalactite. I'm not sure which. Around it were walkways and a control centre.

The Larceny at the controls whipped around as we entered.

Callum fired without hesitation.

Euryale and his people coiled around the walkways, and like a snake launching itself from tree to tree, sprang off, landing on the Larceny and shooting them at close range or stabbing them.

The Restitution fired their weapons, helping me and Callum take out all those in the engine room.

Alarms then started sounding as the last of the Larceny went down.

"No surprises anymore," I warned.

"We have to hurry. It won't be long till the Overlord hears of this," the Restitution said.

Callum picked up some of the Larceny's weapons.

"Don't you have enough?" Euryale said.

"These are for something else," he replied.

As a group, we all moved upwards, climbing this mountain of a vessel as fast as we could before the Larceny onboard could move against us in a meaningful way.

We didn't use the stairs. It turns out that all stairs on the Ark must have been added by Dr. Ghost. Here, the Larceny preferred ramps, which probably worked better with their biology.

As we neared the level where the control centre was a group of Larceny rounded the corner and started firing.

Me and Callum—both wearing shield generators—provided cover and Euryale and the Restitution ducked behind us as we took the hits.

There was no cover in the rampway, and our shields were draining fast.

"Callum?" I shouted over the din of blasts striking the wall and sparks flying.

He was tinkering with the Larceny guns. When he was done, he threw one at them.

"What was that?" I asked.

"Follow my lead," he replied.

I watched as the gun pinwheeled off the wall, then exploded. It was not a big explosion, instead the air shimmered and crackled.

The Larceny near the top of the rampway collapsed as all their machine parts failed them.

The Restitution were not effected. We must have been too far away.

As their parts then started coming back on, Callum fired again, and Euryale and his people followed, using the small window of opportunity.

They overwhelmed the Larceny at the top of the ramp, and we were now on control centre level.

We gathered at an intersection. No Larceny seemed to be around, for the time being.

"Which way to the control centre?" I asked.

"That corridor. Right turn, then left," the Restitution said.

"The question is, what do they have waiting for us?" I asked.

"We're unstoppable so far," Euryale said.

"Let's not get big heads," Callum said, as he checked his gun and gave his sword the once over.

"What will give us big heads?" Euryale asked.

"It's an expression. It means not to get overconfident. We do that, we make mistakes, and the Larceny survive," I replied.

"Humans Maiara and Callum, the Larceny are sending their troops to attack us," the Restitution said, pointing at its scanner.

"We have no cover here," Callum said. "This way..."

He led us and we retreated away from the control centre.

We found a room and ducked inside. It was dark near the entrance. The only light spilled in from the corridor.

Callum flicked on the lights. The room was huge. It had supplies for the Greatlord who usually took this Destroyer out to raid and destroy other worlds. It was a cavernous room with shelves spread out in all directions.

"We need a plan. They can bottle us up in this room if they need to. I imagine more forces are heading this way from the nearby city... Especially if the Overlord knows we're here," Callum said.

"They know where we are," the Restitution said.

"That's their advantage. They have the control centre. We can't surprise them anymore," Callum said.

"Our only strategy now is to fight our way through," Euryale said.

"What about our inside man? Can they help?" I asked.

"I'm afraid I am no longer in contact with our spy. I think they have been discovered," the Restitution Stauffen said.

"I'm sorry," I said.

"They surely sacrificed themselves so we would have a chance," he replied.

"Then let's not waste it," Callum said. He darted his head out of the door, raised his gun and started firing. The blasts from his x-ray gun went through the wall, taking out advancing Larceny before they could reach us.

"They're closing in."

I pursed my lips. It would not be long until we were overrun. We needed an advantage.

"What's in these supplies?" I asked.

"Food and drink from our homeworld," the Restitution said. "Specifically to keep the Greatlord in comfort as they ravage a planet.

Some trophies, some weapons, but nothing more powerful than what we have."

"Wait. Trophies? What trophies?" I asked.

"The Larceny don't just steal water. They take trinkets, baubles... things they find interesting from a homeworld.

"Don't they end up in that museum I was put it in?" Callum said.

"Not everything does."

"This Destroyer stole from Earth. What's here from our planet?"

The Restitution scanned the room. "Artwork, jewels, historical artefacts and some vehicles."

"Vehicles? What type of vehicles?" I asked.

Callum revved the motorbike's engine. "Thank goodness they never drained the fuel from this thing," he said.

I sat on the backseat, a gun in each hand. "This will give us back the element of surprise," I said.

Euryale grasped the hands of his remaining soldiers. "For our ancestors," he said.

"For our ancestors," the others intoned.

"Here we go," Callum said, revved again, released the brake, and took the bike out into the corridor.

"Breakthrough their lines! No one stops until we reach that control centre," I shouted over the engine.

We all nodded to one another.

Euryale and his people burst out and went speeding way down the corridor to the left, while me and Callum headed to the right.

The Larceny rounded the corner, and the snake people went up the walls and onto the ceiling, slithering up, approaching from all sides. The Larceny were surrounded and had to aim in all directions. Euryale and his people attacked from all sides in the chaos.

Callum activated his shield as the Larceny started firing. The first few shots burst off the shield, and they could fire no more as we were suddenly on top of them.

We burst through their formation. Callum held out his sword and sliced through several Larceny as the others were thrown to one side. The bike engine roared all around us in the tight corridor.

I fired at any Larceny I could see.

The Restitution followed behind us, taking out the Larceny that I missed.

Callum braked and burnt rubber as he sped round a corner, then gunned the engine again.

Larceny heading for where they thought we were, had not been expecting us to be coming at them this fast. They had no time to react as Callum scythed his sword into them.

A mass of Larceny took positions at the end of the corridor, forming lines and raising their weapons.

Callum jammed a grenade into a space in the bike's seat, and pulled the pin.

We both leapt off—and if we hadn't been enhanced like One—we would have just ended up as a mass of broken limbs. Instead, we hit the floor and rolled.

The bike managed to stay upright for a moment before wobbling without us to balance it. The front wheel went sharply left and the bike rolled over itself.

The Larceny broke their ranks just as the bike slid up to them and exploded.

A fireball went right towards us. I pushed Callum down and covered his body. The flames reached us and licked the air over our heads before retracting back down the corridor.

The Restitution ran up to us and helped us up.

Callum rolled his shoulders. "Next time I'll wear padding," he said.

"Let's keep going," I said, leading the way to the control centre.

When we reached it, we were met by a huge Larceny. Its putrid yellow eyes glared at us from inside a skull that covered its octopus-like body.

"This is Greatlord Vendak," Stauffen said.

"The one who killed our planet," Callum snarled.

"Wretches," it shouted and lunged toward us.

We fired, and the blasts pinged off its shields.

It fired back and we had to dodge.

Callum lifted a dead Larceny and used it as a shield.

I unleashed the stored-up energy from my shield. The blast pushed Vendak back, but then my protection sparked and fizzled.

My shield was gone.

A tentacle came my way as revenge, and I dodged to the side. The Greatlord swung it back towards me like a whip and I slammed against the wall, knocking the wind out of me. Luckily, this tentacle was not a mechanical one, so I grabbed my knife and stabbed it, slicing all the way through it.

Vendak squealed and reeled back.

Euryale's people then pounced on it from behind.

They took out the Greatlord's tentacles one by one.

Me and Callum joined in by shooting random appendages off.

In minutes, the Greatlord Vendak, destroyer of earth, was dead.

CALLUM

FIRST TRY

Our team took total control of the ship.

Euryale's people ran off to take out any remaining Larceny.

"Are we ready to activate the wormhole?" I asked.

"We are," the Restitution Stauffen said.

"Euryale, Restitution, stay out of the camera's sight. The less they see, the less they know."

I stood with Maiara in the middle of the room and looked up at the screen. "Ready to annoy the hell out of these people?"

"If you think about it, this is what my entire life has been leading up to so far," she replied.

"Huh. You're right. I born to insult these losers. Contact the Overlord," I said to Stauffen.

It took a moment or two. Maybe the Overlord didn't answer the phone on the first ring? Then the screen came on and I was looking at the Overlord, the VP, and some of his most trusted humans.

"Hello, Overlord," I said formally.

"Traitor! What have you done to our Destroyer?"

"Your Destroyer? I think you'll find, its ours," I said and hugged Maiara playfully. "I'm so good at taking these things from you, maybe next time I should just call ahead and make reservations."

The VP's eyes widened when he saw Maiara. Then he composed himself. "You will pay for this," the VP said. "You are a drain on our new society. We've made something of our time here, while you just take."

"We're about to make it a lot worse for you," Maiara said, nodding to the Restitution. "By the way, those cars you used to make back on Earth... They were terrible. My dad said it handled like a drunk octopus. Which is appropriate," she added pointing at the Overlord.

I glanced sideways at another screen. Wormholes were opening up in space above the planet.

In the background, behind the Overlord, Larceny were frantically telling him something.

"What have you done?" the Overlord said.

"Let's see how you like being invaded," I said.

"Yeah. And there's nothing you can do to stop those wormholes. Nothing you can do whatsoever. They are open and you can't close them. Our friends are here now and it's time for you to fall," Maiara taunted them.

On another screen, I saw the Ramothian fleet part the clouds and start firing. The city erupted in explosions.

"Try and stop that, calamari," I said.

"You can't stop those wormholes. We're going to enjoy watching you burn," Maiara said.

The leaders of the humans and Larceny were issuing commands. trying to get a handle on the situation.

The Ramothian fleet was pounding the city, but in the Larceny were attacking in response.

I saw the VP lean down and whisper something to the Overlord.

The Overlord then turned to the screen and looked directly at me.

"I'll enjoy throwing your words back in your face," he said.

The video cut out.

"I think he's fallen for it," Maiara said.

"Humans Callum and Maiara, there's a planet-wide power drain occurring," the Restitution Maier said.

"Here we go," Maiara said.

"Let's hope..." I began.

CALLUM

LITERALLY 5 MINUTES AGO

"By the way, those cars you used to make back on Earth... They were terrible. My dad said it handled like a drunk octopus. Which is appropriate," she added pointing at the Overlord.

I glanced sideways at another screen as wormholes opened up in space above the planet. Then I looked back at the Overlord who didn't seem phased.

"Also, you were clearly terrible at golf. Did any of your 'friends' have the bravery to tell you that?" I added looking at the VP.

I looked back at the Overlord and the VP, and was surprised to see that they were not surprised.

Is this it? I thought. *Have they been warned and are ready? Or did they see this coming through some technological means we didn't foresee?*

"Oh, Callum Tasker, you're so... predictable," the VP said and he laughed with the Overlord.

"They're broadcasting an anti-wormhole wave," the Restitution said. "It will disrupt the wormholes, and they'll close before they fully form."

"You could never beat us," the VP said directly into the screen.

I looked at Maiara and she looked at me.

Then we looked back at the screen.

"Oh, really?"

CALLUM

SECOND TRY

The VP kept smiling. Then his eyes glanced offscreen for a second.

He then frowned.

"Something wrong?" I asked.

"What did you do? How did you—"

"So predictable?" Maiara taunted the VP through the screen, which was suddenly shut down.

"It's done. We've counteracted their attempt to stop the wormhole formation," the Restitution said. "You were right. By getting them to try and close the wormholes, we were able to calibrate them to stay open."

"How long till we catch up with the moment they travelled back in time?" Maiara asked.

"There is no way to tell," The Restitution said. "We don't know when they opened a portal... Wait! There is a power drain happening... and it didn't do anything."

"That was their attempt to send another message back through time to counteract our counteraction. It failed," I said.

"That means they can't change what's happening," Maiara said. She then nodded at the screen. "The wormholes are fully formed. We have our foothold."

Pouring out of the portals came the Ramothians, a host of other ships from species the Larceny had attacked, and amongst them I even spotted the *Vengeance*.

"Success," the Restitution hollered. "We can finally bring them down."

"I wish I could see the VP and Three's faces," Maiara snorted. "They probably thought this was going to a be a minor problem."

"The Ramothian fleet have entered the atmosphere, weapons ready."

"It's time to do things in a way not even a message from the future can stop," I said.

I picked up my communicator and activated it.

"Medusa, Kraken, it's time for the next stage."

I turned to the dome. The Restitution focused the sensors on the coastline next to the city.

On the buildings of the city, weapon installations were deployed. The city was bristling with guns that were about to give the Ramothian fleet a pounding. I assumed they had done that before? Wow... Time travel is really hard to sort out in your head.

This time, though, things would no doubt be different.

The sea along the coast rippled, but not because of a strong sea breeze. It was something else.

"Here they come!" Maiara said.

Erupting from the water came thousands of Medusa's children, creatures born and raised for a single purpose—get their mother's revenge.

They immediately rushed into the city. The Larceny in the streets were taken down without mercy.

A weapon on top of a building turned to fire downwards into the invaders.

The army went straight for the buildings with weapons on top. The serpentine creatures were able to slither straight up their sides.

An army of Larceny managed to organise and rushed for our allies. Medusa's forces suddenly split, leaving a giant gap in their ranks.

The Larceny went to fill the gap in the line, no doubt hoping to divide and conquer, and that was when Kraken burst out of the water.

The giant crocodile smiled as he arced through the air, huge teeth gleaming, water streaming off his body.

The Larceny army faltered. Some fired their weapons, which didn't stop Kraken as he crashed on top of them. The ground shook as he belly-flopped, and the Larceny that weren't crushed went flying.

Kraken opened his mouth to the sky and roared. The thunderous cry shattered all the glass in close proximity.

"For my world, for my people!" Kraken bellowed, and he went snout first into a building next to him. It toppled into the city, and like dominoes more skyscrapers collapsed, creating a giant gash into the city structure, all the way to the Overlord's palace.

That was when, cutting through the clouds, came our allies' fleet.

They poured weapon fire down onto the city, shredding almost all the defences there.

Then the Larceny ships joined the battle in the skies.

"It begins... and the Larceny can't stop it!" the Restitution said. "Your plan worked."

"It's on!" I said.

"Then let's go! The *Vengeance* is docking in the bay," Maiara said. "Time to take back what was stolen."

CALLUM

ALL OUT WAR

We all ran up the access ramp and into the *Vengeance*.

Maiara was behind me, as was the Restitution, Maier and Stauffen. I wondered if I should prepare the others for their arrival. I decided it would be funnier to ignore the issue.

I burst onto the bridge.

"You made it! Welcome to the Larceny homeworld," I said.

"I never thought I would come back here," Lyger said from the pilot's controls.

Maiara was in next.

"Aliens, this is Maiara. She's the one Arkonaut we can trust right now."

"Hi," the aliens said cautiously.

Hippo, Mantis, Antumbra and the Mouth then stood as the Restitution came in behind me.

"Guys, don't shoot them," I said.

"I really want to, though," the Mouth said.

"Lyger, get us back into battle," I said.

Lyger growled at the Restitution, then flew the *Vengeance* out of this Destroyer's docking bay and headed for the nearby city.

"How is the battle going?" I asked.

Antumbra sat down at her station. "The Ramothians have begun their bombardment. The whole planet is erupting in battle."

"We should target their Citadel with the black hole cannons, destroy the Timerod," Hippo said.

"No. That's a bad idea. We have no way to know what that will do," Antumbra said. "We need to get rid of any charge it possesses before we destroy it. Technically, it's connected to the whole universe, so who knows what outrightly destroying it will do."

"We need to get to the Overlord," the Restitution Stauffen said.

"If we kill them, will we win?" the Mouth said.

"No, but what we need to do is gain access to his cybernetics and, in all honesty, he will need to be dead for us to do that," the Restitution said.

"Then what?" I asked.

"His command protocols connect him to every Larceny on the planet. We can kill them all in a single blow," Maier said

"Sounds like a poor system," the Mouth said.

"They wanted control," the Restitution said, and I was sure it just shrugged its tentacles.

"Where is the Overlord?" Hippo asked.

"The central Citadel," Maiara replied.

"How's our army doing?" I asked.

"That giant sea monster of yours has carved a path through the city. The snake-like alien and her children are doing well. However, the Larceny are now getting their bearings. We're fighting a whole planet here."

"Then let's get to the Overlord."

Lyger took the *Vengeance* down over the city. Its weapons fire taking out gun emplacements on a few buildings.

"I'm letting you out here," she said as she came down just behind Kraken, who was stamping through the streets shaking off gun fire that struck his armoured hide.

Kraken took a moment to turn around and stare through the window.

I hoped he could see Maiara, and decide not to close his jaws around the ship.

"Let's go," Maiara said and led the way out of the ship.

"I'm going back up to help the fleet," Lyger said.

Once outside, I could smell concrete dust, and hear the whine of laser blasts and vibration of Kraken's footfalls.

Battle was raging.

The Citadel of the Overlord was before us. It was a building hundreds of meters wide and far taller than the tallest building humans had ever made.

"It's going to take us ages to climb that," I commented.

"Not to mention fight our way in," Maiara said.

"We're going to go through the easy way," the Restitution said. "See those towers around the Citadel? They belong to Greatlords and they are linked to the Citadel. We'll use them for access."

Suddenly, the world sort of shifted, like it had paused and restarted.

"That was the time streams melding again," the Restitution said.

"How much of the power grid has been destroyed?" Maiara asked.

The Restitution accessed the information through its cybernetic implants. "78%. Still more than enough for them to attempt travel."

"Well, they can't go back before now. We have our foot hold," I said.

"They could still change the course of this battle in their favour. Even sending back a complete report of the battle a few minutes will be enough to target ships more accurately, and ambush troops," the Restitution said.

"Then we need to get to them before they can activate the Timerod... Let's pay a Greatlord a visit."

THIRD TRY

So, which Greatlord palace do we try first?" Callum asked.

"Are any empty right now? With no Greatlord home, they might be easier to take… Less security," I said.

"That one," the Restitution said. "The Greatlord was killed recently. In fact, their personal starship crashed into the planet a few weeks ago. Apparently, there was something inside that the Larceny greatly feared."

Callum smirked. "An old 'friend'," he said, but didn't elaborate.

We crossed the city to the Greatlord's palace. Around us, the sounds of war echoed through the metropolis. I thought back to the time I was on the Ammon Ark ship during their short civil war. But that was nothing compared to this. Black hole cannons were firing from orbit down into the areas beyond the city. Larceny were launching ships into the sky and firing back with large weapons across the surface.

It seemed like there were so many things going on, exciting things, scary things, but this is where I needed to be. Me, Callum, and his alien friends were on the mission that was most likely to get me in contact with the Arkonauts, and might be my only chance to save them.

We entered the Greatlord's palace, a miniature, but still huge replica of the Overlord's Citadel. We had to dispatch a few guards at the entrance, but, other than that, it was mostly unguarded. Once we were a few floors up, the lights started to dim.

"The power grid of the Larceny is being drained again. They've activated the Timerod and are preparing to use it," Stauffen said.

"Do we have any idea when they are sending a message back to?" I asked.

"Yes, we do. Three minutes before now. We can determine the message is... Oh, dear," the Restitution said.

"In order to stop the Ramothian and refugee fleet from pouring out the wormhole, they're sending a Destroyer-class vessel through. The Destroyer will slam into Ramothia on the other side."

"They're getting desperate," Callum said. "How do we stop them?"

"We can't. The Destroyer will launch, and not even the Ramothian large guns will be able to target it in time."

"Ramothia will be destroyed. That may help their battle here," I said.

"How do you know this?" Callum asked the Restitution.

"In this chaos, one of our members is now in the Citadel. They can't get closer, but they are witnessing the use of the Timerod."

"So, they hope by sending this Destroyer a few minutes ago, the battle will swing in their favour. Why not send it now?" Callum asked.

"Three minutes of extra time are better than now."

"In the past, we aren't ready to prevent this. They will see the Destroyer launch and not be able stop it," Callum said.

"Wait... How is the message being sent back?" I asked.

"It's a simple instruction, plus some details for the Destroyer's launch," the Restitution said. "Since the Larceny know about time travel in the past, they will be ready to receive it."

"Can your spy send a message through the same time portal, as they do?" Maiara asked.

Callum barked a laugh, "Buy one get one free."

"I see. We piggy back a message on theirs and tell our past selves what to do," Stauffen said.

"But what do we tell ourselves?" Callum said.

The lights around us suddenly dimmed.

"The time travel portal is being opened," the Restitution said. "We have seconds."

"We can't close the wormhole. We have to destroy the Destroyer," I said.

"We need to hit it hard. Can a black hole gun from Ramothia do the job?"

"Not in time."

"What about the gun itself?" I asked.

"It does have antimatter inside," Callum pointed out.

"They're sending their message."

"Tell us in the past to crash a black hole gun into the Destroyer they are sending. And a message to watch out for the same tactic," I cried out.

The Restitution went quiet.

"Err... Maiara, won't a batch of antimatter crashing into a Destroyer mean a big explosion."

"Better here than on Ramothia."

"Still—" he said.

"Message sent," the Restitution confirmed

"What happens now?" I asked.

THREE MINUTES IN THE PAST

"Humans, I'm getting a message," Stauffen said.

"That's not unusual, buddy," I replied.

"It's from me. From the future."

"What?"

"I, from the future, am telling us that the Larceny will launch a Destroyer at the wormhole to crash into Ramothia and destroy it."

"We didn't plan for this," Callum said in desperation.

"But we did in the future. The counter is to crash a Ramothian black hole gun into the Destroyer."

"I trust our future selves. Relay it to the Ramothians," I said.

The Restitution Stauffen went quiet for a moment.

"Won't a black hole gun crashing into a Destroyer literally explode, like, quite a lot?" Callum said.

"Your technical description is beyond reproach," the Mouth said.

"Better here than on Ramothia," I replied.

"It's done. They agree," Stauffen said.

We went to a nearby window in the Greatlord's palace. Far off on the horizon, I saw a flash of light and recognised what it was. When I had been teleported to the Ark years ago, I was holed up in a military base in California. Even across what remained from the Pacific, I saw the Destroyer ignite its engines.

The Larceny were about to launch their colossal ship. Another bright light came down from the sky. It looked like an asteroid heading down to impact the planet, and it struck the Destroyer just as it managed to rise into the sky.

I saw the explosion first. A flash of light that left a sunspot on my eyes.

The planet then shook and every window in the whole city shattered.

Another shockwave washed across the planet.

We all took shelter as the wave toppled the buildings at the edge of the city, and even took the top off the Overlord's Citadel.

"Wow," I said as everything settled.

The boom from the explosion then hit the city, and we all had to cover our ears.

"What's the damage?" Callum said, as things went quiet again. "Is this planet going to explode?"

"No, but our planet has lost 2.5% of its mass," Stauffen said to Maier.

"It's what we planned," Maier replied.

"Do we have to worry about the debris? The tidal wave?" Callum asked.

"No. Thankfully the Ramothians fired a small black hole into the explosion, and more antimatter. The black hole sucked in the explosion and the extra antimatter evaporated it. There will be catastrophic environmental collapse to this planet, so I suggest we be gone in a few hours."

"We only need one," Callum said.

CALLUM

OLD FRIENDS

I led the way into the Greatlord's palace. Behind me, Maiara, Antumbra, and the others followed.

Several Larceny guards stood to attention in the entrance hall. There were two grand staircases leading up to a large room with a vaulted ceiling.

Maiara's Restitution friends leapt over me, and watching an octopus jump into the air, was like watching a football trail ribbons.

The Restitution fired an EMP blast at the first guard, who slackened as half its body shut down. The Restitution then stabbed it with one of its own tentacles.

Another guard moved forward, and the Restitution pirouetted on one of its tentacles and flung its others out, catching the Larceny on what passed for its face.

Me and the others rushed for the remaining guards and took them apart.

One Larceny soldier managed to catch Antumbra off guard, and nearly blasted her head apart, until Stauffen grabbed the Larceny and threw it at Mantis whose energetic scythes cut it to pieces.

Then Stauffen held out a tentacle and Antumbra took it as the Restitution helped her up.

"That was unexpected," she said to it.

The Restitution said nothing and led the way up the stairs.

One floor above was a museum—smaller than the one I remembered stepping out into when I first woke up in the future—but still grand.

In the very centre of the exhibit was a cage, and I smiled when I saw what was inside.

"You," the creature of horror said from within, a writhing mass of shifting dark flesh

I walked up to the cage and swiped my sword at the controls, and the energy field that kept it contained faded.

The creature's skin was covered in scars as well as the eyes, and mouths it typically had. It was on all fours with its front two legs massive and bulky. It stepped tentatively beyond the edge of its enclosure and looked down at me.

"How have you been—? You know, I don't know your name."

"I don't have one, as you understand it. I was captured when I landed on this world, and imprisoned here in this palace by the family of the Greatlord I killed. You can call me Nightmare, as that is what they call me now."

"Okay. Your name is Nightmare. Would you like to do more harm to the Larceny?"

Nightmare peered around me at the Restitution. It sniffed through several slit-like nostrils then huffed. "You are not my enemy," he uttered.

"What is this, Callum?" Maiara asked.

I looked at Antumbra, "A friend?"

"More like ally," she replied.

The palace and the city then rocked again to more explosions.

"We're missing the battle," Nightmare said.

"Then let's keep going," and I pointed my sword to the end of the gallery of exhibits where a giant door was located. Beyond was a bridge that arched over the city below, towards the Citadel of the Overlord.

As if I had commanded it, the door swung open and a crowd of humans spilled through. Most of them were former Arkonauts, dressed for battle, and armed to the teeth.

Behind them, strolling, were a group of richly dressed humans with the VP and Three in the centre.

Me and Maiara raised our weapons.

"These are ours to deal with... But jump in if it looks like we're losing," I said to our alien allies.

We stepped forward among the podiums holding relics of past alien races destroyed by a Greatlord's Destroyer.

The Arkonauts spread themselves out but didn't completely surround us.

This was it. This was all of them. Past friends, past crewmates, fellow survivors of a world killed by the aliens they had allied with.

My blood started to boil as I thought about their attack on Ramothia, of cradling Ada's body. A part of me tried to claw its way into my mind, to go easy on them. Maybe they can be changed... Maybe they could find redemption...

I pushed that thought down.

Humanity was done in my mind.

I was going to end it all.

THE ARKONAUTS

As I walked forward my fingers tightened on the gun I held. I felt my skin go cold. Any moment now I knew I was going to be attacked by my friends, my crewmates, my fellow survivors... all now allied against me.

The last time I had seen them was when the Restitution had helped me escaped years ago. I alone had been able to withstand the Larceny's attempts to turn me to their cause, and when it seemed they would leave me rotting in a cell with no windows, I was given a way out. The Restitution hid me, and managed to get me into a cryo-pod to wait for a time to catch up with the Future Callum.

Now I stood beside him just like I had hoped. But rather than standing together to free our people, we were here to bring them down.

As I looked into their eyes, I saw their revulsion and hatred. However, those faces softened when they saw me. They were comrades who had been through everything they had been through and had still come through intact, still soldiering on.

I felt nothing but hope for them—a hope that they could come back from this brink.

I looked at Callum, who was gripping his gun and sword like they were his whole world. He matched the former Arkonauts' revulsion and bitterness.

How could I change the outcome of this situation I was desperate to avoid?

"I don't know how you got this far, or how you beat us and the Larceny..." the VP began. "But it doesn't matter. Arkonauts, cast that name aside once and for all, and take down these traitors to my new humanity—the humanity I saved with the sweat of my brow, and the..."

"Didn't you grow up the son of a millionaire?" Callum shouted out drowning his words.

"I worked hard to make this all possible," the VP practically screamed.

"Who cares who you are and what you did? You built nothing of any worth," Callum shot back.

"I built a new future for humanity!"

"And I'm going to take it all away," Callum replied.

"Kill them," the VP shouted to the Arkonauts.

"You're going to sacrifice yourselves for... *him*?" I asked them.

Some Argonauts slowed their advance and looked into each other's eyes.

"Yes. I know you don't want to do this," I said.

Koyla stopped advancing and managed to utter, "We have to do this."

"Keep advancing!" the VP ordered.

Koyla didn't move, and he was actually joined by others.

Sandi, however, came in and fired. The blast was absorbed by my dying shield.

I responded, firing back and disabling the gun. Then she was on top of me, and I managed to fling her into a nearby podium that broke under her weight.

Moana was next and she tried to stab me with mechanical tentacles that erupted from her back. I rolled away as they speared the floor.

I sprang to my feet, my body lighter than air as my enhanced muscles lifted me up.

The last tentacle attack I caught. Then I pulled at it and took Moana off balance. I kneed her in the chin and she went stumbling.

"Sorry, but please... please stop," I said to her.

Callum was not being as merciful. Any Arkonaut that came for him suffered several attacks, followed by a disabling blow.

He could not, to my surprise, bring himself to kill them.

"The rest of you, attack," the VP commanded to those who had faltered.

I looked at them and said, "I know you did terrible things, but this is your moment. We can free you. You don't have to be scared anymore."

Some Arkonauts danced around me and Callum, either afraid to move in, or doubting the VP's orders.

Moana came at me again, and I shot each tentacle to pieces. Then she came at me with claws that burst from her fingertips.

I kicked her aside, and then punched Illarion in the stomach when he came for me, pushing him to the floor.

"We don't need to do this!"

Callum had Saibu on the ground, with his gun pointed at the Arkonaut's head.

Moana stood up and wiped her chin of blood. "We do Maiara," she said, her arms open wide.

"No. stop," I said, dropping my gun.

Callum whipped his head around to me.

"Maiara, what are you doing?" he said, his eyes darting around and his voice nervous.

"Arkonauts, I have at my back aliens ready to help. Ramothians and others are here to end this."

At that moment, a titanic explosion destroyed a building outside.

"We're going to win... finally win. I understand that you did what you thought you must. It was just us, without One, at the mercy of the Larceny and them," and I pointed at the VP and his entourage.

"That will all be over if you just help us now," I pleaded.

No one moved.

"Kill them," the VP said, spittle flying from his mouth. "You must not let them take what I—what *we*—built," he ordered.

"It doesn't have to be like this" I shouted back.

"Maiara, this is our path now," Koyla managed to mumble.

"Let's make a new path, together," I said.

"No," Moana screeched at me and she gripped her head. "This has to be the right way. We've followed it for so long. We're alive the human race is safe."

Callum backed away from Saibu, then raised his gun at the others. He sidled next to me. "Maiara, please pick up your gun. We need to defend ourselves."

"No, Callum. Choose your own path. This is mine."

"Arkonauts, One never wanted us to be this way. He was supposed to protect us, to shield us from this darkness."

"He's not here, Maiara," Illarion said, holding his stomach.

"And who took him from us?" I asked.

All the Arkonauts, for a moment, almost turned their heads to the VP, but didn't fully do it.

Callum stepped past me, gun raised.

The Arkonauts looked at him, then looked down at the ground, shame covered their faces.

"No, Callum. Look, they're not brainwashed. They're terrified," I said.

He paused, his gun quivering, but not firing.

"It's time for us to be like One. It's time to take up the burden of facing the darkness and realise it's not the cold emptiness of space, nor the invaders of our world, but ourselves. Finally, I have found a way out for us. They can't hurt you anymore. You don't have to do their bidding anymore. The VP, the Larceny, they're going to lose at last. You can walk away from them and their failures."

It was at this point that the aliens joined me and Callum, walking forwards to stand by our side.

Nightmare sniffed the air.

"You are not my enemy," he declared.

"Please," I said. "Take this chance."

"Listen," the VP began, then his voice softened. "I understand how hard it's been. But this is the way forward for humanity..."

"Are you even human anymore?" I asked.

"Do as I say," the VP said.

The Arkonauts appeared to shudder away from him.

"You don't have to fear him," I said.

They looked at the floor and did not move.

"I need you to do this. Prove to the Larceny you're on their side," the VP said.

"Callum, say something," I whispered to him.

Callum kept his gun raised, the barrel bouncing from one Arkonaut to the next. Then he lowered the gun. He didn't say anything, though. Maybe he didn't believe any words of hope if he said them.

"Please, Moana, Illarion, Gerlinde, Waris, Ivaylo... everyone. Don't you remember the murals? The future we were going to build together? I know that desire is deep within you. Dig it out from wherever you buried it. Embrace it, and join me and Callum."

"You cannot turn away from the Larceny. We..." and the VP gestured to the wealthy humans around him. "We helped you to be just like us, and you have helped the Larceny and us to show this galaxy the true way forward."

"You don't need his way anymore. You don't have to feel like change is terrifying. You don't need to think about where your next meal is coming from. You don't have to be afraid of the future. That's what he and his kind has always wanted. They've always wanted you to be afraid. Don't be afraid. Be like One. Here. Now. Because of him I have no fear... Callum has no fear...

"Let's all be like him," I said, and fell silent staring into the eyes of my former crew.

Koyla dropped his weapon, then Gerlinde, then Cortez.

All the Arkonauts started dropping their weapons. A wave of acceptance radiated out amongst.

"Yes," I cried out.

"I don't believe it," Callum whispered.

"Maiara..." Moana began her voice breaking.

"It's ok my friends, it will be ok."

"Oh, well," the VP said, and he pulled from the pocket of his trousers a small device.

He pushed a button.

Instantly, a pain flared in my head, in the heads of all the Arkonauts, including Callum.

"Dr. Ghost wasn't the only one to give you nanite implants," the VP said.

The Arkonauts dropped to the ground.

Me and Callum fell to our knees clutching our skulls. The pain then died away, and we were left panting hard.

We looked up, and every former friend, crewmate, and survivor was dead.

"Why aren't you dead?" the VP said to us.

I didn't know exactly. Maybe the enhancements to our minds had nullified what the VP had just tried to do. I ignored him as my gaze swept over the bodies of the Arkonauts. Tears filled my eyes. I felt as though someone had ripped something from my very flesh.

Callum looked around at the Arkonauts, and turned his face from them, crying.

Through watery eyes I looked up at the VP.

I grabbed my gun where I had dropped it.

The doors to this museum closed at a gesture from the VP, just as the blast from my gun pinged off the metal.

"Get that door open," Antumbra ordered.

Nightmare roared like a lion from its many mouths at the same time, and bolted for the door. His claws tore great gouges in the metal.

I brought my hands to my eyes and wept.

Callum put his arms around me and wept too.

MAIARA

REVENGE

"I'm sorry, Maiara," Callum said.

"They're gone," I replied and I sniffed as I stared at my crew all dead before me. They weren't moving, and their cybernetics were all silent.

"I tried for so long to save them, and now it's all gone. We're all that remains."

Callum didn't speak. He just looked out over the crew. Tears rolled down his cheeks like a waterfall.

"I wanted to kill them, Maiara, I thought there was no hope for their redemption. I killed Ogwambi and... others. What have I done? How could I have given up on them?

"When it started with Matthieu, all those years ago, he was supposed to be safe. He was supposed to be free of the past. And he died for nothing in that cargo bay. I have always wanted them all safe. How could I have forgotten that?"

"Nuan died because of a trap set by the General." Maiara said.

"I died because of Turso."

"Then so many more at the hands of the VP and the Larceny," Maiara finished.

As we both languished in our grief, Nightmare continued to claw at the door.

"In a minute that door will open. On the other side is what is left of our people—the worst of our people," Callum pointed out.

"I know."

"Are you angry right now?" he said.

"I am."

"Do we press on?" he asked.

I remained silent, unsure if there was really anything left for me to do.

I had failed my people. And for the humans that remained I felt nothing but hatred.

"I say we take this anger and finish it right here, right now," Callum said through gritted teeth.

I stood up and he stood with me.

My eyes scanned the room one last time.

Moana lay with an almost serene expression on her face, right in front of me.

I looked down at my gun. Is this the right way to honour her?

"Is this revenge?" I asked Callum. "Is that all that's left?"

He primed his gun and hefted his sword.

"Maybe it's justice. Maybe it's wrath. Either way, if you ask me it has to be done."

I nodded.

It did have to be done.

This was going to be the end.

The humans beyond the door had brought down the whole human race... like they always do. We would return the favor.

Nightmare gripped the door and tore it off its hinges at last. He waited by the door, panting.

My alien friends gathered around me.

"It is time,." I declared.

THE CLIMB

The door led to a short covered skywalk that led to the Citadel.

On the other side was another set of doors.

"Beyond those will be guards, Greatlords, and the Overlord," Maier said.

"Do we have a plan?" Antumbra asked. "If we just burst through that door, they're going to be all over us."

The whole building then shook and the group stopped.

"Look, it's that big thing," Hippo said.

Kraken was outside, climbing the Citadel of the Larceny.

"That's our ride," Callum said.

He fired his gun at the window, as did the others, blasting a hole big enough to leap out of.

"Maiara," Callum nodded towards the beast. "He's your friend. Ask him for a lift."

I leant out of the hole and bellowed, "KRAKEN!"

Kraken paused. Some gunfire from a nearby Greatlord's palace hit on his left flank, and he roared in pain. Then his tail lashed out and knocked the gun turret from the building.

Kraken then clambered over.

"We need your help to get to the top," I shouted at him.

He nodded and turned his body towards us.

"Let's go," Callum said and he was the first to climb on. He hit Kraken's back and held on tight to the rough scales and spines.

Hippo was next, and his landing actually made Kraken wince. Hippo was having a hard time holding on since he was so bulky.

Then the Restitution leapt down and used their mechanical tentacles to secure Hippo.

Everyone else leapt and held on without difficulty.

I clambered down Kraken's back and held onto a spike near one of his working eyes.

"Let's go," I said.

The crocodile started scaling the building. After ascending a few floors another turret on the Citadel started firing. We all had to take cover near spines.

"Do something about that," Kraken called to me.

The aliens were returning the fire, but their weapons were too puny to hit the turret.

"Lyger, can you give us air support?" Antumbra said into a communicator.

A few seconds later, the *Vengeance* came screaming out behind a palace and fired at the turret, blasting it to pieces.

The aliens waved as the ship went flying past.

Kraken kept climbing.

I took a moment to take in the scene before me.

Half of the Larceny city was blown to pieces. The other half was still being contested by Medusa and the other Ramothian forces.

It looked like we were winning.

On the horizon, I saw something strange. It looked like Larceny ships all lining up instead of fighting, creating a chain. Even my enhanced eyes had trouble making it out.

I moved down to the Restitution.

"What's that over there?" I asked pointing out over the city.

The Restitution focused its lens-like eyes on where I was pointing.

"The Larceny are laying power lines. It looks like they've scavenged them from other areas of the city," the Restitution said.

"What? Why?"

"They're going to use the lines to reconnect those that were severed earlier. If they do they'll be able to use the Timerod again."

"Surely, we don't have to worry about that anymore... What could they possibly do to change the situation?" the Mouth called out.

"They can change time up to thirty minutes ago. What can they do in that time? What tactical moments can be altered to their benefit?" Callum asked the group.

"More importantly are our past selves going to be ready for it?" Antumbra added.

"They could try launching a Destroyer again?" Hippo said.

"No, the Ramothians are ready for that."

"What does our spy say?" Callum asked the Restitution.

"I'm afraid I am no longer in contact with them. The Larceny must have discovered them."

"We must be able to work it out. Come on! What could they be attempting to do?" Callum said.

"I've noticed something about the power lines. They've connected every power source on the planet," Maier said.

"They'll need as much power as they can muster, especially after we severed the other power lines," Antumbra commented.

"It's more than they need though," the Restitution said. "They've connected all their available ships. Even old Ark-type ships."

"Antumbra, what could more power mean? Could they have developed a way to break the limit of time travel?" Callum asked.

"No. No way. They only just learned about it. More power is only used for one thing when it comes to the Timerod."

"What's that?" I asked.

"The ability to open more portals to the past... Or one big portal to the past."

"Why would they need a bigger portal to send back information?" Callum asked.

"They wouldn't," Antumbra said.

"So why would they would need multiple portals?" I asked.

"To send back an army!" Hippo said.

No one spoke.

"Can they do that?" Callum asked Antumbra.

"Yes. With more power, they can. They can also open the portals up wherever they need them."

"Right now, there are Larceny on the other side of the planet, away from the fighting," the Restitution said. "They can't get to the fight."

"That's their plan. They're going to open portals up to where there are Larceny. They will then go back in time and add those numbers to their forces. We'll be massively outnumbered in seconds," Callum said.

"How many Larceny can they send through?" I asked.

"Millions," Antumbra replied.

"They cannot be allowed to use that Timerod," Callum stated.

I crawled up Kraken's back.

"Buddy, we need to go faster," I told him.

CALLUM

THE FALL

Kraken picked up the pace as he ascended the Citadel.

I looked down and my head spun. I think it was vertigo because we were almost a mile from ground level.

"Do we know how long until they can activate the Timerod?" Maiara asked.

The Restitution shook its torso.

Just then, I heard a wailing noise.

"What is that?" the Mouth asked.

I scanned the sky and spotted the source of the noise. Three Larceny ships soaring down toward us.

"We can't take those down," Antumbra said. She raised her communicator. "Lyger, we're on the south side of the Citadel. Three ships are heading for our position."

"On my way," Lyger said.

All we could do is watch as the ships descended, then started firing.

Their beams raked the side of the Citadel, then struck Kraken on his side and tore at his leg.

His lower body lost its grip on the building and he slid down. As his claws dug in the structure , they left huge rents in the glass and stone.

"Hold on, Kraken," Maiara called out.

His lower legs scraped at the side of the building, then managed to gain purchase.

The ships arced back around. Then, suddenly, one was blasted out of the sky by the *Vengeance*.

The second ship continued onwards trying to escape the *Vengeance* as it chased it down. Lyger managed to clip the ship with its weapons, and the ship went spinning out of the control.

"Erm," Hippo said.

We all watched as the ship careened toward us.

"Brace yourselves," Antumbra called out.

The ship struck the Citadel just above Kraken. Glass shattered and metal groaned as the superstructure started to buckle and break.

Kraken slipped down some more.

"We need to get off," I called out.

"What?" Maiara said.

"Kraken might fall and we need to keep going," I said.

"He's right," Kraken said. "Go on." He lifted a leg and punched his way through a wall. His leg now acted like a bridge to the hole he had made.

"This way," I said and darted down the leg.

Antumbra and the others followed me, and I helped them through the hole.

"Come on, Maiara," I called to her. She was hanging onto Kraken's side.

"Kraken..." she said.

"Go," the crocodile said, as he slipped again.

Maiara reluctantly walked across Kraken's leg, and I pulled her inside just as the exterior of the building gave way, and Kraken fell with it, roaring as gravity claimed him.

Maiara tried to look over the edge, but I pulled her deeper into the building. It started to collapse around us.

"Kraken," she called out.

I ushered everyone deep into the core of the building, as the floors cracked and crumbled around us. I was worried the whole building would collapse and we'd be done for.

We scrambled to a safer area where everything was more stable. Still, the whole building shuddered, metal groaned, and then quieted down.

The floor in front of us was gone. There was a gouge in the building like a giant had taken a bite out it.

Maiara stepped forward to get a look. Hippo grabbed the back of her shirt.

"I wouldn't, human Maiara."

"I have to see..." she began.

"If he survived, we'll have to find him and help him later," I said. "Right now, we have to stop the Larceny."

Maiara nodded and stepped back from the edge. She then turned around and wiped her eyes. "You're right. Let's go."

I hugged her with one arm as the others rushed for the stairs.

"Come on, Maiara. We'll win this for him. Kraken would want us to go on."

"Yes, he would," Maiara uttered. He wanted to see this battle through to the end, and so should we.

CALLUM

FOURTH TRY

The stairs led up several levels until we broke out into a completely open cavern. This entire floor had no pillars or support structure. It had a domed roof, and windows around the perimeter. An arched doorway at the far end led to a bridge.

In the middle was the Timerod, connected to an array of wires and conduits.

Beyond was a terminal for operating it. Larceny were furiously manipulating it. Arrayed around the room were the Overlord and his Greatlords. They all wore an extra layer of mechanical armour and appendages. Like mech suits for an octopus.

Amongst them were the remaining humans—the VP, Three, and his cronies. As we entered, they slowly backed away, putting the Larceny between them and us.

My alien allies spread out from the doorway we had entered.

The Overlord turned slowly towards us, his mechanical tentacles tapped at the floor as he turned his bulky, skull-like face to meet us.

"Kill them all," it said without fanfare or monologue.

The Greatlords looked at each other, no doubt slightly worried about facing us.

"Antumbra, get to the Timerod and prevent them from using it," I said to her. "Everyone else, it's time to bring the Larceny down."

We charged, as did the Greatlords.

Shots were fired and shields were hit as both groups closed the gap.

I met one Greatlord one-on-one. Its tentacles shot out to spear me and I dodged and bent away from them.

Shots from my gun flared against his shield and gradually they wore it away.

Then a tentacle snaked out and tripped me up. I rolled away as more tentacles struck the ground.

The hair on my body stood up as a wave of energy passed over me.I realised I was under the Greatlord's shield, within it. So, I sliced with my sword and took out the ends of two of its limbs.

It howled in shock and backed away.

Its shield was passing over me again, so I dived forward and fired.

My blast burnt a hole in its skull, and another hit its jaw, and it tried to scramble away again.

It fired wildly with the weapons on its remaining tentacles.

My own shield virtually collapsed from the damage.

The Greatlord kept its distance, learning from before and keeping me outside of its shield.

However, one of its guns moved out beyond the shield as it aimed down at me.

I brought up my gun.

"Can't break my shield, traitor human."

Instead, I shot at its unshielded gun, which exploded and ripped down the whole tentacle, blowing a hole in the Greatlord's side.

Its shield then collapsed, and as the Greatlord seethed at the pain of its burst limb, I was up and leading with my sword.

By the time it turned back to me, I was inside its shield again, and the sword tip went right through its skull. I wrenched the sword free as it died beneath me, and looked around at the battle.

Mantis' skeleton was cracked in several places yet he was still swiping away at a Greatlord.

Hippo's bulk was protecting him as he charged at another.

Antumbra and Maiara were working together.

The Mouth was holding on for dear life as he clung to the back of a Greatlord's skull, trying to eat his way through while the Greatlord floundered, reaching round to its back to try and dislodge the little alien.

Nightmare was devouring his second Greatlord.

The Restitution who had come with us were struggling with their own nemesis.

I leapt down from my kill and tore off one of its mechanical tentacles.

Stauffen was pinned to the ground and the Greatlord stood over it, shield down, but totally in control, I whipped the tentacle at the Greatlord. The bladed end caught it on an eye, and it screamed, letting go of its quarry. Then the Restitution speared it through its one remaining eye and into its brain.

I was about to celebrate with our allies when the room started to hum.

Power conduits feeding into the rod were flowing with energy.

As I helped the Restitution to its 'feet' it said, "They've done it. I'm detecting portals opening around the planet. Their Army can step through. Victory is theirs."

There was pause in the fighting as the whole room turned towards the glowing Timerod.

"It's over. The portals are open. The army will go through once they have locked in the time coordinates. Our past selves won't be able to stop them," it added.

"When the universes re-join, we will be victorious," the Overlord shouted across the room. Images appeared above it showing multiple time portals opening across the planet with Larceny preparing to march through.

"Can we shut down the power?" I asked.

"No. We don't have anything strong enough," the Restitution said.

"Get down," Lyger's voice suddenly said over our comms.

"Lyger?" I said.

"Get away from the Timerod," she shouted.

Me and my friends did what she said, and he backed away from the centre of the room, leaving our Greatlord enemies to flounder where they were.

The Greatlords raised their limbs in triumph mocking the retreating aliens. They thought they had won.

That's when the *Vengeance* smashed through the windows.

Lyger had rammed it into the building and now the ship was inside.

She banked left as the ship came through and the wings cut through the thick power conduits.

The Greatlords left behind were torn apart, squashed, or ended up clinging to the ship as it passed through the building.

"Lyger!" Antumbra called out as the *Vengeance* went right out of the other side of the Citadel, smashing the walls and glass, and tried to climb back into the sky.

Lyger said. "Finish it my friends."

The *Vengeance* flew away, trailing smoke and fire.

I turned back to the room. Nearly all the Greatlords were dead, and the humans had disappeared.

The Timerod was dull. Without its power, the images above the Overlord showed the portals closing.

Lyger had done it.

"No," the Overlord shouted out.

His army stood uselessly where they were, unable to affect the battle here, or in the past.

CALLUM

SACRIFICE

The Overlord, in his cybernetic suit, and the remaining Greatlords in theirs, towered over me and Maiara.

There were no words, no grand statements about how we were killing their species and bringing down their planet, their world, their genocidal ambitions.

The mechanical tentacles were ready to spear us both. That's when I felt rumbling through my feet.

I looked at Maiara, who no doubt the felt the same thing.

"That's big," I said to her.

She grabbed me and pulled me away.

"Stop them," the Overlord yelled.

That was when the floor cracked open, and Kraken's snout erupted through the floor and snapped wildly.

Four Greatlords were crushed under his bulk as the Overlord screamed and moved away from the monster. Leaping from the croc's head was Nightmare, his many teeth sank into the nearest Greatlord. Kraken hauled himself onto the floor, and his remaining four eyes stared down the Overlord. The Overlord threw his mechanical tentacles forward in rapid succession and speared the beast in the belly.

Kraken roared and snapped at him again. He caught some tentacles in his mouth and they sparked and fizzled as they were crushed.

The Overlord ejected them from his suit and backed off.

The Greatlords struggled to try to help their leader, but Nightmare was inside their shields, and he was tearing them apart.

Kraken took fire from large weapons the Greatlords had attached to their suits.

Maiara took a grenade from her belt and chucked it at a Greatlord's feet. When it went off the Greatlord went flying upwards from the explosion.

A Greatlord charged at me and I danced and ducked away from its tentacles and weapons fire. My own shield was nearly gone. The Greatlord was suffering, too. A hole in its shield had opened up on top of its head.

My shield had stored some energy for the concussive blast, so I aimed it down at the ground and fired.

Newton's Third Law sent me flying upwards right over the Greatlord, and I shot downwards through the gap in its shield... and through its head.

It slumped over as I landed on my enhanced legs with only a mild shock through my bones.

Kraken groaned as he took more hits from the weapons fire. His snout was a mess, his face was burned on one side and he was now missing another leg. He panted as blood trickled down and pooled all around him.

"Die, creature. Die," The Overlord said as he speared Kraken with the combined force of all his tentacles.

Kraken coughed and he slumped. The floor rippled like water as his bulk hit the ground, near the edge of the room.

"Kraken!" Maiara screamed.

The croc opened his last remaining eye and managed a weak smile before his eye lids drooped.

The Overlord then turned to me and Maiara.

Nightmare came at him from the side, but the Overlord's shield deflected it away, and he shot him point blank. Nightmare was nearly blasted to pieces, and what remained crawled away too injured to help.

The Overlord turned its weapons back to us.

There was no way to dodge. He had us.

Then Kraken lunged and snapped forward, and his mouth grabbed the Overlord's tentacles.

"Let me go! I am the Overlord of th—"

He didn't get to finish his sentence as Kraken rolled out over the edge of the building.

The Overlord screamed as they plummeted. He tried to fire at Kraken, but the croc's jaws slammed shut forever.

Maiara and I ran to the edge.

Kraken and the Overlord fell, locked together. His tentacles flailed around to grab the side of the building. Some managed to get a grip, but Kraken's weight pulled them free of the building.

The Overlord desperately struggled to free himself, but to no avail.

"Kraken," Maiara called out.

I watched as the beast and the Overlord—locked in a final battle—hit the ground near the base of the Citadel.

The impact was like a small meteorite, and clouds of debris and dust plumed upwards.

We had to turn away and shield our eyes.

Once it cleared, we looked back down.

Kraken lay still, his body broken.

The Overlord was next to Kraken—his skull shattered, a dirty, bloody mess with just one putrid yellow eye remaining.

I looked across at Maiara. Her chest was heaving. She was weeping. She stared down at her alien friend.

"Maiara?"

She didn't respond.

"Maiara."

She finally turned to look at me. Anger and grief mixed together on her bruised face.

"We need to get to the VP," I said.

She looked away, then back down at Kraken. Then she growled and powered up her gun.

"He's mine," she said and ran off in the direction the VP and his entourage had gone.

"Yep. I'm not going to argue," I replied and chased after her.

THE END OF HUMANITY

"How are we going to catch up to them?" Callum asked me.

The VP was far ahead, as was his daughter, Three. They were running down the huge bridge connecting the Citadel of the Overlord to his personal vessel behind the city.

Me and Callum were running as fast as we could, but the VP and Three had similar enhancements to us. We were not going to catch them.

"Got anything that can slow them down?" I asked.

"Let's see how far I can throw?" he said and took a grenade from his belt.

He burst forward, planted his feet, and threw the grenade with all his might. His aim was true and the grenade flew forward. However, it fell short, landing in the midst of the human billionaires running just behind the VP.

It exploded, and sent some of them flying over the edge of the bridge.

The VP and his daughter stopped and turned back at the explosion.

Callum raised his x-ray gun, aimed, and fired.

The VP ducked behind another human—a woman who had once owned a social media empire. She took the blast.

I fired at them with my gun, and took down a former prince.

The VP set off running again.

"Callum, they're still too far away!"

Callum took a radio off his belt, "*Vengeance,* you still flying around?"

"We're here," Lyger replied. "Barely."

"The man who caused this is on a bridge heading for a ship. Can you blast the bridge?"

"Shall I just shoot him?"

"No. Not this time. He's ours," I screamed into Callum's radio.

"Okay, okay" Lyger said.

The *Vengeance* swooped in from our right and fired, strafing the bridge. It collapsed ahead of the VP, right over the pit that housed the vessel.

The VP looked over the edge then back at us.

"Thanks, Lyger. We'll take it from here," Callum said.

We slowed down as we neared, wanting to catch our breath.

The VP watched us approach, then looked over the gap ahead of him. He seemed to be judging the distance. Then he looked back at us. He was red in the face, sweating, and his suit was disheveled. He gritted his teeth, and his arms became tentacles, transforming into whips. Three loaded a gun of her own, and a sword popped out of her back, which she grabbed and held in front of her.

From a hundred meters away, my enhanced ears caught the VP ordering the remaining human lackeys forward.

Men and woman who preferred the power of money cautiously stepped forward. They all had cybernetic implants of their own. But they had never been in a fight.

Me and Callum took them down easily, and the *great and the good* fell before us.

That left only me, Callum, Three, and the VP.

"You have to help us escape," the VP said.

"Why is that?" I asked.

"We are now the only humans! We are all that's left!"

"So what?" Callum said.

The VP backed away a little. "Wha-what are you saying? It's just us. Our race ends with us."

Callum looked at me.

I shrugged.

"We're ok with that," he replied.

"Father, let's just kill them. Look at what they took from us," his daughter said.

"Quiet, daughter. Now is not th—"

Three ignored him and stepped forward.

"Words won't help us," and she walked forward, a cruel smile on her lips."

"Is this for revenge? Revenge against us for killing your crew?" she taunted. "I've taken you both out before, even that machine, the freaky, static alien. I'm going to take you down again, here and now, and get my own revenge."

Callum raised his gun, but Three blasted it out his hand. He seethed, clutching his burnt hand.

Three moved in with a sword and Callum deflected it with his own.

She kicked him, and he reeled backward.

That was when the VP came in to help.

"Take him," Callum called out, and he backed away drawing Three in.

I went for the VP, and he sent tentacles my way. I had to leap sideways to avoid them. I fired at him and his own personal shield absorbed the blows. Four of the writhing limbs had guns on their tips. He aimed and fired. My own shield, weak as it was, took the shots. I fired back with concussive blasts.

The VP's enhanced body took the blast well, and he dug his limbs into the bridge to stop himself from being thrown over the edge.

"I can't believe it has come to this," he said. "I can't believe that everything I managed to earn for our species has been taken away from me like this."

"Now you know how so many others have felt as you stepped over them—on top of them—as they held you up. And you called it *hard work*," I replied.

"No. I made all of this happen!" he shrieked. "Me!"

"Only on the backs of those you deemed less worthy," I snarled.

I leapt at him to continue our duel.

CALLUM

THREE

Three was right. I didn't know how, but her enhancements were better than my own. Dr. Ghost may have left behind a way for me and Maiara to get stronger just like One, but Three's father must have been able to pay for something far greater.

Our swords clanged against each other, and, in all honesty, she was winning. She wasn't using a lot of effort while I was. I was dancing the edge of my limits.

It was only a matter of time.

Come on, Callum. Think! I yelled to myself.

I thought about everything that got me to this point. The allies, the fights, the time travel. And it was all for naught, because soon I was going to get it, and then Maiara was going to be facing both of them alone.

Wait... Time travel?

"This is hardly a challenge," she suddenly said.

Then I smiled.

"You really think you're better than me?" I asked.

"Sweetie, I'm better than you in every way. Before this enhancement I was still better than you. I was born better."

"Then why aren't I already dead?" I said.

That's when I let my sword parry wide on purpose.

Her smiled faded, and she snarled and lunged at me. Her sword thrust forward faster, taking the advantage of the opening.

An opportunity I had created.

That's when I smiled.

I dropped my sword, and twisted out of the way of her blade because I knew where it was going to be.

Just like we had defeated the Timerod—the Larceny's and VP's supposed trump card—I gave her exactly what she wanted. Like all people who want everything, she took it without question.

I brought my arms down, and my leg up, grabbing her thrusting arm and breaking it in two places.

She screamed and howled, and backed away, cradling her useless limb. She then straightened it out, and seethed in pain.

"Heal. Heal," she commanded, as the nanites in her system went to work.

I dived for my sword, took the hilt, rolled towards her, and plunged it through her heart.

She gasped.

I twisted the blade for good measure.

Enhanced or not, she wasn't coming back from that.

With her dying breaths, Three tried to claw at my head.

I just pushed her aside.

She died with a look of disbelief on her face.

MAIARA

THE VP

A tentacle went right through my left lung.

I didn't pause to register the pain, and simply hacked down at the tentacle as I fell backwards.

The VP was missing half his appendages, thanks to me. He stood over me ready to stab me in the head.

Callum then came in, and the VP retreated back a few steps.

I stood up and Callum and I faced the VP down.

We both ducked and weaved, dodging whips and blasts and then destroying the VP enhancements.

He leapt backward, putting distance between us and him. Then he reformed the tentacles on one side of his body back into an arm.

He then raised the remote he had—the one that had just killed the Arkonauts.

"That doesn't work against us," Callum said.

"The kill switch doesn't. Well done for realising it was there in your minds and getting rid of it. But this remote doesn't just kill. It also educates."

He pushed a button.

Instantly pain flared in my head. I went down on my knees. It was too much.

Callum went down too, into a fetal position, screaming.

"One thing you should know about me, children... I plan ahead."

He dropped the locked remote, and his arm became those spiked, weaponized tentacles again.

He went for Callum first, ready to stab him. Callum was in too much pain to do anything about it.

I was about to watch him die, again.

I tried to raise the gun to shoot, but then I dropped my arm. The pain in my hand was sapping my strength. I could only get my hand up a little.

"Good luck, girl, but you can't strike me. I've always been untouchable."

My hand shook as I raised it as far as I could, and moved it to the left.

"See," he taunted me. "Untouchable."

I managed to turn my head to look at him. I hoped it was a look of complete and utter contempt.

"You should never discard things when you think they have served their purpose," I managed to say. "Someone else can always make use of them."

I fired my gun downward, right at the remote, which was blasted to pieces.

The VP's eyes went wide.

He turned back to face Callum, who was already rising.

Callum was bleeding from his eye sockets and nose. He looked like an angry avenging angel. He charged the VP. His sword sliced all, but one of the tentacles.

The VP, in one last desperate act, lunged forward, trying to spear Callum.

But I grabbed the VP's flailing limb first.

Callum kicked at the VP's legs, taking him off his feet.

I planted, and pulled at the tentacle, bringing my arms around, fully extended.

My strength, and the VP's momentum, carried him over in an arc, and after almost one full turn, I let go.

He went flying off the bridge, and fell through the gap the *Vengeance* had made.

He screamed—his eyes wide, his head darting around—and looked for any way out, as he fell into the pit below.

Me and Callum limped to the edge and watched him disappear into the darkness.

THE END OF THE LARCENY

I stood on the edge of the ruined platform, looking down into the depth of the pit. I grasped my chest as my nanites healed my wounds.

I felt a relief, a sort of completion. It was over for humanity now. The man had tried to have it all—keep his claws on his money, his position, his power—and he deserved absolutely none of it. Now I had taken it from him and it felt good. Even better, it didn't feel like revenge. It was justice.

Behind me, Callum sat on the ground panting hard. He stared off across the city. The forces of the Ramothians and their allies were mopping up some ships belonging to the Larceny. I heard, but barely registered, the gunfire in the streets of the city behind me.

"We still have a whole planet of Larceny to deal with or capture," Callum said. "The Ramothians, and the others, will need our help."

"They won't. Soon it will all be over," I replied.

"What do you mean?"

"Wait for it," I replied.

One of the Larceny ships passed above me. I looked up just as it suddenly went drastically off course. It pinwheeled in the sky like it had lost power, but I knew otherwise.

The ship crashed into the Overlord's vessel in front of us, smashing apart on its hull.

Callum looked up. "What was that? It just fell out of the sky!"

He got up and joined me on the edge of the platform. We looked out across the city and saw all the other Larceny ships in the air drop like flies. A large scale army of the tentacled aliens still fighting, despite the death of their Overlord and Greatlords council, collapsed in the middle of a fight with Medusa's children. Even from this distance, my enhanced eyes showed me her army, looking confused, then cheering at their victory.

"They all died?" Callum uttered.

"The Restitution have killed every Larceny left on the planet," I explained.

"I don't understand."

"Even though the Overlord is dead, his robotic parts are still connected to every other Larceny. It's how he partially controlled them. The Restitution have tried over the years to bring about the end of their people. One long shot was to use that connection to infect every Larceny with a virus that shut down their cybernetic systems, killing them all. Only with the Overlord dead, and gaining access to its circuitry, was it possible."

Callum looked back at the Overlord's citadel. At the base of the mountainous building was Kraken's corpse, which I could not look at, and the dead Overlord, his skull shattered on the ground in Kraken's jaws.

"They just ended all the Larceny on the planet."

"Good riddance, I guess," Callum said.

"Follow me," I replied.

It took us both half an hour to walk back to the Overlord's Citadel. We didn't talk along the way. There was plenty to talk about, but maybe we were just too tired to talk. The entire human race was now dead, not counting me and Callum, of course. The VP and his chosen ones were dead. The VP had killed the Arkonauts. I flashed back for a moment to watching them die. My heart ached at the thought. My dream to return them to who they once were had been snatched away cruelly by the VP and his failsafe.

He was in God's hands now, and that would not be good for him.

I cleared my head as we entered the top room of the Citadel.

Strewn about were the fallen Restitution. Most were my friends. I could barely look at them. Callum couldn't either. He kept his gaze fixed across the room where his alien friends stood, two missing, and the others wounded, but alive and smiling at him.

The massive room was filled with aliens all gathered around the edge. The last remaining Restitution stood in the middle, surrounded. The Ramothians and their refugee allies seemed to regard them with curiosity and the same hatred they had reserved for the Larceny. Mixed emotions for those who looked like the destroyers of their world, but also the architects of their victory.

Then Stauffen stepped away from his fellow resistance members.

I dropped my weapons, and approached him arms out.

Two of his non-cybernetic tentacles pulled my hands together and he held them.

"It is time, Human Maiara," he said.

"I understand. Forgive me. But I must say this even though we have talked it through a dozen times. You don't have to do this. You are at these races' mercy, and they have not hurt you. They have watched you kill the Larceny. They know you to be friends."

"This is how it must be. My race's time must come to an end. We have wrought much destruction on the galaxy. Even within us is the possibility of such evil rising again. We must pay back the destruction of countless peoples."

I felt a tear run down my face.

"Please... You can work through this."

He stepped forward and knelt down to my ear.

"Humans are not like us, Maiara. It doesn't have to be the same for your kind. You love your people. We curse our name. It can be different for humans, but not with us."

He squeezed my hand once more, then let me go. I gasped as he walked away. I knew what was going to happen. I was going to see it for a third time. It was more than I could bear.

He turned back to me before he rejoined the other Restitution.

"Always honour our choice, Maiara," Stauffen added. "Now, and for all of time."

He was then lost in the throng of Restitution standing resolute and tall.

Callum stood by my side. Out of the corner of my eye, I saw the confusion in his face. With added senses just like his, I felt his shame and concern. Had he guessed what was going to happen?

His arm came up slowly, reaching out for me, tentative at first, then he went for broke and wrapped it around my shoulder.

I let his embrace comfort me.

The Restitution formed together, their mechanical tentacles interconnecting.

Then as one they called out, "We were once a part of the destruction of civilisations. We are covered in a great shame. Today we give Restitution. Today, hopefully, in those that remain, we have found some honour. In accordance with a justice known only to that who can judge us, we end the Larceny for good. Forgive us if you can but learn from us, you must.

"Thank you for bearing witness to something no species has done before."

The Restitution all stood straighter, their non-cybernetic tentacles finding each other and holding each other tight.

The crowd gathered around the room's edge and muttered, wondering maybe if this was some sort of prelude to an attack. Understandable, considering what the Larceny had done to them.

In a second, a flash passed through the Restitution. I watched Maier shudder then they all collapsed. Their cybernetic implants dulled and went dark.

I walked away from Callum, and he let me go. I walked through the rows of the dead—of a species within whose hearts I had seen both utter darkness and oppression, as well as duty and honour.

None of the other aliens said anything. They watched me in silence. I was a stranger to most of them. Yet I was thankful they let me have this moment.

I found Maier and crouched down and held her tentacles. There was no life in them, no warmth. It had gone so quickly from her mollusk shell.

I wept for her and her race. Everything they had been was now gone. In a few short generations in the memories of the aliens around me, it would be like they never existed.

Would the aliens here write down this sacrifice and remember it?

Would I ever have to go through this again?

The Ammon, the Arkonauts, the Restitution... Three times I had watched a race fall.

How many more civilisations would I have to see end forever?
With teary eyes I walked out of the room.

CALLUM

FIFTH TRY

In high orbit above the Larceny homeworld, me, my alien friends, the Ramothians, and other refugees stared out of a viewing window. I was on one of the Ramothian capital ships, and we all looked down at the planet below—the source of much misery and sadness across the galaxy.

Maiara was the only one not standing. She was sitting by the window gazing at the planet with a faraway expression.

I wonder what she felt about what was going to happen. The world beneath her was one she had spent the longest time on, far more than even Earth. The bodies of her friends, of Kraken, of the Arkonauts, lay on that planet.

I thought about the Ark, of the remains of my former crewmates, of so much history that was about to disappear.

The president of Ramothia then spoke, "Begin the bombardment."

I watched as Ramothian black hole cannons moved into view ahead of our ship.

There was a pause as they took up their positions.

Then they fired.

Each shot threw a black hole at the planet, all of which crushed and sundered a small part of the planet. An antimatter shot right behind then blew the black hole up. The planet suddenly erupted in multiple craters. Each shot erased a city once belonging to the Larceny.

The firing stopped.

"There. Not even the pieces will be able to bear a record of the Larceny," the Ramothian president said. "The Destroyers will be reaching ignition now."

Across the world, steadily growing balls of light expanded outward. The light cast silhouettes on the planet's surface of the many Destroyer-class vessels .

Each ship was simultaneously firing their engines.

Usually, a Destroyer firing its engines on this world would not have harmed it, as they sat in cradles designed to absorb the energy. But, with so many of them firing all at once, the system could not handle the pressure. The planet blew apart. Some of the Destroyers almost got away. Then the flying giant shards of the planet crushed even their mighty hulls. Not one made it beyond the Larceny planet's dying atmosphere.

The explosion petered out and that was that. The Larceny were gone for good.

Maiara pressed her hand against the window. She muttered a goodbye.

The throng of aliens broke up, and the fleet arrayed around the planet started to head towards the wormholes they had arrived through. There were cheers and celebrations, as now all the races could rebuild in peace, knowing no more ships would rain down on them to steal their water and erase their civilisations.

I wandered over to Maiara and sat with her by the window.

We both looked out at the dead world. Its iron core exposed.

"I saw it this time, a world ending," she said.

"I'm sorry," I replied, but not taking my eyes of the remains.

"The first time—with Earth—I missed it. We all did... Apart from you."

"I remember. You all fell down, and I gripped the rail and stayed standing. This is my second time seeing this kind of destruction."

"You got what you wanted," she said.

I looked away from her, and from the planet.

"It wasn't what I wanted. Only what I felt was... Restitution," I said.

"We didn't have to go like them. We were not like the Restitution. Humanity could have had another chance."

"Like so many others we destroyed," I shot back. "Sorry, Maiara," I added quickly.

She didn't reply, just gazed out of the window.

"I suppose our chances run out."

We both went quiet.

"What do we do now?" I asked.

"We're the last two humans. We can't rebuild. We're no Adam and Eve. It doesn't work that way for us."

"I know, but we still have each other, and there're things we can do. We, technically, have a ship, and we have a galaxy we could explore. Maybe in this big old universe we can find a new home, a place where we can settle down."

A tear rolled down my cheek.

Maiara wept too.

"Oh, Callum. Everything's gone. Everything we knew," she sniffed. "We have nothing left. No crew. No remnants of our world."

I sniffed too. "That's not a reason to give up. We're still here."

In that moment, we both leaned forward, glancing at each other's lips. We hugged at first, and it felt like a blessed relief to do so. The warmth of her body, the contact with another human. There were so many emotions to release, to deal with.

I cried into her shoulder.

She did the same into mine.

Then we came apart, then kissed again.

I realised that her warmth was the only warmth that was left of my kind.

We kept kissing, ignoring the aliens muttering at something maybe they didn't do.

We separated when, across the room, a strobe like pattern of light danced around and caught our eyes.

Antumbra had opened the Timerod and was inspecting it.

"What's she doing?" Maiara asked.

"I don't know. She can't go back in time," I said.

Maiara's hand went to a pocket on her left thigh. I wondered what she was reaching for, but I didn't push it.

I helped her up, and with one final glance back at the dead world, we wandered over, holding hands in our mutual vice-like grips.

"What are you doing, Antumbra?" I asked.

Gathered around Antumbra were my other alien friends.

"I have to destroy this too. The Ramothians won't allow it to exist. I'm just checking out what the Larceny did to it before I do. I can't let there be unanswered questions."

"Learn anything interesting?" I asked.

"The Larceny understood its functions quickly, which made sense as they are—*were*—an advanced species. It seems they added some upgrades of their own, mostly to further understand its functions."

"They still never figured out it couldn't send someone back past the last time travel point," I said and laughed.

"Well, the Timerod is incapable to reporting that information. I merely deduced it from experience. This new update is certainly illuminating, though," she answered. Antumbra splayed a hand open in the midst of the energy field.

The Timerod now displayed a single line. As it expanded a bit more, I saw that it was four lines intertwined. One was purple and only started wrapping around the others a little way down the line. A green line went a little further. A blue line went further back. A red line continued back into the past, presumably to the very beginning of time.

"Four timelines?" I ask tentatively. I was no chrono-scientist, or whatever.

"Exactly! The Larceny were able to expand the Timerod's ability to scan the universe. They must have discovered evidence of the four merged universes that were created every time the Rod was used. The blue one, here, is yours."

"Can we do anything with this?" Maiara said, her hand squeezed mine tighter.

I knew what she was thinking. She was hoping for another chance to travel back in time.

"No, Maiara. It won't help. We still can't go back," Antumbra said and her gaze drifted away from her device.

"What does this mean?" I asked.

"It means that the timelines that were created are still sort of there, forever bound with this timeline. Still following it into the future," Antumbra said. "Something of the past, of universes that no longer exists, perseveres. Bound is perhaps the wrong word. This image is misleading. The correct word is stacked."

Maiara let go of my hand and gasped.

"Did you say *stacked*?"

"I did," Antumbra said.

"Explain what you mean by that?"

"Well, simply put, the universes are actually on top of each other." She tapped at the floating controls and the intertwined image of the timeline rearranged itself to show the red line from the distant past joining with the blue line. It was like different types of toothpaste from a tube. The green then lay on top of the blue, close to the present, and the purple went on top. All four lines continued into the future.

"In this representation, the new timeline is made up of elements of all four timelines, and will be forever."

Maiara reached into her pocket and pulled out a scrap of paper.

"Can this help us get back into the past?" she said.

Antumbra took the piece of paper. She looked confused for a moment, then shook her head.

"Sorry, Maiara. I don't—"

She frowned then turned it around. "Sorry. I had it upside down."

Antumbra stared at it again then her eyes went wide.

"Where did you get this?" she asked.

"The captain of my crew came up with it. He wondered for ages why Future Callum never sent a message back through time more than once. He figured out what you figured out... that returning to a point in the past before the last time travel event was impossible. I thought this might be a solution."

"Is it, Antumbra?" I asked.

"It might be."

"Might?"

"This is a theory from a human who had never seen the Timerod, but if I understand it correctly, then yes, we can. However, it is extremely risky."

"Why?" Maiara asked, grabbing my hand.

"We can't technically travel to the past because those universes don't exist. The Timerod can't extrapolate the past of what doesn't exist, then open a portal to it," Antumbra began.

"But this calculation and data... I've been looking at it all wrong. Whoever wrote this worked out that the stacked universes are on top of each other and also merged—all at the same time. Knowing this, I can re-program the Timerod to extrapolate the past."

"Huh," Maiara said "One's still saving us from beyond the grave."

"You said it was risky?" I asked.

"This reprogramming will allow me to open a portal to the past, however it will only go as far back as the first time we changed the past. That's where this stacking begins. While we will be able to open a portal, I'm kind of forcing the Timerod to accept it. For all we know, I'm aiming you at the wrong place in space and time."

"So, we could die?" I said.

"Yes, Callum. That is the risk."

"Can you give me odds?" I asked.

"I cannot."

"Open the portal. I know exactly where and when," Maiara said.

"Wait, Maiara. What are we doing?" I asked her.

"We're going to go back, Callum. We're going to save them," she said.

CALLUM

LOVE

I stood to one side with Maiara as Antumbra worked the Timerod, calibrating it to One's calculations.

"Maiara, what will this accomplish?" I asked her. "You know that nothing we do will stop time from recombining and the universes becoming one again. Whatever we change, the universe corrects. We can't create an alternative universe where everything is better."

I turned her by the shoulders to the window.

"This is the future now," pointing at the destroyed planet.

She turned back to me. "Callum, we have a chance to save them. Yes, we can only go back to a point in time where we exist. But that's enough time to stop this. We can stop the Arkonauts from ever falling."

I turned away from her and ran my fingers through my hair.

"It won't work," I said. "Look, Maiara, I don't want them to be dead, but look at what they became. That's still in them. Heck, it's even in us. Look what happened to them here. Look what they did. The remnant of humanity took part in genocides, they were helping the Larceny of their own free will."

"Because they had the VP for inspiration. They were blinded by a greedy self-important person. They were brainwashed into protecting him when all he ever wanted was to cling to power and wealth, to keep himself safe from the disasters that he helped create.

"We can give them a different inspiration."

"And what if they fall again? Humanity became a blight on the universe just as we were a blight on our own homeworld.

"The Restitution saw their kind for what they were and ended them. Now they can never again hurt anyone. Is it not time to finish the human race and end any possibility of us hurting anyone again?" I asked.

"I spent years with the Restitution. I tried to get them to see that they didn't need to end their lives, too, but they couldn't give themselves that grace. They hated their kind. They hated themselves."

She put a hand on my chest.

"Callum, do you hate the Arkonauts?"

My mind flashed back to moments of Ogwambi trying to kill me, of Sanna's gunfire ripping into my side, of Illarion trying to strangle me. I saw the hatred they had for me for trying to take away their position they had come to enjoy. In their dying moments, though, I also saw their pain and suffering. I saw them grasp for life I had taken.

And I pitied them for it. In them, I also saw my own hate, and my own pain and suffering. I was no different. I wish they had turned out differently, because if they couldn't, then what could my future hold? Could I end up like them too?

I looked into Maiara's eyes.

"I don't hate them. I love them. I wanted so much more for them."

"I love them too. That's why we're different than the Restitution. We still love our crewmates, our captain, and our species' legacy. We're going to give them another chance because we love them."

I sniffed, stood straighter and nodded at her.

"Come on. Why don't we go somewhere only we know, and change our fate?"

MAIARA

SALVATION

My spirits were lifted like never before. I watched, all giddy and filled to the brim with hope, as a time portal opened in front of us. Beyond was the best possible time and place for us to give humanity another chance, and save many, many lives. I rotated my shoulders and checked my weapons.

"Are you sure this is the right time period?" Antumbra asked me.

"It is. It's our best shot. When it's done, if we complete our mission, then other races destroyed after humanity joined the Larceny will survive, too. Including yours, Antumbra."

"Human, take this device," the Ramothian President said. He held out a small crystal attached to a Larceny network connector. "This will set off all the Destroyers on their planet. All you have to do is push the button. Since we're ahead of the time period you're travelling to, they won't be able to override it. We know their systems back-to-front now. It will destroy the Larceny homeworld, and the Larceny in the time where you're going."

I took the device. "What about the Restitution?" I asked.

"We can't separate them out," he said. "I'm sorry."

"Can you modify it to send a message to them ?" I asked

"Since it's connecting to their network, I don't see why not? What should the message say?"

I thought for a moment, then said, "Upload any information on time travel you have, and records of the battle today. Then add a personal note. *You succeeded. This is your Restitution.* That will be enough."

Callum checked his weapons to be sure they were still working. He then turned to his alien friends.

"Callum, this is a one way trip. You won't come back. You won't even be able to age back into our timeline. If you succeed, you will finally create a new timeline," Antumbra said. "After this, I will destroy the Timerod. This is the last time we will see each other."

"I understand."

He went up to the Mouth. "I recreated it as best I could. It should switch them back on like you asked." The little alien handed Callum a small remote.

"Thanks, Mouth," he said to him.

I watched as Callum moved through the group of aliens. I looked around and found no one to say goodbye to me. I was saddened at that, at first, then I realised where I was going and I smiled. All my friends were on the other side.

Callum stood before Hippo and the Mouth. "This is something we do on my homeworld when we're saying goodbye."

He embraced them in a hug. Both aliens imitated him. Hippo's huge arms nearly smothered them both.

"Good luck in battle, Callum," Hippo said.

"Live as long as you are able. Then live again," the Mouth said.

The hug lasted a little longer, then they were released.

Callum then embraced Lyger. "I like hugging you. Your purring is nice," he said to her.

"Thank you for freeing me, and giving me a fresh start, Callum," Lyger replied.

"I hope you meet some of your people again, the ones who might still be out there," he said.

"I will never stop looking."

"Take care of my ship," he said.

"It will need a new name. How about *the Ada*?" she said.

"That sounds perfect," he replied, and squeezed her one last time.

Callum stood before Antumbra. She let go of the controls to look at him.

He broke the silence first.

"I tell you what. When we succeed, I'll come and look for in the new universe," he suggested.

Antumbra smiled. "I won't know you in the new universe."

"I know your wife's name, your children's names. I know your favourite foods. I know you are dedicated and willing to sacrifice anything for your people. I'll know you, and we will be friends again."

"Thank you, Callum. My house will be very untidy. My family never quite got the hang of being ready for guests."

"You should have seen my room," he replied, and he and Antumbra gave each other a nod.

"Don't ask my other self to cook for you. I'm terrible at that," Antumbra added and barked a laugh.

"I never told you this, but you are the person I have been friends with the longest. You are my best friend. I would never have made it this far without you. I was truly blessed to know you," Callum said.

Antumbra whipped a small bead of light from her eyes then leapt forward and hugged him.

"Ow, ow, ow," he said and she let go quickly.

"Sorry. I had to do that," she apologised.

Callum brushed his partially singed clothes and skin.

"I will miss you so much, Callum," she said. "Goodbye."

"Goodbye, my friend," Callum said.

He wiped his eyes of tears and stepped up to my side.

"You ready?" I asked him.

He nodded back.

Antumbra took one last look at the pair of us.

"Do we have a plan?" Callum asked.

"No, not exactly. Any ideas?" I replied.

"I suppose our goal is to save the Arkonauts."

"That's a good plan."

He nodded and extended his sword, holding the remote Mouth had given him by its hilt. His gun was powered up in his other hand.

Antumbra widened the portal.

"Go," she said.

"See you in another time," Callum replied.

Then we leapt through.

BACK TO THE PRESENT

11

MAIARA

ONE FOR ALL

Me and Callum landed right where I told Antumbra to send us. We now stood on either side of One, who was on his knees rocking gently. In front of him was the Overlord and their Greatlords, as well as the VP and his cronies—the privileged of Earth who joined him in becoming part of the Larceny.

The look on their faces was priceless.

All their eyes widened and their jaws dropped.

Callum pointed the remote at One and pressed a button.

I threw a modified shield generator ahead of us, and the shield expanded, cutting the room in two.

I turned to face the Larceny guarding One and took them out, while Callum got One onto his feet.

Decades ago, I had seen One walk away from us to try and save us.

This is where he made it to, despite his child like state, and his fear and confusion. He had made it this far to try and save us. And now my heart leapt as he came back to us, restored and with a fire in his eyes once again.

12
CALLUM

SAVE THE ARKONAUTS

I watched as One returned to us. The nanites I had reactivated patched those areas of the brain the VP had stolen from him. He rose to his feet, and stood in front of me.

"Callum?" he said and he touched my face tracing the scar.

"Future Callum," I said.

Suddenly the shield was assaulted by weapons fire.

The Larceny on the other side were trying to break through.

"Good to have to have back, One," Maiara said.

"Maiara... Wait. You're older. You're from the future."

The shield around us pinged with each blast. It would fail very soon.

"Fast as ever, it worked. Your plan worked. Even when you had lost yourself you were still looking out for us."

I hugged him.

It was so good to see him.

Maiara hugged us both.

We separated and One turned to the Larceny, and the traitorous humans beyond. "Well, then, let's end these enemies of humanity."

"No, One," Maiara said and she held up two guns for him.

"What?" he said.

"Go save the Arkonauts. We'll handle them," she answered.

"Get them back to the Ark and off this planet," I said.

"You're my Arkonauts too. I have to help you. Especially when I failed before."

"You didn't fail." I said.

"We survived. Go help them, One… like you helped us," Maiara told him.

He took the guns, slowly.

"Go, One. Go! You did your duty. You saved us. You really did. Go save the others," I said.

He nodded, then smiled at both of us. He ran down corridor, back to where the Arkonauts were waiting.

Maiara smiled after him.

"It's done. They'll be safe," she said.

"The shield will fail in a moment," I pointed out.

She brought out the device the President of Ramothia had given her. "They'll have fifteen minutes. Is that enough?" she asked.

"More than enough for One," I said.

She paused with the finger on the button.

"Will the Restitution know what's going on?" I asked.

"They will. I wonder if they will feel betrayed? Will they understand?" she said.

I shrugged. I had no idea what they would feel.

She pushed the button.

It took a few seconds, but a low rumble passed through building and up my legs.

It had begun.

Behind the shield, the Larceny were going crazy. Their most powerful ships had just turned against them.

The VP was already heading to the door along with the Overlord.

"They're trying to get away?" I said.

"Then let's go after them," Maiara declared.

We ran forward, our shield failing, and chased down the Thieves.

13
PRESENT MAIARA

ESCAPE

I paced within the security barrier.

The Arkonauts were muttering, frightened and scared. We had just discovered that everything we had known had been a lie. Dr. Ghost had condemned us to die to try and stop these Thieves, to stop those privileged and selfish humans from becoming a blight on the galaxy. His son was trying to save us. It was such a cocktail of emotions, and I had no way to deal with it.

We were stuck on this planet, under the power of these Larceny.

Was there any hope for us?

We all staggered as a giant rumble rippled across what seemed like the whole planet. Light shot into the sky around the nearest Destroyer vessel, just on the horizon. The planet started to shake continuously. The shuttle nearby rocked on its hydraulic legs.

The Larceny surrounding our pen turned this way and that, unsure of what was going on.

"Maiara, what's happening?" Ogwambi cried out.

"I don't know," I shot back.

"Maiara, look," Luciana said, pointing over my shoulder.

I spun.

"Oh, my," I said.

One was running back to us. He held two guns in both hands. He was covering ground extremely fast. His eyes were fixed on us.

"He's back!" Illarion said.

"How?" Sanna added.

"Who cares?" I said.

One raised the guns, and the Larceny around our pen got their act together and started firing. It didn't matter. One blasted each of them apart in rapid succession. He jumped high into the air and fired from above. He spun and ducked and weaved in a brutal display of force I had never seen before.

When they were all dead, he raised a gun and fired at the device projecting our prison. The whole thing shut down immediately. But we didn't say anything. We just stared back at our captain, our mouths agape.

"Arkonauts, I don't know about you, but I don't like this planet. Let's go find a new one," he said.

We all cheered.

"Climb aboard the shuttle! Let's get back to the Ark," he ordered.

Me and some of the others ran up to him.

"What happened? How do you have your nanite memories back?" I asked.

One looked down at me and smiled.

"It's thanks to you, Maiara. You never gave up. You came back for us."

"What does that me—"

A planet wide earthquake rippled across the world.

"No time now. I'll explain later. Get on board. We're leaving."

One practically pushed us up the ramp and into the ship. "Maiara, Koyla, you're helping me fly this ship. Go get the engines started. Illarion, Gerlinde, Moana, and Ogwambi man the turrets. Shoot down anything that tries to stop us."

"Everyone else, strap yourselves in," One ordered as he made his way down the length of the ship barking out his orders.

I got to the cockpit ahead of One, and me and Koyla started activating the systems.

One marched in ten seconds later.

"Fully powered, One," Koyla reported.

"Hold on. This is going to be one heck of a ride."

Me and Koyla sat down in vacant chairs and manned our consoles, which included shield and sensors.

One checked a final read-out, telling him everyone was strapped in. Then he activated the communications.

"Who are you calling? We don't know anyone on this planet!" I asked.

"Yes we do. And we're going to need their help. Now, hold on," he announced and launched the ship forward. It flew out across the city.

"Anything following us or coming at us?" he asked.

"Not as far as I can tell. It's chaos down there," Koyla said. "Every single Destroyer vessel is starting its engines. If they fire at the same time, this planet is gone."

"Then we'd better hurry. Koyla, connect to the Ark using the remote access from this ship. Open the docking bay doors and start the launch sequence. We need to make a quick exit from this planet."

"Will do."

One increased power to the engines. "Let's just hope we can make it."

"We'll make it" I said.

14
CALLUM

HELP FROM THE FUTURE

Me and Maiara were a whirlwind of weapon fire and sword slashes.

The Larceny were in disarray and unable to coordinate, falling to us as we chased after the Overlord, the Greatlords, and the VP and his ilk—the thieves of our future.

We burst out of the rear of the building and found ourselves just next to a staging area. Various Larceny spacecraft were everywhere, including one of their capital ships.

"They're heading for the ship. They can fly that out of here," Maiara said, pointing at the leadership of the Larceny and the VP crossing the runway towards it.

"We need to destroy it. We can't let them escape."

"Callum," she replied pointing at a nearby fighter craft. "I can fly that."

"Let's get aboard."

The ship was being boarded by Larceny and one of the VP's allies. He had separated from the VP's group, wanting his own vessel, no doubt. Typical.

He was trying to order the Larceny about.

We wasted no time. We took the Larceny down and left him standing amongst their dead bodies.

"Good! Help me. We can escape together."

Maiara hit him in the head and he fell off the ramp onto the tarmac.

"Sorry, but this is ours. We already paid for it. I'm sure you understand," I said after him, closing the ramp.

Maiara took the ship into the air and towards the capital ship.

I activated the ship's sensors.

"The Arkonauts are on their way back to the Ark." I reported.

"Good," Maiara replied.

She lined up the ship and started firing.

Our fighter's weapons struck the ship at multiple points on the hull. Maiara took out weapon emplacements before the ship could respond. She took out the struts holding it vertical, and the ship collapsed onto its side.

"Well done," I said and kissed her on the side of the head.

"We should go after the Arkonauts, and make sure no one tries to take them down."

Before she could lift the ship up and turn it around, the Overlord and its subordinates rose up reaching out with their tentacles and managed to the grab onto our fighter, pulling it down.

"The engines are stalling," Maiara reported.

The ship crashed onto the tarmac.

I pushed a button and the canopy snapped open, partially dislodging a Greatlord who had moved on top of our ship. The putrid yellow eyes inside the skull were bloodshot, and it was snarling. I shot it through its head and it dropped away. Another took its place, and Maiara stabbed its eyes with two blades.

It fell screaming.

We stood up in the cockpit, weapons pointed out at the circle of traitorous humans and Larceny leadership arranged around our ship.

"Who are you?" The VP said.

"Does it matter?" Maiara said, holding her fire.

I looked around. The VP's daughter was glaring at us. Her usually perfect blonde hair was a mess. The Overlord was breathing deeply, its eyes filled with anger.

"How could you do this to us?" the VP said. "We saved the human race forever."

I suddenly had a brain wave.

"But this was the plan, right?" I said loudly.

"What?" the VP replied.

"Callum?" Maiara whispered out of the corner of her mouth.

"This is what you told me to do. Activate the Destroyers all at once and prevent the Larceny from leaving the planet. This was the plan all along, Mr. Vice President. Now, the Arkonauts can get away and the enemies of humanity are destroyed."

The Overlord and Greatlords rounded on the VP and other humans.

"That's a lie," the VP called out.

"There is no other explanation," the Overlord said. "This was your plan. I still don't know how they appeared out of nowhere, but how dare you! We saved you from your dying planet."

"Why would we do this?" the VP said. "I'm telling you it's a lie."

The Overlord spluttered.

"We're trapped here with you, too," the VP added.

The Overlord looked confused. It still wasn't sure. So, I tipped the scales.

"Get on board, sir," I said patting the aircraft, then I fired at the nearest Greatlord.

That started a frenzy.

Greatlords and the Overlord rushed the remaining humans. Those who had sold humanity down the river for a chance to escape Earth—the richest of the rich, the ones who had paid off politicians and saved themselves—went down at the tentacles of the Larceny.

Weapons fire started striking our ship, and me and Maiara ducked down into the cockpit.

"Well, that will do it," Maiara said as we crouched down together face to face.

"Do you think we can fight our way out of here?" I asked.

Maiara primed her guns. "Probably not without help," she said.

"Blaze of glory?" I asked her.

"Blaze of glory," she nodded then leaned forward and kissed me on me.

I returned the kiss.

"Let's go," she said after breaking free.

We leapt out of the cockpit, side by side, attacking. I stabbed a Larceny right in the eye while Maiara did the same, but shoved a grenade into one's eye socket and then backed away as it exploded.

Some of the humans screamed at us and charged, angry we had taken everything from them.

They were not able to fight back in any way, but they had guns and the blasts peppered us with weapons fire.

We ducked behind the wing of the ship.

I had a blast in my chest and my left lung was struggling.

Maiara had taken several hits and her clothing was charred, but her nanites were taking care of the wounds.

"You alright?" she asked.

"My body's trying to take care of it," I said, coughing up a little blood. "But I don't think we have enough time to heal."

"Callum, look," Maiara said.

I turned my head as a bunch of new Larceny ran across the landing area towards us.

"This is it, Callum," she said as the hoard of Larceny bore down on us.

I closed my eyes. There was no point to resisting. We had done all we could. I was prepared to—

The new Larceny, surprisingly, ran past us, and came down on the Greatlords instead, heading for the Overlord.

"What?" I exclaimed.

Me and Maiara were left untouched as these new Larceny stabbed, shot, and bludgeoned their leadership, pulling the Overlord to the ground and spearing him with tentacles in the eyes.

"It's the Restitution," Maiara realised.

One of the attacking aliens stopped by Maiara on its way to the carnage. "Thank you for bringing about our end," it said and then joined the others.

"No. Come with us," Maiara said.

"Maiara, it's what they want. We have to let it happen their way. Besides, we have a human problem we still need to take of," and I pointed across the landing area.

The VP and his daughter were heading for a small ship on the end of the row of other Larceny ships.

"Where are they going? Every ship that can leave the planet is about to destroy this whole world?"

My face fell. I knew exactly where they were going.

"Not all of them..." I pointed out.

"The Ark! The Arkonauts," Maiara gasped.

15

PRESENT DAY MAIARA

RACE TO THE ARK

One flew the ship across the planet at top speed.

"One, we have Larceny ships closing in on us," I reported.

"Hold on!" he warned, and he dove the ship into part of the cityscape below us. The ship dipped and weaved as One took it around the buildings.

"We can't lose them," I said.

"Their ships have better tech than ours. Fire when you get a clear shot," One said over his shoulder.

The Arkonauts in the turrets gave their affirmative.

"Here they come," I said.

I heard the turrets fire and the enemy ships fired back.

The buildings around us were blasted apart as the weapons hit all around us.

"We're going to have to break cover from this city to get to the Ark," One said.

"We'll be sitting ducks," I said.

"Keep firing. Don't let up," One commanded as the ship broke out of the city. The Ark was coming up fast. Behind us, the sky was turning red and dark brown. The city was collapsing as violent tremors shook the planet.

"This planet's going to blow," I said.

"But not with us on it," One promised.

The ship rocked as the enemy weapons fire finally struck us.

"Shield down to 88%" I said.

"Turrets, focus your fire on these coordinates. Fire on my command," One said.

"That's just empty space," Moana called back.

"Please do it," One said, and he got an affirmative back from the others.

He tapped the controls in front of him then turned the ship banking it onto its side.

Arkonauts screamed and whooped as the g-force threw them to the side of their chairs.

I looked out of the window as we banked, and I was forced into my seat. We were followed by the pursuing vessels and they grouped together as they tried to keep up with our maneuver.

"You're funneling them," I said.

"Fire," One called out.

The turrets fired into a spot right behind the ship, and the alien ships flew right into the blasts.

"Got them," One cried out, as he corrected the ship's course and headed straight for the Ark.

"How are we going to break the Ark loose from the clamps holding it?" I asked.

A screen in front of One switched, on and I saw Doc's face.

"Doc," I called out.

"Hello, Maiara. What can we do for captain? You have awoken the Ammon early."

"I have no time to explain. The Ammon have the means to fight. The Ark is clamped in place and we need those clamps destroyed. Can you do it?"

"We can. Sending fighters out now."

"Have them return to the ship as soon as possible. We're taking off," he added.

Doc's face disappeared. I looked out the forward viewscreen and saw objects leave the top section of the Ark.

"Will they get back in time?" I asked.

"They will," One said.

"There's another ship passing us," Koyla said.

"They're going for the only ship that can escape that planet," One said.

He gunned the engines and chased after them.

Once our course was steady, we continued onto the Ark.

The console beeped at me.

"One, another ship is coming in with weapons armed."

"Track that ship and fire," One said.

"Wait," I shouted out. "It's not attacking us."

16

MAIARA

THE VP

"The VP has full control of the Ark. He's heading for the docking bay and I'm guessing he can open it," Callum said.

"He can close it behind him too, and keep the Arkonauts out," I said. "Speed up."

"We're going as fast as we can," Callum said.

"The Arkonauts are far behind. They lost ground trying to escape those Larceny ships."

"It's up to us," Callum said.

"Go faster," I said.

"How?" He asked.

"There has to be a boost on this ship!" I said.

"Nope. Wait... We could lose weight," he said.

"You're not thinking of throwing me out are you?" I joked.

"Hold tight," Callum warned, and he pressed some buttons and the canopy of the ship blew itself out.

The wind assaulted my face. "More warning next time," I shouted at him.

"I'm dropping the missiles we have on board, plus the spare seats."

Behind me, two of the seats ejected.

"Not mine please," I shouted.

We sped up.

"Taking power from life support, since we're not using that now," Callum added.

We picked up more speed.

The docking bay on the top of the Ark opened as a small hole on the massive flank of the ship, just visible between the Ammon part of the Ark.

"They're going to make it before we do," I said.

The VP's ship entered the docking bay, and the door started closing.

"Faster, Callum."

"It's not me! It's the ship," he said. "Hold tight! This is going to be close."

We closed in on the gap in the docking bay.

"We have one minute to get that bay door open. That's how far behind the Arkonauts are."

"The VP has a remote. We have to get it! Hold on!" he called out.

The docking bay door was nearly a slither. We burst into the docking bay and lost the tips of the wings along the way. We lost the landing gear, too. The ship slid on its belly, and Callum fired two thrusters on the front end. Sparks flew around us, and we skittered towards the VP's ship, just as he and his daughter were climbing out.

Callum pressed a button and fired a blast at their ship. The two of them dived out of the way as their ship exploded.

Our ship slowed down, and we crashed into the wreckage, coming to a jarring halt.

We both leapt from the ship.

I burned my hand on the hull, but ignored it as we ran for the pair of them.

"This isn't your ship," Callum bellowed at the VP.

The VP backed away from Callum, his eyes wide and his bottom lip trembling. He raised a remote control and pressed a button.

Callum smiled. "Won't work on me," he said.

The VP pressed the button again then seethed and threw the remote away, making the same mistakes again. I scooped up the remote, pressed the buttons, and the docking bay door started to open again.

When I turned back, the VP's daughter, Three, threw herself in Callum's path. He had to turn to face her. She had a knife and had the same upgrades as me and One and Callum.

Callum gritted his teeth and fended her off.

"Get to the VP," he shouted.

I ran right for him.

He stretched out his arms and I remembered that, by this time, he had already had cybernetic surgery by the Larceny.

His arm split into those tentacles of his, and he threw his arm forward at me. I dodged away as the space I had been in filled with spiked tentacles that would have flayed me alive. He withdrew his arm for another stab at me, and I flung my sword just like last time. He didn't know that I had been in this exact fight before.

The sword cut five of the tentacles from his arm, and he gasped as they flopped to the floor, wriggling there like worms in morning rain.

He turned his other arm into a gun and fired.

I managed to duck behind the ship. I glanced out and saw him turning the gun on Callum, to help his daughter.

That was when the shuttle came flying into the bay, and whoever was in the gun turrets fired at the VP.

He ran on his mechanical legs away from the gunfire that blasted apart the decking.

One settled the ship down. That was it. Game over for the VP. There was no way he could take on One and us.

The ramp out of the back extended straight out. It was me, another me, on the ramp.

From behind the ship I was using as protection, I gazed across the bay at myself, younger, traumatised, but not nearly as much as me.

I stepped out.

Despite the chaos, despite Callum fighting the VP's daughter, despite the sky outside the Ark tearing itself apart and the planet below cracking and shaking itself to death, I had to see her this girl I once had been.

She saw me and paused.

I smiled, knowing that I saved her decades of pain.

A rumble vibrated through the ship and the Ark listed. Earthquakes caused by the Destroyers all over the planet were causing titanic destruction to the core, and they must have dislodged the Ark in its landing zone.

The three ships in the bay slid across the deck.

One pulled up the shuttle to give it stability in midair.

Callum and the VPs daughter cried out as their feet lost balance without warning. Callum dug his sword into the ground and created a hold for himself.

The VP's daughter did the same with a blade from her wrist.

The VP however slid away.

I was forced to follow, as the ship I was behind went sliding towards the bay doors, taking me with it. I dropped the remote I still held, and it slid away, as I tried to grab something to hold onto.

My younger self also lost her footing, and joined us as we slid towards the entrance to the docking bay.

We were going to go tumbling out and down the Ark's hull.

The Ark then fired its own engines.

I felt the ignition through the deck plates. The deck went flat again just before me, the VP, and my younger self went flying.

The two other ships were less lucky, and out they went, crashing down the side of the Ark.

One brought his vessel down to us, and the turrets swiveled our way.

I looked up into the cockpit. There was One, smiling at me.

"Maiara... old Maiara... Back away," One said.

As I steadied myself I saw that I was in the firing line with the VP right behind me.

"Wait," the VP shouted.

He held up in his hand, which held a small rectangle box, then he pointed it at the ship.

I knew what it was, and I knew it was all over.

17

CALLUM

THE BEST OF HUMANITY

As the ship lurched back to virtually upright, the floor levelled up and I leapt to my feet.

The ship's engines were on and the ship was heading up, slowly, like a Saturn Five rocket first bearing its own weight. Soon, it would rise like a bullet into space.

My attention turned away from the VP's daughter for a second. Out of the corner of my eye, I had seen both Maiaras and the VP go falling towards the open bay doors.

I breathed a sigh of relief realising that both Maiaras were on their feet and One's ship was beside them.

I heard a foot step behind me and turned.

Damn she's quick, I thought as I barely managed to deflect Three's knife away from my eye socket. Unfortunately, the other blade she had went right into my chest and into my lung.

I cried out in pain as we went rolling. Then I kicked her away. I grabbed the knife hilt and pulled it free. I tried to breathe, but my lung had collapsed on that side. I scrambled away on my back, on all fours, like I was imitating a crab.

She rose to her feet. Her once lustrous blonde hair dangling over her face like she had just gotten out of bed.

"I was going to be a queen," she shouted at me.

Come on nanites, I said to myself. But they were taking their time fixing my lung. At least the flow of blood had slowed.

Three dove at me with the knife.

I kicked her in the chest and away from me.

She was quickly on her feet again, and brushed her hair from her face, which wore a bestial snarl.

She shouted at me again, but I couldn't really make it out as the engines fired again for another burst of speed. Air was whipping around as the planet below fell away.

In minutes, we would be in orbit.

"I wish I could carve your face off in front of that pretty girlfriend of yours," she shouted as she came at me with the knife.

I had no way to stop her.

That was when Ada slammed into her side.

One had woken Ada.

Three slashed with the knife.

The blade opened up Ada's face, but the robot just kept coming.

"Get away from my crew," Ada shouted.

The girl lunged and Ada took the knife from her.

"I command you t—"

Ada stabbed her in the chest. Right where her heart was.

She managed to gasp and back away. Three then pulled the knife out.

Her own nanites started closing the wound.

"I command you t—" she said through bloody teeth.

Ada then shot her in the head. Down she went.

"You don't command me," Ada said.

From my prone position on the floor, I looked up at her, and she looked down me.

"I thought you were dead," she said.

"Nope," I replied.

There was a whine from the other side of the bay. One brought the ship down and cut the engines.

I saw the VP waving something about and said, "What's going on down there?"

18

PRESENT DAY MAIARA

THE SACRIFICE

The VP smiled.

"You know what this is?" he cried out.

I turned to One, who was scowling through the glass window of the ship.

He looked ready to kill the VP, but he made no move.

"In case it's not clear... If I just press this button, your crew will die. Set that ship down and give me control of this Ark," the VP said.

I was mere feet from the VP. My other self was staring daggers at him.

I stared across at myself, and saw a face etched with trauma. She looked at One, then across the bay at... at an older Callum. And he was safe. Two was there and she was protecting him. I then looked back at myself.

I saw her smile. She was happy.

Then, suddenly, I was in her mind. I saw all she had been through.

Her eyes went wide and she turned to me.

Somehow the nanites in my brain and hers were connecting.

We were sharing memories.

I felt her pain. Some of it old. Some of it new, but all mine.

I looked at the VP as he held the remote, brandishing it like it was ticket to a new life. He smiled "I say, you obey me or this crew dies," he said. "I am your future. I always was. I am the only one who can lead you. I, who helped fix this ship. The man who built businesses! The only one with vision that guided so many..."

I looked at myself, then the ship with my friends, One, Two, and Callum.

All were safe. The Ark was away. These Thieves were falling by their own swords.

A future that had been taken from them was nearly theirs, again.

There was only way to make sure.

How to describe this decision... these thoughts.

The only thing I saw was him. To see him gone and everything he stood for.

I didn't think of the pain that would follow.

I didn't need to. For I knew I would still live.

I looked into my own eyes.

"No," she said to me.

But it was too late.

Out of the corner of my eye I saw One shout, "Maiara!" from within the ship.

The VP turned. His eyes widened.

I barreled into him.

He screamed, as his legs were lifted off the ground, and over we went

The wind whipping around the Ark as it rose took us both. Even if he pushed the button, it wouldn't matter, the remote was now out of range. I had saved them all.

All he could do was scream in terror as he lost everything.

I closed my eyes as I fell.

I lost contact with myself.

I felt her grief in that last second. But I also felt a moment of pride and admiration.

The crew were finally safe...

19

MAIARA

ESCAPE

I dropped to my knees, staring out into the sky that was growing darker. The docking bay doors started to close.

One landed the ship.

For a moment, I couldn't move. The voices around me were dull and my eyes were locked on the space where my younger self had once stood. Two hands grabbed my shoulders and Callum practically shouted my name into my left ear.

I broke from my spell and stared back at him.

"Callum, she—"

"I know. You are always amazing. No matter who you are," he said to me, and hugged me.

When we broke apart, the Arkonauts were gathered around, crying, hugging each other, and mourning Maiara's passing.

The ship shuddered.

"The planet... It's going to explode," One said.

"Are we clear?" Callum said to One.

"No. I need to get to the control centre."

Despite the emotional turmoil, everyone rushed after him.

Despite what I was feeling, seeing myself die, I managed to follow.

Me, Callum, Two, and One reached the control centre first.

The dome and floor showed us what was going on.

The Ark was in high orbit.

The planet below was cracking apart.

"Are we going to get away?" Callum said.

"Our engines have more power in them now than when we left Earth," One replied, his fingers moving in a blur over the controls. "We even have enough to use the wormhole drive."

"Wormhole drive?" I asked.

One typed and talked rapidly. "The ship had the ability to create wormholes for faster than light travel. We never had enough power to use it before, but now we do. We'll find a new home much faster now."

"The planet is destabilizing. It won't be long till it blows, we need to go," Two reported.

The rest of the Arkonauts crowded in, all staring upwards watching as the home of the Larceny broke apart.

"It's going to be close," One said.

The Larceny homeworld had a giant gash across its surface. Balls of light peppered the surface as the engines of several Destroyers fired at once.

The Ark was really moving now. The planet shrank from our view.

Then, it exploded.

The second time in less than two hours I had seen the Larceny homeworld get annihilated.

Some of the Destroyers almost escaped. The exploding planet released them from their pits, but even they were soon crushed when the pieces of their homeworld smashed into them like the jaws of a car crusher.

Chunks flew after us. A camera shot of the tail of the Ark, where our engines were, showed pieces of the planet almost chasing us.

A particularly large piece was coming right for us.

"The Ark's not supposed to do this, but—" One said and he tapped a control.

A lateral thruster on the side of the Ark erupted at full power.

Everyone, even One, lost their footing briefly as the Ark lurched sideways.

The piece of rock barely missed us, and a few building sized rocks ricocheted off the hull.

The whole crew went silent.

Then One said, "We've outpaced them. The Ark is clear."

After that, there was another explosion. One of celebration. Every Arkonaut was cheering.

Two and One embraced.

I stood next to Callum, my hand finding his, and we watched the remains of the Larceny homeworld slowly cool in the cruel vastness of space.

Their species was done.

We were safe.

"I am now the only human to see a planet burn three times," Callum said.

"They say the third time's the charm," I replied.

Callum smiled.

"That they do."

The Arkonauts were cheering. Some were kissing and hugging one another all around us.

"Did we really do it?" Koyla asked me.

I stared at the dead world.

Seeing myself die, seeing a world die for the second time, seeing my crew alive safe and happy... it overwhelmed me. I was unable to think.

"We can only hope," I whispered.

THE FUTURE

EPILOGUE

I woke two hours before daybreak.

Decades had passed, and today was a special day.

It wasn't a birthday, not Christmas, or our new, new years.

No. This was the day... The day that made everything worthwhile.

I turned my head and, in our bed, Maiara lay awake, too, with her eyes staring up at the roof of our log cabin.

I stared up there with her.

We didn't speak for what felt like hours.

"I'm afraid," I finally said.

"Me too," she replied.

We both sighed.

"Let's go and see," she said.

We slipped out of bed and dressed. Gone was the military style clothing of our past, a past that also happened to be our future.

We chose our light, airy clothing made from local plants. Maiara added her Arkonaut hoodie, and chose a light blue colour for today. We went down the small hallway to the room next to ours. In two smaller beds, a boy and a girl slept soundly.

I went in and knelt beside them, lifting their hands and squeezed them. They didn't wake. Instead, they groaned and scrunched up their faces in an adorable way.

Maiara joined me. She bent down and kissed them on the forehead.

Then, her face went pale.

"What if they disappear?"

I only stared back at her. I had no answer.

"Don't go anywhere," she whispered to the boy and the girl.

"Come on. Let's go see," I said.

We stepped out of our small house, onto the main street of a growing town. The sun's rays had not reached us yet for the day. At this time of the year, the sun cast the shadow of the Ark on us, and kept the air chilly.

Down a silent, grassy street filled with the houses of our fellow Arkonauts, Maiara and I strolled barefoot. My hand was holding Maiara's tight.

No one was up. We were the first risers, or so we thought.

The street led to a hill overlooking the colony: humanity's first. At the end of the street, we found One watering his plants.

He rose as we passed by and I frowned at his working so early.

"When the sun falls, it will be a warm day," he explained. "They need their water now."

"You weren't waiting for us?" Maiara asked.

He smiled. "We'll be here you when you get back," he said.

We both wiped away tears, hoping that was going to be true.

We kept walking.

A path had been worn into the hill. It led to benches at the top. Half way up, the hill had been levelled. In this area, four gravestones marked the resting place of friends.

One read, Mattheu. The other, Nuan. The other two read, Callum, and Maiara.

We stopped for a moment, and picked some leaf litter off the graves. Then we continued on.

At the top of the hill, we sat on a bench, clutching each other's hands, and an arm wrapped around each shoulder.

The Ark loomed over humanity. The pyramidal shadow was shrinking as the sun rose, casting light to either side, illuminating a sparkling sea, and green continent.

Maiara looked at her watch.

"When the sun rises over the peak, we'll know."

I nodded.

"Do you think we did it?" she asked.

"I have no idea."

"We might be about to see everything disappear," she said, her voice barely a whisper. It was as if saying the words meant they might come true.

"Please, please, let this stay," I said out loud.

We watched as the tip of the pyramid's shadow reached the outskirts of town.

"Any moment now," Maiara said.

We hugged each other closer.

"I want you to know that you were right," I said.

"What?"

"You were right. We gave our people a second chance," I said. "I should have never questioned it."

"They didn't deserve it, but we gave it to them... Because we love them," Maiara replied.

"And now, we'll see if it saved them," I said.

The sun crested the top of the Ark.

The light reached the town. On the beach nearby, Kraken burst from the water and beached himself on the sand, basking lazily.

Maiara stood up and stared out, then looked at her watch.

"It's all still here," she declared. "A new future, no joining together of old and new, just a separate new universe."

I got up and looked over a town, waking up. Doors opened as Arkonauts and their children rose to greet the sun and start the day. Chatter and laughter filled the air. The remnants of humanity continued their new lives.

Maiara turned to me, tears in her eyes. She walked forward and wiped the ones on my cheeks away. I did the same for hers.

"We did it. We're free."

We hugged each other.

"Let's go and see what has been gifted to us," I said.

As we walked down, our son and daughter ran for the hill.

"What do you think the others are doing right now?" Maiara asked.

"Others?" I asked.

"Our friends, all across this universe. They're out there somewhere."

I looked up at the sky, past the moon where the Ammon and Ada had made their home, and out into space.

"They're living their lives. Content, happy, and free," I replied.

Maiara turned my face to hers.

"Just like us?" she asked.

I smiled back and said, "Just like us."

We strolled back to the colony, hands intwined. We gathered up our children and rejoined the rest of humanity.

The future was ours again.

ACKNOWLEDGEMENTS

A big thanks to everyone at Spaceboy Books for travelling with me on this literary journey, and helping me to finish my first book series.

ABOUT THE PUBLISHING TEAM

Nate Ragolia is a lifelong lover of science fiction and its power to imagine worlds more hopeful and inclusive than the real one. His first book, *There You Feel Free*, was published by 1888's Black Hill Press in 2015. Spaceboy Books reissued it in 2021. He's also the author of *The Retroactivist,* and *One Person Can't Make a Difference*—featured on Tor.com's Can't Miss Indie Press Speculative Fiction list. He founded and edited *BONED*, a literary magazine, has created webcomics, and pets dogs.

Shaunn Grulkowski has been compared to Warren Ellis and Phillip K. Dick and was once described as what a baby conceived by Kurt Vonnegut and Margaret Atwood would turn out to be. He's at least the fifth best Slavic-Latino-American sci-fi writer in the Baltimore metro area. He's the author *Retcontinuum,* and the editor of *A Stalled Ox* and *The Goldfish* for 1888/Black Hill Press.

www.ingramcontent.com/pod-product-compliance
Lightning Source LLC
Chambersburg PA
CBHW061532210726
48287CB00006B/1917